MISCHIEF INDEED

"You have a twinkle in your eye, my lord," Marianne said. "If I knew you any better I would say it was mischief you had in your mind." She sighed. "It seems there is little way out, now that the banns have been posted. . . ."

"There *is* a way," his lordship said. "Marry me instead."

"Surely you cannot mean it!"

His lordship composed himself solemnly. "I do. My good family is positively hounding me to marry. There is no reason why the lady should not be you, my dear."

"Then . . . it is more as a favour to you than to me that you make me this offer?" It was a hard truth, but the only one Marianne could live with.

My lord, correctly divining the direction of her thoughts, bowed decisively.

"I'd be most obliged to you, my dear. My Lady Sinclair . . ."

Marianne blushed. "We are not yet wed, my lord."

"But we shall be before the day is out." He drew closer and extended his arm. Gently, very gently, he pulled her toward him and touched her chin lightly. Marianne had never felt anything so gentle and giddyingly breathtaking at one and the same moment. It was fortunate that she did draw breath then, for a second later she could not. Her mouth was entirely enveloped by that of the personable gentleman before her. . . .

BOOK YOUR PLACE ON OUR WEBSITE AND MAKE THE READING CONNECTION!

We've created a customized website just for our very special readers, where you can get the inside scoop on everything that's going on with Zebra, Pinnacle and Kensington books.

When you come online, you'll have the exciting opportunity to:

- View covers of upcoming books

- Read sample chapters

- Learn about our future publishing schedule (listed by publication month *and author*)

- Find out when your favorite authors will be visiting a city near you

- Search for and order backlist books from our online catalog

- Check out author bios and background information

- Send e-mail to your favorite authors

- Meet the Kensington staff online

- Join us in weekly chats with authors, readers and other guests

- Get writing guidelines

- AND MUCH MORE!

**Visit our website at
http://www.zebrabooks.com**

SEDUCING LORD SINCLAIR

Hayley Ann Solomon

Zebra Books
Kensington Publishing Corp.

http://www.zebrabooks.com

ZEBRA BOOKS are published by

Kensington Publishing Corp.
850 Third Avenue
New York, NY 10022

Copyright © 1999 by Hayley Ann Solomon

Zebra and the Z logo Reg. U.S. Pat. & TM Off.

First Printing: June, 1999
10 9 8 7 6 5 4 3 2 1

Printed in the United States of America

One

The bandbox hit the cobbled street with a tremendous thud. Several windows opened at the unexpected sound, but my lord, having executed an uncommonly neat side-step, simply stared at the offending object with a benign curiosity that spoke volumes for his temper.

Not by the flicker of an eyelash did he appear perturbed, or in any manner reveal sensible relief. On the contrary! The fact that he'd so recently avoided having the living daylights squashed out of him seemed of no great moment.

He looked skywards and was rewarded by the sight of an intriguing pair of ankles making a most unladylike appearance beneath, the lord noted with appreciation, petticoats of an intricate point de nil. Fascinated, the man adjusted a cape of his box coat and watched as the ankles made their precarious descent. It was refreshing, for a change, to see someone other than himself fall into a scrape.

He was shaken from his reverie by the dawning notion that the lady's legs—though delightful—were nevertheless too short to reach the box she had thrown down. They dangled precariously from the knotted rope of bed linen and simply *invited* aid.

This the gentleman did find perturbing. He supposed

she'd expect some help and he would be cozened into giving it. He sighed. Very well, simply for the sake of peace he would lend her a hand, bow *very* civilly, and resume his amble across the street.

He would *not* embroil himself in conversation, he would *not* succumb to her bountiful charms, no matter how appealing they might be. My lord was a reformed man. For him, a life of celibacy and saintliness. He was done with his share of womankind. Done for good.

"Help me!" The young voice high above his head seemed cross rather than panicked. This pleased the lord, who perceived at once that he was not likely to succumb to *this* female's charms, luscious ankles or not.

"How the devil did you get into such a state?"

"Let me down and I will tell you!"

"What if I weren't here?"

"Well, you *are* here, aren't you?"

The question was unanswerable. With a deft movement, the gentleman placed his elegantly gloved hands about her waist and lightly lifted her to the ground. Her bonnet narrowly missed being caught in the trees, but apart from the odd ribbon, appeared becomingly intact.

"That is better! I thought you would *never* help me! I've been sitting on that windowsill for an age!"

"You mean you *deliberately* aimed the bandbox at my head?"

The young lady grinned, her lips rosy and annoyingly inviting to one so recently sworn to the single state.

"Not your head, your feet! Of course, if there had been another way of getting down . . . but there was not, you know. I could never have touched down on my own. I measured the distance the other day. I would have broken an ankle at least."

The gentleman stared. At four and twenty he considered his experience of the female sex to be vast, but this seemed to be the outside of enough. His voice assumed a pompous air that did not sit right upon his normally cheerful shoulders.

"And serve you right, too, you young minx!" He frowned, then shook his head. For the life of him, he could not understand why he'd not stuck to his original intention and continued on his walk. The lady had already imposed too much on his time. Still, she was such a slip of a thing, and for all her bold words seemed to have no idea whatsoever of the predicament she had placed herself in.

Even now, the gentleman could see several impertinent young bucks eyeing her up and down. He noted, too, that the windows that had opened on the bandbox's collision with the ground had not, subsequently, shut. Only his presence, he knew, had saved her from some embarrassing encounters.

The lady fluttered her eyelashes appealingly and peeped up at him. Her eyes were wide and soulful, and the colour of honey.

"I suppose you are going to start on a great scold! I would have taken my lady's maid if I could only have convinced her to come!" Her face puckered in remembered frustration. To her annoyance, her rescuer was not sufficiently sympathetic.

"The fact that you could not so convince her means you must be in some very terrible scrape, young lady!" He tried to sound stern, then realised, to his utter mortification, that he sounded exactly like his own stultifying tutors. He smiled wryly to himself. Imagine himself, Alistair Raoul Griffin Sinclair, growing old and stuffy. *Horrors!* He relented, but only, he told himself, because the silly chit was in trouble enough, and he'd not have it on his head.

"I suppose I cannot persuade you to return from

whence you came? This jaunting about is not at all the thing, you know!"

The lady cast reproachful eyes at him. The honey, he noted, was tinged with flecks of green.

"I thought better of you, sir! Of all the gentlemen I saw walk past today, you, at least, seemed the most likely to help!"

For an instant the gentleman doubted. Had she recognised him then? Had the young Lord Sinclair's notoriety for falling into scrapes actually recommended itself to her? Was it his decidedly murky reputation that had caused her to cast her worldly goods at his feet? The uncomfortable thought vanished almost as soon as the suspicion had arisen. Her face was gratifyingly blank.

"Why me?" He asked.

"Because you look neither top lofty nor . . . nor . . . leery."

At least she had the grace to blush, he noticed. So the wee poppet was not as innocent as he had feared. Well, she would need to keep her wits about her, at any rate. He sighed and took up the box.

"You need not think I feel grateful for your choice, young lady! I get into enough pranks of my own making without having to be cast knee deep into yours. However, since the damage is done, let us repair to that inn. I know the landlady. She will secure for us a private parlour and keep us from the eyes of the curious."

Instead of fainting with gratitude, the young lady fixed him with a stare of hostile suspicion.

"I am not a light-skirt, you know!"

"You will be mistaken for one if you persist in making such unladylike references!"

She squirmed a little and wished she had chosen some- one else upon whom to foist her troubles. Still, he'd looked so jaunty and carefree that she'd felt certain he would understand.

The gentleman saw the doubt in her eyes and took up his advantage. "Do I look to you like the seducer of young maidens?"

She eyed him squarely. True, his cravat was impeccable and his buckskins perhaps a little tighter than they strictly ought to be . . . his shoulders were strong and patently devoid of padding . . . his exasperated look was most unloverlike. . . . She made her decision and grinned. He noted how the corners of her lips tilted upwards and how merrily her bright eyes sparkled.

"I won't look too deeply upon that point, sir! I have, after all, a brother!"

He wagged a finger in her face and again felt the alarming sensation of being an octogenarian rather than a bright young man of four and twenty.

"There you go again, young lady! Your implication is most improper! Most!"

"But true, nonetheless."

He ignored her. It was bad enough being lectured to by his mama and his loving, though misguided sister. He didn't need this little widgeon of a thing to start up, too. Still, since her scrape must count as the master of all scrapes, he was relieved to consider that she was in no position to start calling the kettle black.

He bowed and took her hand, glad that they were finally making progress. She dimpled at him, and he found himself cursing.

"Sir!"

"Beg pardon, ma'am. Just clearing my throat."

"That's a tarradiddle if ever I heard one! Still, we're all entitled to our vices, I suspect. Shall we go in?"

The gentleman was of two minds whether to strangle her then and there and have done with it. The lady was infuriating! What was worse, he strongly suspected he was about to become embroiled in yet another problem of the petticoat kind. His mind wandered to his greatest friend, mentor, and champion. Lord Raphael Delaware would likely throttle him for this. Especially so soon after narrowly disengaging him from the clutches of a scheming adventuress with superb golden hair.

Then there was the Miss Dunning affair. He'd been five seconds away from a duel. If it had not been for Raphael's timeous intervention . . . He shuddered. Still, Miss . . . Lord, he did not even know her name! Miss so and so looked harmless enough. He'd settle her in the lodging, pay her shot, and be on his comfortable way.

The lady smiled charmingly. "May we hurry? I would not like to be seen out here, you know. The Mershams are out driving but any moment they might surprise us by an appearance."

His lordship's heart sank. More and more this was sounding like trouble. His step quickened. He did not know the dreaded Mershams, but whoever they were, he had no wish to encounter them. He held out his hand. "Hurry then, ma'am!"

She pulled her hand away. "No need to manhandle me! I told you I am not a—"

"Light-skirt. Yes, you mentioned that once before." His voice became grim. "Do you wish me to help you or not?"

"Of course I do! Only, I can walk myself. See here." She quickened her step, then let out a yelp of pain.

"Now what?" The gentleman seemed resigned to his fate.

"It is nothing. I may have sprained my ankle, that is all." She winced but held her head up high and carried on bravely.

"Oh, for heaven's sake!" His lordship let the bandbox he had been carrying clatter to the ground without ceremony. He whisked the lady up in his arms and marched towards the entrance of the Cobbler's Inn.

"What about my bandbox?" Her voice was dangerously close to a wail.

"I'll send my groom after it."

"Put me down! We will be a spectacle."

"Be quiet!" His voice sounded as stern as that of any of his dreaded tutors. His next words surprised him as much as they outraged her.

"Another word from you and I'll set you inside and give you the spanking you deserve!"

"I'll scream!"

"Scream, then. Do you wish me to set you down and leave you here?"

The young lady looked about her and mutely acknowledged she did not. The taproom was stuffy, smelled suspiciously of spirits, and the people frequenting it were staring at her with most unhealthy interest. Besides, she could feel her ankle slowly swelling beneath her petticoats, and there was something very warming about the feel of the man's arms about her. Her thoughts became somewhat improper, and the man was amused to note she was blushing.

His voice softened. He could not, after all, resist a young woman of such eminent charms. Even if she *was* a termagant and most unladylike in her behaviour. He exchanged a few words with the innkeeper, but the lady in his arms did not interfere. Truth to tell, she had quite given herself up to the marvelous sensations she was now experiencing and had most unaccountably lost interest in paltry particulars. For some reason she felt certain the young gentleman in the debonair box coat would come up trumps.

Trumps it was: a first-class private parlour with a fire cozily made up and a most appetising tray of steaming delights carried in only minutes later. The lady had forgotten how hungry she was in her anxiety to make good her escape. She set to with gusto, hardly minding the pain as her rescuer felt her ankle and bound it tightly after applying liniment procured from the housekeeper.

So good did she suddenly feel that she was compelled to grin. Her rescuer put his hands behind his back and grinned good naturedly in return. She was intriguing, even if a little infuriating. Raphael would no doubt know what to do with her even if *he* did not.

"I suppose we ought to be introduced."

"Strictly speaking, sir, that is correct! Since there is no one about to do the honours, should we do it ourselves?"

"I expect so, my damsel in distress! I suppose there truly was a need for a rope of linen? Most dramatic, you know, but hardly necessary, one should think."

The lady bridled. "Most necessary! How else could I make my escape? I got the idea out of *Frangeline.*"

"I could have guessed that. Only a novel could employ such a foolhardy mode of escape!"

She looked at him crossly, her eyes narrowing to a glare. "Do you want to be introduced or not?"

"I am not sure, ma'am! I suspect our introduction is going to lead me into trouble!"

She pouted, but cheerfully acknowledged the truth of his statement. "Very likely, I'm afraid! The Spencer-Pultneys seem to attract trouble to them as a matter of course."

"No more, surely, then the celebrated Sinclairs? My lord extended his hand. "Lord Raoul Sinclair, Viscount Hansford, at your service!"

She inclined her head and dimpled merrily. "I would curtsy if I could, my lord! Miss Marianne Spencer-Pultney in your debt."

"The Spencer-Pultneys of Caversham?"

She nodded.

"My father's kin." He smiled. "How do you do, Miss Spencer-Pultney?"

"Very well, I'm sure, my lord!"

They smiled at each other in perfect amity as she handed him some confection of sugar pastry.

"Not bad for an inn. French cook, you can tell."

"I'm not that discerning, your lordship. Only starving."

"Starved by the wicked Mershams, whoever they may be."

She peeped at him suspiciously, but his features did not look patronising or mocking. She relaxed a smidgen and helped herself to a stuffed mushroom.

"Exactly, my lord. Or rather . . ." She was anxious to be just. "Not wicked, perhaps, but definitely misguided."

"And what are they misguided about?" He could not help noticing the bouncy jet curls that peeped out from under her bonnet.

"Practically everything, I'm afraid!"

"Enlighten me."

"Well, there is Lila. She is my stepsister by marriage. She wears only pink and lilac, and all her gowns are hideously covered in flounces."

"Flounces are the fashion."

"I know, but she is a trifle on the stout side. How do you know?" Her tone became suspicious.

His lordship choked on a piece of jellied ham. "How do I know what?"

"That flounces are the mode?"

"I just know. Flounces are the mode and that is all there is to it." What *was* it with the girl? She seemed determined to remind him of his lights-of-love. Many a ruffle he'd bought them, to be sure.

She cupped her hands and looked at him. "I won't tease you, my lord! You're in the right of it, of course, but on Lila, flounces are just too overpowering to imagine."

My lord winced. He knew precisely what the young lady meant. Half the young damsels selected for his matrimonial inspection looked like little pumpkins decorated with yards of lace. Still, he did not see the need to agree too readily with the insouciant young lady before him, so he merely managed a sarcastic, "So flounces are the sum total of your troubles?"

She glared at him. "Do not be so wretchedly *idiotish*, your lordship! As if I would take flight for a mere trifle like that!"

He looked at her wearily. "I don't know you, ma'am, and who knows *what* maggot might have got into your head? By the by, I don't think 'idiotish' is a very respectable term for a young lady like yourself!"

"Good lord, no! I would never use it in company, of course, but you don't count, after all."

His lordship the Viscount Hansford was unused to being told he didn't count. He was not sure that he liked the sensation it engendered, especially when the young lady doing the telling was as fetching as this one.

"What do you mean, I don't count?"

She did, at least, have the grace to blush under his blustering scrutiny.

"Well, I mean you are not likely to ring a peal over my head or turn your nose up in haughty disapproval and give me the cut direct. I'll wager you've used a few choice terms in *your* lifetime, my lord. Why I know you do! I heard you say—"

"Be quiet, ma'am! I do not wish to have my indiscretions thrown in my face. Besides, I am a man. That makes all the difference, and you know it."

She sighed and removed her bonnet. "You are right, of course. My wretched tongue. Will you forgive me, my lord?"

Her eyes were so expressively contrite that he had no

option but to forgive her instantly. "Very well, cry friends, shall we? And now, my dear, you really had better tell me what is on your mind."

She nodded and her shoulders drooped.

"The fact is, Lord Sinclair, I am in the most dreadful coil."

"I gathered that! Why do you not start from the beginning?" His encouraging tone had a soothing effect upon the vivacious young lady beside him. Apart from twining her long, slender fingers around and around, she seemed to have taken a grip on her agitation and settled down to begin her story as logically as she could.

"In a nutshell, dear sir, I am being forced to wed the most curmudgeonly man on the face of this earth. He has nothing to recommend himself to me. Nothing whatsoever!"

"I am amazed your family would countenance such a match. He has no title or fortune, this specimen of pulchritude?"

She grinned at the term despite her unenviable predicament. It seemed she had chanced upon a kindred spirit. The gentleman before her was a model of all she could dream of, if she dared. Exceptional looks, youth, vitality, and obvious humour. If only *he* had been the Earl of Glaston, she might have been more reconciled to her miserable lot.

"Oh, he is blessed with all of those things, dear sir! The wretched man is an earl and reputedly extremely rich."

"Sounds like a dream come true for any young lady. What is the hitch?"

"The hitch?" She glared at him. "The hitch?" Her voice was almost a squawk. "Nothing, my lord, if you happen to consider a man in his dotage with the manners of a . . . a . . . barracuda and the habits of a miser admirable qualities in a husband!"

His lordship's lips curved slightly at her flashing eyes and obvious indignation. "And is he handsome, this paragon of yours?"

My lady issued something curiously close to a snort. "If your taste runs to something very akin to a cross between an owl and a pig!"

"Sounds disgusting, I admit, but there must be many young maidens eager to become a countess. Surely the rank outweighs these other trifles?"

She looked at him in disgust. "You have obviously not met him, my lord. I would not marry him if he were the king himself!"

"Fair enough. Why, however, do you not simply refuse him and have done with it? No one can force you to marry him, you know."

She stared at him in despair.

"There's the nub of it, my lord. Unless I take active precautions they can and will."

The viscount released his cravat and looked at her with sympathy. It seemed that he would have to be her knight in shining armour, after all. He only hoped he could untangle the chit's troubles without becoming too embroiled himself. He'd had enough scandals for a lifetime.

"Begin at the beginning, my dear."

She sighed. "Very well, I will try to order my thoughts. I am always being told what a harum-scarum miss I am, and I suspect that is the right of it. I have begun at the end, rather than the beginning, of my woeful tale!"

"Never mind, start again. I will interrupt you if I need to."

She nodded. "It all began with my great aunt Harriet. She was a conniving old soul, slightly malicious and the bane of all her nieces' and nephews' lives. Come to think of it, she was an exact replica of my scurrilous husband-to-be, only in female form. *They* should have made a match of it!"

"Mere speculation, my dear. Stick to the point."

She glared at him, then relented. "Very well, but it is not easy, such a tangle as it is!"

"How does your great-aunt Harriet feature in your extraordinary escapade?"

"She left me a great deal of money in her will. I am, in fact, an heiress."

"My felicitations. I am still, however, in the dark."

"There was a stipulation, the old witch!"

"Let me guess. You were to wed this mysterious earl."

Marianne nodded seriously. "The will, I suspect, was half spite, half malicious meddling. There was talk that *she*, you know, was in love with this earl in her heyday. He scorned her and she became . . . well . . . eccentric. Rich, too. She invested in the new railway, and what with the war and all, her money doubled and trebled and multiplied before her very eyes."

"Why would she want you to marry him?"

"To gall him, I suppose. To manipulate him even in death and wreak some sort of pitiful revenge upon his person. She was the meddling sort."

"He need not take the bait. If he is as rich as you say he is . . ."

She looked at him pityingly. "A miser, you know, is never rich enough."

"I see."

"Besides . . ." She blushed. "He has no direct heirs. His nearest heir is a cousin from whom he is estranged. I am certain he would wish for a son simply to spite this young man."

The viscount nodded. *"That* I understand. I have exactly such a cousin, and he would spit in my eye if he could. My parents named me for him, and do you know what he did? Caused a public scandal and announced that I, a mere babe, was simply trying to flaunt my right to supplant him in his face. Can you believe such codswallop?"

She nodded. "You understand me exactly, sir! He will marry me to spite his cousin and get his hands on Greataunt Harriet's fortune. I, however, have no intention of succumbing to my aunt's machinations! I believe that in a strange and awesomely muddled way she meant well, concerned that I may not be able to catch a husband, with my lack of figure or fortune of my own."

The viscount's eyes rose. The lady's figure was enviable. It was a wonder she did not know it.

"She could have left you the sum unfettered."

Miss Spencer-Pultney's eyes flashed a deep, honeyed gold. "Exactly so, sir! But that was never her way. She could not resist poking her meddlesome finger in, even at the very end! I suppose she thought I'd fritter away the capital where she knew the earl would not. He lives in a mausoleum with no heating whatsoever, just as she did. Not even the tiniest fire in the parlour. Servants cut to the bone, too. What good is a fortune if you refuse to use it?"

The young man grinned. "Exactly my thoughts, my dear! I do not hesitate to squander my own fortune, much to the despair of my mama! She is forever bringing me to book for my frittersome ways."

Miss Spencer-Pultney rolled her eyes in sympathy. My lord thought her attractive despite the obvious trouble she was causing him.

"Shall I continue?"

"Pray do! What happens if you do not wed this spectre of a man?"

"The money goes to the preservation of pugs. I am serious, my dear sir. The woman was animal-mad, as the smell in her house—*my* house, I should say—attests!"

The viscount's eyes twinkled. "I will help you escape!

You cannot be permitted to reside in such a house and in such odious company! Let the money go to the dogs and be damned!"

"That is exactly my sentiment, sir! My stepsister Lila and her mother unfortunately do not share your views. I am troubled, too, about my brother. He is at Eton, and the upkeep is exorbitant."

"One thing at a time. Why does the dear Lila want you to marry the earl?"

"It will increase her consequence beyond measure to be sister to a countess! Her mama would take over the running of the household, and the earl would not complain about getting a free housekeeper. She will launch her daughter into society under the aegis of an earl's residence, and no doubt Lila will do very well for herself. No doubt she does not realise how mean-spirited and clutch-fisted the earl actually is. I can't see him sponsoring grand come-out parties for the fair Lila, but there! Perhaps my judgment is clouded."

"I think not, but I see how your mama can be misguided."

"Do not call her that, I beg! She was my dear papa's sorriest mistake, and he lived to regret the connection, believe me!"

The viscount eyed her with a new and softer pity.

"Would you like a drink, my dear? You look parched."

She smiled at him gratefully. "Some ratafia, my lord. I am dreadfully sorry to have embroiled you in this coil!"

He eyed her wickedly. "No, you are not! You selected me especially, if I recall!"

She smiled and swallowed genteelly. "Maybe so, but still I regret the necessity! I am not *all* hoyden, you know!"

The viscount's eyes twinkled. "Now you disappoint me! Tell me about your brother."

Her eyes clouded. "He is the best of brothers! I am just

concerned for his welfare. After Eton it is Oxford; then I had hoped he could buy his colours into a fine regiment."

"Can he, if you default the will?"

"I hope and pray so, dear sir! I was left some money of my own when Papa died, and he has an annual stipend, but I am not sure we can do it. I am not troubling him with this at the moment. I was just hoping something would turn up." Her face brightened visibly. "Perhaps I can become an opera dancer or an actress. . . . I hear they earn prodigious sums."

"Not for their singing, however. I would advise you strongly not to take that course!" The viscount's tone became almost high-pitched in alarm. Clearly, this enterprising young lady was out of the ordinary way. She needed protecting from herself, the little innocent.

"Well, what do you suggest?"

"Tell me the name of your intended."

"He is not my intended!"

"Oh, all right, then! Your *intended* intended!"

Her lips curled up in an unwilling smile. "You are the outside of enough, dear sir! All right then, my *intended* intended is none other than his lordship the Earl of Glaston."

There was a pregnant silence in the room. He looked at her narrowly, then smiled, closed his eyes, and muttered something very like "Fate."

The lady herself seemed unfazed. As she helped herself to a delectable-looking sugar plum, she had no idea that her world was about to be turned upside down.

Two

"His lordship the Marquis of Slade." The butler bowed politely and withdrew as a tall, exceedingly personable gentleman entered the room and made a raffish bow.

"My lady Sinclair!"

The dowager viscountess Sinclair looked up from her needlework and gave the gentleman a smile of welcome. The young lady seated demurely at her side paled somewhat, then also extended her hand in greeting.

"Miss Amber, my felicitations. I think between the pair of us we may have spared your impetuous brother a somewhat embarrassing encounter!"

"I hope that may be true, sir! I fear, however, that he may not yet have learned his lesson. The last I looked, Miss Marston seemed set to lay siege to him, and you know how it is. . . ."

"Indeed I do, silly cub. For the life of him he cannot resist a pretty face. He must be a very indulgent relation indeed, for he has before him two perfect examples of grace and beauty. You'd think he would have a surfeit of such charm."

Lady Sinclair raised her eyebrows languorously and smiled. Her daughter, she noticed, had started fidgeting with the tea things and did not look up.

"Thank you, my dear Raphael! You have a real gift with

words, but such flummery before dinner is rather too much, you know!"

"Not flummery, my dear Lady Sinclair! London would be hard-pressed to find two prettier or more complaisant women than yourselves."

If he noticed the blush that rose to the cheeks of the young Miss Sinclair, he showed no sign. In truth, his thoughts wandered to the brother, his dearest and most scapegrace young friend in all the world.

"Is Raoul within? There is a spanking-new hunter I've just acquired, and I thought a turn of thoughts might cheer him somewhat. I'm afraid I gave him a thundering scold the last time we met."

"And so he deserved! You're a good friend, my lord. Unfortunately, Raoul stepped out a number of hours ago. He left no indication of his likely return, and I did not quite like to press him. So *trying* to have to answer to one's mama, you know!"

Lady Jane smiled charmingly, and Raphael felt his mouth curve in warm response.

"He'd get along a sight better if he did! Ah, well, no harm done after all. I'll not keep my horses waiting, then."

"You will not stop to have some tea? Amber has acquired a special way with this bohea flavour. Really refreshing, although I know you men are more prone to stronger drink."

"Not if Miss Amber's concoction is the alternative!" He threw a friendly glance in her direction and she was moved, at last, to speak.

"Thank you, my lord. Do not, I beg you, hold your horses on our account. I'll have Petersham send round a sample for your delectation. That is, Mama, if you do not think it improper?"

Lady Sinclair secretly sighed at her obstinate but beloved young daughter. It was clear how the wind lay with her, but she persisted at every opportunity in sending the marquis on his way.

"No, my dear, it will not be improper. Peterson shall send the tea around if his lordship is sure he will not stay."

The Marquis of Slade bowed his thanks and flashed an extraordinary, quite magnificent smile at both ladies. If his appreciative eye lingered on one young lady in particular, her eyes were too downcast to notice.

"Until tomorrow evening, then!"

"Tomorrow evening?"

The Duchess of Cardamon's ball. I had thought you attended."

The young Miss Sinclair threw an anguished glance at her mama.

"Good gracious, Amber! I had quite forgotten!"

"I cannot go, Mama!"

"But we have sent in our acceptance. It will be highly uncivil if we do not!"

"I will feign a headache, then. It is much for the best. I am perfectly certain the duke will be most discomforted by my presence, and I bear him no ill will whatsoever."

The Marquis of Slade looked mystified, and it was left to Lady Sinclair to explain something of their dilemma.

"You must think us bedlamites, Raphael! The truth is—"

"Mama!"

"Do not be so missish, Amber! Lord Delaware can be relied upon to keep a family confidence. After all, he has done so admirably in the past!"

"Yes, but this is different!"

My lord noticed the lady's high colour, and though he was intrigued, puzzled, and more than a little curious, he took pity on her.

"Hush, ma'am! Though I hope I am no tattlemonger, your daughter obviously wants this confidence kept. I will spare her blushes and look to my horses at once."

His quiet, deep tones did little to soothe either lady. The dowager viscountess was confirmed in her desire to keep him with her a while longer, and the younger Miss Sinclair suffered private agonies of her own. The voice was wonderfully masculine and only confirmed her deepest, most secret heartache.

There could be no doubting it; she was in love with the utterly unattainable. Raphael Delaware, the Marquis of Slade, was a confirmed bachelor and a noted connoisseur of womankind. There could be no place in his heart for a handsome but not pretty woman of five and twenty, long past the age of marrying, and a bluestocking to boot.

Lady Sinclair sighed. There was nothing for it but to send the man on his way. After her daughter had so rudely rebuffed him, she could hardly, after all, insist that he stay. She inclined her head politely and bestowed a warm smile on the incomparable before her.

"Thank you, Raphael. Your forbearance does you credit. I trust we shall see you soon, if not tomorrow night."

He bowed, cast one last shadowed look at Miss Amber Sinclair, and took his leave.

Miss Sinclair set down her teacup and prepared to withdraw herself. The dowager viscountess forestalled her sternly.

"Amber!"

"Yes, Mama?"

"I think it is time for serious discussion, my dear. Now is as good a time as any."

Miss Sinclair cast an anxious look at her mama. The tone brooked no argument, but she felt the first stirrings of an almighty megrim. She pressed her hands against her forehead, but it was cool. Lady Sinclair indicated the chair with a firmness that allowed no opposition. Her demeanor, however, was softened by a gentle smile. Amber knew that smile all too well. None of the family could ever resist it, which was how it came to be that Lady Sinclair ruled her roost despite being the most gentle, amiable soul alive.

Miss Amber moved resignedly to the tea tray and poured herself a cup of the aromatic bohea. She was surprised to find her long, graceful fingers trembling just a little. Lady Sinclair felt a deep sympathy mingled with ineffable irritation at this further proof of her daughter's agitation. What had she done, she wondered, to be saddled with two such adorable yet muttonheaded children?

She would need to take a hand in this particular problem, for she suspected that this was one coil that Raphael would not be able to untangle on his own. Heaven knew, he'd had enough of a time with her son. Really, the panic Raoul's capers could cause were the outside of enough! Still, this was not about Raoul, and she realised the conversation would need a good deal of tact and circumspection.

"The Duke of Cardamon is not the first admirer you have rejected, although certainly he is the most eligible."

"Mama, I—"

"Wait! Do you so despise him that you cannot see fit to wed him? More than half of London would die to be in your position."

"I am not half of London!"

"No, but the question remains, nonetheless."

Amber blushed, and Lady Sinclair could see a small tear sparkling in the corner of one wide and normally merry eye.

"Freddie is a dear, and I am most sorry to have disappointed him."

Her mother threw her a sharp glance, then continued ruthlessly. Rejecting the season's premier suitor needed a little more in the way of explanation. There was only one that would satisfy her, and she'd get to the bottom of it. "I can understand your rejecting Fishingham's suit . . . he is old enough to be your father. Browning . . . not of your rank nor, I fear, your mental agility."

Amber's lips quirked at this small understatement. "Denville . . . certainly your social equal but a trifle portly . . . Reed I do not consider. He is a gazetted fortune hunter and I am surprised your brother countenanced his suit in the first place."

"No doubt he knew I'd send him the rightabout more effectively than *he* ever could!"

Lady Sinclair's lips twitched but she went on remorselessly. "Lord Reefton—"

"Mama, is it necessary to go through my suitors as if they were groceries on a shopping list?"

"I had hoped not, my dear, but now I find it most necessary. The duke has impeccable rank, style, amiability, and looks. There can be no possible reason for your rejecting him unless . . ."

Amber did not wish her perceptive parent to dwell too much on the *unless*. Loving the debonair Marquis of Slade was humiliating enough without having to admit to it. She decided to take her mother up playfully upon the matter of the duke's good looks.

"Good looks, Mama? He is too blond, I am sure! My taste does not run to the fair, you know."

Her mother looked bland. "No! I believe I know exactly what your tastes run to, my dear. Tall as a willow, hair as black as ebony, a bewitching smile, twinkling dark eyes, and a tiny, almost imperceptible dark patch above his mouth. I daresay I'd be in love with him myself, if I were only half my age."

Amber had grown pale, her gaze wavering listlessly as her mother spoke.

"I am right, am I not?"

"Is it that obvious?"

Her mother shook her head gently. "Unfortunately not,

Amber dear. I think you would be surprised at the results if you *did* display your attraction more openly."

"Wear my heart on a sleeve? Mama!"

"Nothing so vulgar, my dear, but a little encouragement would not go amiss."

"There is nothing to encourage."

"No?" Lady Sinclair arched her brow effectively.

Amber looked perplexed. "Do not look so horridly *knowing*, mother!"

The dowager viscountess relented. "Your secret is safe, my dear. I do not mean to tease you with it, only to prod you into a little action."

"What do you mean?" Amber replaced the teacup in its saucer carefully. She could not quite catch her watchful parent's eye.

"You can hardly expect to advance your cause if you hustle the good man out every time he alights upon our doorstep!"

"But his horses were waiting. . . ."

"A plague upon his horses!"

Amber's eyes widened at this uncharacteristic use of cant.

"I am sorry, Amber; my language is execrable, I know, but desperate times call for desperate measures."

"What is so desperate, Mama?"

"*You* are, my muddleheaded infant! You are five and twenty, a diamond of the first water, and practically on the shelf! If you will not have anyone else, at least have the goodness to make a match of it with Slade!"

"He has not asked." Amber's tone was low.

"Nor will he if you persist in caring more about his pesky cattle than the man himself! Next time he offers to escort you to the opera or Lady Faversham's or—"

"He does so only out of kindness to Raoul."

Lady Sinclair emitted a most unladylike snort. "I suppose it was out of kindness for your dear, absent brother that he accepted a cup of tea just now?"

"You heard him say he wouldn't keep his horses waiting."

"What I heard, young lady, was his accepting the tea the instant he heard it was your blend."

Amber's eyes flashed. "Just because the man is courteous—"

"Have done, Amber! You are giving me the headache. There is no talking with you. If you persist in being blind, there is nothing to say to it. I suppose I shall have to endure the sight of unrequited fulminating glances between the pair of you till the end of my days."

Amber was indignant, though a rising hope was soaring through her heart. "His lordship does not cast me fulminating glances!"

"Does he not? Then it is I, my dear, who must be blind. Now if you will excuse me, I think I will tidy myself a little before the dinner gong."

Lady Sinclair left behind her a very thoughtful, silent daughter. She nodded her head decisively as she moved towards the stairs. She was not repentant at all for initiating the little talk that had just taken place. It was as plain as a pikestaff that the pair needed a little gentle prodding. If Lord Raphael Delaware, noble Marquis of Slade, was not halfway in love with her daughter despite his raffish reputation, she would eat her last hatpin.

My lady was a very fashionable sort. She would not trifle with a hatpin unless she was quite certain upon her subject. The Marquis of Slade might be famed for his mistresses, but in her daughter he'd undoubtedly met his match.

Lila Mersham pouted in the mirror and pressed a large solitaire emerald against her pudgy neck. Unfortunately, the gem was paste and fashioned in so vulgar a manner that the artifice was obvious to anyone in the least bit discerning. Since neither Lila nor her mother, Delphinia Spencer-Pultney, could be described in these terms, the gem was permitted to remain. It was a regrettable choice, for Miss Mersham's attire was closer to puce than the lilac she traditionally affected.

The glittering green looked slightly dull against her sallow skin, but her dresser did not dare demur. Instead, she clucked round both mother and daughter and showered compliments where none were deserved. Still, she had her position to think of and several mouths at home to feed. The dresser could not afford to be too particular in her choice of employers.

"La, you look splendid, Miss Lila, you do!"

Miss Lila managed a satisfied smirk. "A little more powder and that will be all, Tate."

The dresser dabbed another layer of the scented talc upon the young Miss Mersham. If she had not been afraid for her place, she might have suggested a bath. Now she bobbed a curtsy and was only too thankful to be dismissed.

"It is too bad I don't have a string of diamonds like Lady Cressingham!"

Mrs. Spencer-Pultney nodded her head in sympathy. "Of course it is, Lila, dear. I'd suggest you borrow Marianne's pearls, but they are too plain, I feel."

Lila nodded. "So prissy! This emerald is more the thing, I know, but I do so long for a decent tiara!"

"You shall have one when Marianne is wedded."

Lila's mouth drooped in discontent. "Why does *she* get to marry an earl and inherit a fortune? I'm sure I was *very* caring of Great-aunt Harriet whenever I saw her."

"Life is very unfair, Lila, dear. I am positively vexed myself. I do declare, it must have been at least three times that we visited Caversham!"

Three

His lordship the Viscount Hansford ran his perfectly manicured hands through his much ruffled hair and sank back in despair.

"You are not going to be an opera dancer!"

"I tell you, I am not going to marry the Earl of Glaston, and that is final!" Marianne glared at the impeccably dressed man before her and tried not to be dazzled too much by his handsome and extremely personable countenance. It occurred to her that he might have more than passable attractions if he were not so pigheaded and arrogantly high-handed.

Lord Sinclair sighed loudly and tried once more. "I did not say you were to marry Glaston."

Miss Spencer-Pultney's features lightened considerably. "Then you will help me find a position on the stage? I *knew* you were a prime one!"

The viscount's face mirrored his frustration. Had Lord Raphael Delaware been privy to the interchange, he might well have found it comical. For once, Raoul was on the side of propriety.

The lady, blissfully unaware of the ire she was arousing, continued in soothing accents. "Do not worry, my lord! I have a prodigious fine voice, you know!"

His lordship was momentarily diverted. "Have you?" He

eyed her suspiciously. "All those gloomy drawing room arias, I suppose!"

"No such thing!" Miss Spencer-Pultney turned her nose up in indignation. "I can't abide them, though I've been forced to sit through a good many in my day."

His lordship cast her a sympathetic grin. "And I, my dear. The opera, I assure you, is more diverting!"

Marianne seized her advantage. "What did I tell you?" Her voice was eager and her eyes hopeful as she turned upon her victim.

His lordship had to prevent himself from squirming under her gaze. He pulled himself up to his manly height and uttered sternly that the opera was all well and good, but not for gently bred females like herself. "What is more," he added for good measure, "do not try to cozen me into saying something I do not mean. I have a sister at home and am quite awake to such tricks!"

His tone was so dampening that Marianne lost hope and sat back with a small sigh. "What then? I can't marry the earl, and opera dancing is out of the question. All very well for *you,* my lord!"

"No need to glare at me! You are not, I hope, addicted to fits of temper or the sullens?"

"Certainly not!"

"Good. I can't abide females who nag at me."

"What has that to do with anything? In a few minutes you will never see my face again."

"*Au contraire,* Miss Spencer-Pultney." He reached out and briefly kissed her hand. Marianne felt as though she had been burned by fire. Certainly, her cheeks blushed becomingly. The viscount noticed this and smiled.

"You have a twinkle in your eye, my lord. If I knew you any better I would say it was mischief you had in your mind."

"Would you? Not far off, Maid Marianne. My friends

call it the mischievous twinkle. They know to beware when they see it."

"I must count myself among your friends. I find I am *most* wary, my lord!"

"Good. Tell me, Maid Marianne—"

"That is most improper, my lord!"

His tone took on a surprisingly serious note. "None of this is very proper. Would it be taking very great liberties if I called you Marianne?"

For some curious reason, Miss Spencer-Pultney felt a second flush rise to her cheeks.

"I suppose not." She cast her eyes downward so that he could not see the sudden embarrassment reflected in their depths.

"Good." Raoul's tone was tender. "If we are going to cobble a plan together, you had better call me by my first name, too."

"So you *will* help me?" She looked up, her tone joyous with eager expectation.

His lordship liked the sudden light that sparkled in her expressive honey-colored eyes. He found himself noticing, not for the first time, her ruby red lips, and the slender frame that hid such gentle and becoming curves. Not an antidote, at least, this unusual little minx that had tumbled so unexpectedly into his already complicated life. Of one thing he was certain: she had none of the missish airs and graces that so bored him to tears. She might be a trifle bossy, a smidgen high-handed, and altogether improper, but she was, after all, a lady. Her bearing was courageous, her lineage impeccable, and her heart, if not her head, in the right place.

My lord was not so inured to the ways of the ton that he did not know of the temptation sent her way. Many, he knew, would die to be placed in her position, set up for life as the Countess of Glaston. This little snippet flashed fire at the very thought. He thought the better of her for it. Now he sighed dramatically.

"I suppose I will have to help, Marianne. I never could resist a pretty damsel in distress."

She smiled at him pertly. "I warrant not, my lord!"

He laughed, quite undeterred by the impertinent meaning behind her words. A diverting little lass, and understanding at that. She would serve the purpose. If the dowager viscountess and his eager sibling persisted in badgering him to wed, then wed he would, if not quite where fancy took him, then at least where inclination did. He quite surprised himself to find that he was anxious to help the diverting Maid Marianne. Better yet, the chance of disobliging the curmudgeonous Earl of Glaston seemed too good to resist. A great jest it would be, to be sure. He choked, then coughed as his future wife glared askance.

"I'm glad that you find the situation mirthful, my lord!"

"Raoul. And so will you, when you hear the truth of it!"

"The truth?"

"Yes. Have the banns been posted?"

"To my wedding? Yes. A fortnight yesterday. There seems little way out now, which is why you find me in such a coil!"

"There is a way." His lordship's tone was suddenly emphatic.

"What is that?" She leaned forward eagerly, cupping her face in her hands.

"Marry me instead."

She looked at him pityingly. "Surely you can come up with something better than that, my lord? Your family will have fits, I'm sure. Besides, the banns are out. I cannot wed another man."

"What is the name of the man you are to wed?"

She sighed, as if speaking to a very stupid infant. "I

told you. The Earl of Glaston, though what that is to the purpose—"

The viscount's tone was patient, but his eyes twinkled as if at a great joke.

"I remember, that, my wee love. But I asked you what *name* was written upon the banns."

"Name? Lord Alistair Sinclair."

"The same name indicated in your great-aunt Harriet's so generous testament?"

"Yes . . . but—"

"Well then, behold, before you, Lord Alistair Sinclair!"

"What are you talking about, my lord? Your name, as you have several times told me, is Raoul."

He bowed. "True, my dear, but christened, to be precise, Alistair Raoul Griffin Sinclair."

There was a moment of shaken silence, then a peal of the most delightful laughter that Alistair Raoul Griffin Sinclair had ever heard.

"You cannot mean it!"

His lordship composed himself solemnly. "I do. Here is a handkerchief; you look as if you could do with one!"

"Thank you. What an unholy tangle this is, my lord! I take it the cousin who so disobligingly cut you is—"

Lord Sinclair nodded approvingly at her quick wit. "One and the same, I am afraid. The odious Earl of Glaston. I am his scurrilous heir, though he shuts his eyes to the fact whenever he can."

"Marrying you would be poetic justice, my lord, if this were not real life."

"I think it is the very thing *because* it is real life!"

His eyes grew suddenly serious. For a moment Marianne's heart fluttered wildly. The man had a bewitching way about him. She could be reconciled quite easily to his merry ways and handsome features. She could happily come to grips with the core of kindness she detected beneath his happy-go-lucky exterior. Oh, yes, there was no question that the viscount could pose a temptation of the strongest kind. . . . For a moment she suspected the impossible. He had come to admire her . . . possibly love her— She was being foolish. This last thought was confirmed by his next dampening words.

"My good family is positively hounding me to marry. Since one female of good breeding is much like another, there is no reason why the lady should not be you, my dear." His tone was well-meaning, but Marianne felt ready to throttle him. The words brought her, however, to sober reality. My lord was not finished.

"A lady of good standing is what the pair of them require, and you would fit the bill tolerably well, I daresay."

He looked at her a trifle doubtfully, and Marianne felt her hackles rising.

"I *can* be a lady if I wish to be!"

He grinned, unaware of the wrath he had caused. "Yes, but I wager you do not wish to be often!"

She acknowledged the truth of this hit with a wry but intriguing smile. "You have the right of it, I am afraid, my lord! Being a lady is so insipid, I find, so you see, marriage to me would be quite useless."

"Not so! It will have the decided advantage of balking old Alistair in his malicious desire for an heir."

Marianne looked blank. When enlightenment dawned, she was indignant. "You mean—"

"Yes. If Glaston is fortunate enough to have a son in his dotage, I am supplanted."

"Then it is more as a favour to you than to me that you make me this offer."

He looked at her twistedly, then inclined his head.

Marianne swallowed. It was a hard truth, but the only one she could live with. She could accept such a proposal on no other terms. A marriage of convenience—convenience truly on both sides—she could possibly countenance. One born of chivalry? She knew she could not. My lord, correctly divining the direction of her thoughts, bowed decisively.

"I'd be most obliged to you, my dear."

Marianne was not convinced. "The earl might still marry someone else!"

"I think not. Without the sweetener of your fortune, I doubt the earl would ever have contemplated matrimony. Your great-aunt Harriet was shrewder than you know when she wove that particular plot."

"Why should he not wed?"

He raised expressive brows and grinned. "Too expensive, I warrant! A house in town would become essential, the holland covers of his wretched mausoleum would have to be removed, dinners would become just a tad more elaborate, a nursery would need to be set up, more servants . . . carriages. Marriage, I've been told, does not come cheaply!"

"But *you* are ready to undertake it!"

"Only think how economical I am being. You come ready with your own fortune. I need hardly even dip my fingers into mine!" He grinned obligingly, removing all sting from his words.

"I forgot. If you are Lord Alistair, I stand to inherit."

"So you do, my little maid."

"Great-aunt Harriet will turn in her grave."

"Very likely. Serve the old meddler right!"

Marianne smiled. "You tempt me!"

"So I should. You're in the devil of a fix, and by some stroke of luck I can help. What is more, *I* rid myself of nagging relatives and the spectre of an heir. It is a bargain both ways."

Marianne sighed and tried to ignore the hollow pit rapidly descending into her stomach. It was hardly the stuff of dreams, this match, but his lordship had the right of it. She *was* in the devil of a fix. "If your parents agree, it is a bargain."

"My father is dead. My mother will no doubt come round."

"I want her to be *pleased.*"

"She will be when she makes your acquaintance. She'll heave great sighs of relief that you are not some high flier or . . . or—"

"Opera dancer?"

"Exactly, my dear!"

His lordship flashed her such an utterly charming smile that the normally imperturbable Miss Spencer-Pultney felt breathless. "A merry song and dance you seem to lead her, sir."

He looked most unabashed. "Poor Mama! I am a wicked scapegrace, and so she will tell you, no doubt. Still, you look a game one yourself, my little maid, what with your linen rope and all."

"Will I never live that down?"

"Not if I can help it. I give you fair warning!"

"Thank you. I shall remember it."

He bowed. "Do not take it to heart, my love. We all have our wild oats to sow, after all."

"And are all yours sown?" Marianne regretted the words as soon as they were out. My lord's eyes shuttered infinitesimally for an instant, and she sensed a withdrawing.

"I can't promise you that, Marianne." His tone was surprisingly serious, a painful blend of the rueful and the tender.

Marianne nodded. It was all she could do not to bite her lip. "It is better to be started on the right footing, my lord. You can no more promise to mend your ways than I can mine!"

"Not a conventional basis for a marriage, but perhaps sound nonetheless."

"Perhaps." She smiled at him. "If I am not dreaming and we really are to do this wretchedly crazy thing—"

"Then I must hurry up. Yes, I know, my own dear shrew! You need to be safely wedded by nightfall. I'm not perfectly certain of all this, but I expect a special license will do the trick."

"Will it be issued?"

"To a peer of the realm? I expect so, especially since the banns have been posted this age. No one need know I am not the *original* Lord Sinclair, you know."

"True. I will wait humbly in this anteroom and not stir an inch."

"You had better not! By the by, do you prefer yellow or violet?"

"Beg pardon?"

"The posy, you know! Daffodils or violets?"

Marianne was much moved by this evident display of thoughtfulness. It seemed an age since anyone had taken her personal tastes into account. "Violets, I thank you."

His lordship nodded. "A good choice. The vivid purple will complement your sultry eyes. I will have a bouquet sent round."

"Not a bouquet! A simple posy will do."

The viscount raised his brows. "Not penny-pinching already, my dear?"

She smiled. Despite the gravity of her situation, his humour was infectious.

"Scrimping and scraping to the manner born! Perhaps I should, after all, be marrying the miser Glaston!"

"I think not. The very thought sends me hastening to do your bidding. Before I leave, is there anything else of great moment I should know?"

"No, I don't think so . . . Oh, good lord!"

"What?"

"Hide me!" Miss Spencer-Pultney dived off her chair and made for the drapes behind the recess.

My lord, understandably puzzled and astonished, looked out of the open window and caught sight of a scrawny, sallow-faced man, slightly effete with tall starched collar points and a unique combination of purple-and-plaid striped vestments. "Who the devil is he?"

"Hush!"

"He cannot hear us from here, Maid Marianne. Who is he, anyway?"

"Peter Mersham." Marianne hissed the words faintly.

"The fair Lila's sibling?"

She nodded. "Despicable little creature. If he were not terrified of Glaston, he would have importuned me no end."

"But he would be—"

"My brother by marriage. Sickening, isn't it?"

The viscount cursed under his breath. "I cannot leave you here, Marianne. The man may divine your whereabouts at any moment. You are safe while you are under my protection."

"I cannot gad about the countryside in search of a preacher!"

"Why not?"

"Think how it will look! I am not chaperoned."

"You may hide under my carriage rug. No one need know you are there. When I have procured the license, we will travel directly to the city and have the ceremony performed."

"No. I am not going to my wedding day looking like something the cat has dragged in."

The viscount sighed, an obstinate scowl descending upon his rugged, carefree features. "I am not leaving you at this dubious inn in the hands of a possible lecher!"

Marianne folded her arms.

"Come out from those curtains, you widgeon!" Reluctantly she did so.

His voice took on a coaxing tone. He was well versed in the art of gentle persuasion. "I will buy you a pretty dress. You may change at my grandmama's house. She was ever a one for a lark, Lady Caiting!"

"I am glad you think this sorry predicament a lark!" Marianne refused to be drawn by bribery. She was just about to say there was nothing wrong with the gown she was wearing, when she caught sight of the deplorable hem and the furbelows that sadly needed refurbishing. Her feminine heart relented.

"Very well, my lord. You may buy me a gown. I will reimburse you when I have consulted my bankers."

The viscount's eyes twinkled, but he was circumspect enough not to reveal his mirth. "Very well, my lady Sinclair!"

Marianne blushed. "We are not yet wed, my lord."

"True, but we shall be before the day is out. There is just another thing that I shall preempt, if I may."

"What is that?"

He drew closer and extended his arm. Gently, very gently, he pulled her toward him and touched her chin lightly with his fingers. Marianne thought she had never felt anything so gentle and giddyingly breathtaking at one and the same moment. It was fortunate that she did draw breath then, for a simple second later she could not. Her mouth was entirely enveloped by that of the personable gentleman before her.

If she felt the former sensation heady, it compared not in the least with what she felt now. The man was sultry and fragrant and beguilingly firm. To her horror she realised her lips were yielding with giddy abandon. Worse, the gap between them had narrowed dangerously, and she had the most lowering feeling that it was she herself who had caused the decreased distance between them. Not that the viscount was objecting, it must be said. His hand was just straying to take advantage of the opportunities cast his way when dawning panic beset his bride to be.

"Stop it at once!" Her eyes sparkled and anger slowly replaced the lazy, wanton contentment of the moment before.

The viscount eyed her warily. His body urged for more slaking of the sudden desire that had sprung up between them. But his chivalrous upbringing and his instinct for self-preservation scolded him. When he spoke, his voice was ragged and slightly self-mocking.

"Beg pardon, Maid Marianne. I had thought my approaches not entirely unwanted."

"Well, they are. Unwilling and unwanted." Shame suffused Marianne's being. She yearned for nothing more than to run from the room and never see the face of this charming, rakish rogue again. She very much feared her feelings were running away with her rationality. Heavens, she could hardly think when he looked at her with those smouldering eyes of passion. Her normally irreproachable body was playing games with her senses, and he, quite villainously, was not playing the part of a gentleman.

Marianne scolded herself for her shamelessness, and her face flamed crimson. The man had made his reasons for the marriage perfectly plain: her fortune and the prevention of an heir to supplant him. He'd as good as told her that any female would suit, since it was his duty to marry. He'd made no promises of fidelity, quite the contrary, and he had compounded these sins by having the brazen effrontery to suggest that she might be shrewish.

Well! He need not think she was some plaything designed solely for his amusement when he happened to have the odd spare moment. If a marriage of convenience it was to be, then so it would be. Nothing more, and certainly nothing in the physical sense. Her eyes met those of her intended, and her body cried out against this unfair edict. To her chagrin, she could see that he read her thoughts, and the coolness in his manner changed subtly to one of amused triumph.

Marianne hated him for that.

"You do not amuse me, my lord!"

"No?" He placed a caressing hand upon her arm. His voice was silken and low. Marianne felt as though his glove were boring through the thin silk of her dress to the creamy, untouched skin beneath.

"Let me go!"

He removed his hand but his searing blue eyes held a slight twinkle. He bowed. "As you wish, my lady."

Marianne suffered silent pangs of desolation. She wanted his warm hand back and the vile man knew it!

"Thank you." She stood upon her dignity, her head held very high. "I trust you shall importune me no further. Not now, nor when we are wed."

For a moment anger sparkled in the man's eyes; then he remembered her yielding lips and revealing blushes. He grinned, confident that her scruples revealed more of her inner desires than the haughty lady might quite have wished. At four and twenty, his lordship the Viscount Hansford had been most fortunate in his dealings with the fairer sex. Truth to tell, he had not been scorned in all his tender years. He did not intend to be now. Not by a bossy little snip of a thing who did not even know how accurately to aim a bandbox.

His smile changed to a slight frown. He would give her a taste of her medicine and make her *beg* for his favours.

He bowed distantly and shuttered his eyes. "Very well, madame. If such is your wish."

Marianne felt her heart sink at his coldness. Then she

brought herself up sternly. If the marriage was consummated she could not ask for an annulment. The only way of securing my lord's freedom—and her own—was to stand firm.

Marianne sighed. She had never before had problems with celibacy. Now she wanted him to smile at her provocatively and lay siege to her senses, as he had but moments before. Instead, she curtsied politely and murmured something rather innocuous about rain.

Four

The viscount masterfully ignored her commonplace utterances. With two swift movements he gathered up her few possessions and rang the bell. He was just issuing instructions when the sound of raised voices entered upon his consciousness.

The startled chambermaid's eyes widened at the sound of the landlord. She dropped her hand from the door frame and stood back a fraction, the better to view the fracas taking place in the corridor.

Miss Spencer-Pultney, wrapped up in her own misery, did not pay much regard. A moment later, however, her reverie came to a rude ending. The door was prised open and her despised relative stood upon the threshold. Fortunately, he had not seen her, so she wisely pulled the bonnet down hard over her face and turned her back to the intruder.

"I told you there was a spare room up here! Why should I have to mingle with the common taproom crowd when there is a cosy fire and a decent collation for the asking?"

My lord stepped forward, and the wrath he felt for Marianne was heaped roundly on her stepbrother's head.

"Perhaps because the intrusion is grossly rude, an assault on my privacy, and infernally bad manners to boot." Marianne had to stifle unbidden laughter at this outrageous set-down. It was so haughtily delivered that she felt, for a moment, that she did not at all know the man who was that day to be her husband.

Peter Mersham's eyes boggled as he looked at his lordship askance.

"And who the devil might you be?"

"That is not to the purpose, sir. I am rather fastidious in my acquaintances."

The landlord gulped. "Beg pardon, my lord, the gentleman was most insistent."

"So I see. I'll not hold the intrusion against you. If you can send down to my grooms I'd be most obliged."

The landlord bowed in visible relief. A spat between gentry was not what he wished to become embroiled in. Most unpleasant. Most unpleasant indeed. He withdrew, the better to disassociate himself from any such goings-on.

Mersham's eyes were boggling in chagrined disbelief. Marianne nearly gave the game away with ill-suppressed merriment. It was an age since she'd seen Peter Mersham receive the comeuppance he deserved.

Her stepbrother glared at Lord Hansford and placed two feet squarely in the door.

"I am a gentleman, sir, and I demand to share this parlour!"

"Unfortunately, it is already occupied." Raoul refused to budge.

Mersham's eyes wandered to the lady at the window, and his mouth turned upwards in a silent sneer. "I see that, my lord! Your bedding had best be done upstairs, however. There is no need to waste a private parlour upon a light-skirt."

My lord's eyes darkened and he felt his hands clench. If it were not for the fact that for the first time in his life he virtuously wished to avoid a scrape, he would have milled the man down without a backward thought.

"Thank you for your advice. Now if you will excuse me, I am about to shut the door." He advanced two paces, and the man was forced to step back a little. Mersham eyed the viscount narrowly and decided from the cut of his coat and the hauteur of his bearing that he would do well to placate him.

"No need to stand upon ceremony, my lord! I tell you what. Leave me with the collation and possibly the filly over there and I will reward you handsomely." Peter Mersham had the strangest notion that all gentlemen were as heavily in debt as he. The thought simply did not occur to him that a pecuniary bribe of this nature might not have an instant appeal.

Despite herself, Marianne gasped. The man was outrageous! In a twinkling the viscount was at her side. She felt a painful pinch, surreptitiously placed, and knew that he meant to warn her. This was no time for missish indignation, no matter how self-righteous.

"I thank you, but no. My answer remains firm on this point." The viscount's voice was quiet, but dangerous lights flashed into his eyes. Peter Mersham, ever one to stubbornly root his feet where they had no business, did not take up the hint. Instead he cast an experienced eye over Marianne and announced that he could not see what the fuss was about anyway.

Miss Spencer-Pultney emitted an undignified hiss under her bonnet. His lordship's lips twitched. He was convinced that his bride could deliver a veritable tongue-lashing if she chose. He would have been quite diverted to hear it, but the risk of unnecessary scandal would be too great. For her own sake, the Viscountess Hansford must be beyond reproach.

Drawing himself up to his full, not inconsiderable height, he addressed himself to the interloper.

"Enough of this, my good man! The conversation fa-

tigues me more than the sight of your face." He turned
to Marianne, who still faced the window. "My dear, if you
are ready, we shall leave this . . . this . . . *person* to the rem-
nants of our repast."

Mr. Mersham was taken aback. He had not expected
such a sudden capitulation. Worse, the thought now occurred to him that it might be *he* saddled in the end with
the tab for this meal. He was just composing an inarticulate
but nonetheless blustery response when the viscount
stepped forward, took Marianne in his arms so that her
face was wholly obscured, and moved with remarkable
swiftness towards the open door. Down the hall, several
housemaids had found it necessary to commence a frenzy
of dusting and polishing.

Marianne found she liked the warmth of my lord's chest
as she nestled in a trifle deeply. Only, she told herself
firmly, because she did not want the odious Peter Mersham
to catch a glimpse of her face. Nothing could be more
lowering than that, she was convinced.

If my lord's heart beat a trifle faster at the feel of her
evident charms, she was none the wiser, never before having had the felicity of being so close to a gentleman such
as he.

"You cannot simply remove yourselves!" The bluster became more voluble. Mersham's panic increased a smidgen.
His suspicious little mind was perfectly certain the pair
meant to do a runner on him, leaving *him* to pay the shot
for the night's entertainment. He moved menacingly toward Lord Raoul. It was true that his bulk was prodigious,
but more, his lordship reckoned, from overindulgence
with sugar plums than from months of scientific training
at Jackson's boxing saloon.

He pulled at his lordship's sleeve. Marianne buried her
head in his chest and willed herself to stop trembling. His
lordship might scorn Mersham's capabilities, but she did

not. She had, after all, lived in hourly fear of them, and old habits certainly died hard.

"Unhand me this instant or I shall not answer for the consequences!" His lordship's tone was biting.

Mersham, already a trifle in his cups and made bolder by the combined forces of blue ruin and the obvious fact that he was bigger than his quarry, squeezed all the tighter. Roused to fury, Raoul set Marianne down. The chance for a mill seemed unavoidable and, truth to tell, his eyes gleamed with sudden devilment. The man needed a lesson, and his knuckles were itching to give it.

Marianne saw what was about to happen and stepped back out of the fray. Her bonnet had been loosened as she was set down, so it was urgently necessary to set it to rights. The last thing she needed was Peter's prying eyes upon her.

Mersham rolled up his sleeves. His eyes strayed for an instant to Miss Spencer-Pultney, who was engaged in the annoying task of untangling a knot, keeping her wits about her, and at one and the same time looking as inconspicuous as a noisome fly on the wall. When she accidentally knocked over a salver of Westphalian ham in her urge to step into the shadows, she found she'd spectacularly failed in all three. Mersham's eyes came to rest upon her, and her bonnet was looser than ever, her wits entirely scattered and the focus of the room directed fearsomely upon herself.

"Marianne Spencer-Pultney or I will be damned." The look in the man's face turned from astonished surprise to calculating cunning. "A lover's tryst, I see! I knew you were no better than you ought to be!"

Marianne glared at him. "It is not what you think, Mr. Mersham."

"No? What else can I think of a slut like you? I'll take

this gentleman's pickings when he is through, or the Earl of Glaston shall be apprised of this day's work."

Marianne was just formulating a biting retort when her admiration for her intended increased a thousandfold. It had been with a deft sidestep and hardly any show of force that he landed the brawny Mersham a facer he'd not soon forget. Her good opinion further increased when my lord the viscount followed this piece of violence with a delectably deft left hook.

Peter Mersham staggered, then sank to his knees. His nose was bloodied and his menacing lips did not look quite as threatening as before. In a matter of seconds he emitted a sonorous groan and fell flat upon his well-padded stomach.

Marianne clapped. "Excellent, my lord! A regular out-and-outer!"

He looked up and grinned. "I had expected to find you in a swoon upon the floor. Beg pardon, ma'am."

Her eyes lit with infectious laughter. "No pardons required, I assure you. Is that odious man awakening?"

His lordship looked at his prey. "No, but I think we had better do something to set him to rights."

"Whatever for?"

"I need to have a little talk with this wholly inebriated piece of devil's work."

"What sort of talk?" Marianne was aware that the coldness between them had vanished, and she was glad of it.

"You will see. Fetch me that pitcher, if you will."

Marianne understood and was well pleased with the projected plan. She tripped over to the side table and selected the Sevres jug filled with lemonade.

"May I?" she asked.

His lordship grinned, then shrugged. "Little shrew. You are enjoying all this, I'll warrant!"

"Indeed I am, sir! Peter Mersham has deserved his comeuppance this age."

Something in her tone sobered him. He determined that the lady most truly needed the protection of his name. If a tiny thought niggled that he was once again in the very depths of a scrape, he ignored it.

"By all means, then, do the honours."

Miss Spencer-Pultney's eyes gleamed with mischief as she poured the lemonade over her victim. There was a shocked gasp in the corridor, indicating very surely that the dusting was getting less attention than possibly it deserved. Raoul moved to shut the door while the step-brother Mersham gasped at the newest outrage against his person. He sat up, suddenly very sober.

"I'll kill you for this, you and your little piece."

"Call the lady anything of that sort ever again and the boot will be on the other foot. As surely as my name is Alistair Raoul Griffin Sinclair, Viscount Hansford, you shall answer for it."

The name meant nothing to Peter. He was too angry and too pained to make the obvious connection.

"The little vixen is no better than she should be, and so I shall inform Glaston when next I see him. She shall be sorry for this day's work, I assure you!" Mersham's tone was recklessly defiant. He was still too foxed to detect the dangerous light in his lordship's sapphire blue eyes.

"Your impertinence is unspeakable. I forgive it only in deference to your ignorance. The *lady*, I take leave to inform you, was this day married."

Marianne looked up sharply. He could feel her quick intake of breath and willed her to be silent. She was, but the effort was considerable.

Mersham's eyes widened in disbelief and something akin to horror and mirth combined.

"Never say you *married* the chit?"

"The *lady*. Mind your manners, Mersham. I will not warn you again, and you've had only a *taste* of my brand of punishment."

Mersham fingered his chin. A bruise was already faintly detectable beneath the skin.

"I'll say not a word more, my lord. 'Tis a rare joke, that is all. If you married her for her fortune you can whistle *that* to the wind. She inherits not a ha'penny unless she weds the Earl of Glaston. If you'd done your homework a little better you would not now be shackled with a dowerless bride."

"You are dangerously close to another taste of my fist, sir! Let me assure you, however, that you are not to disturb yourself on my account. The viscountess inherits quite a fortune under the terms of her great-aunt's will. I am, as I have already mentioned, Alistair, Lord Sinclair."

This time the implication of his lordship's birth name truly sank into the injured man's addled brain. The look of triumph that had momentarily crossed his face gave way to impotent fury. Marianne moved instinctively toward the viscount.

His arms responded instantly, cradling her in such a warmly instinctive manner that it seemed her hips moulded to him of their own volition. In truth, the closeness was unexpectedly strange to the innocent Miss Spencer-Pultney, who found her concentration diverted most unaccountably from the matter at hand.

My lord, too, felt the stirrings of a passion not altogether directed at Mr. Peter Mersham. An inner voice warned him he was in a heap of trouble. A marriage of convenience was one thing if it was convenient. It was another thing altogether if disturbing sensations kept arising to confuse otherwise clear-cut issues. He would have to keep his wits about him and his wandering eye firmly in check. The lady would be his wife, but he would not be leg-shackled to her. In the future, he would keep his distance. For now, he took leave to hold her closer, the better to shield her from the ravening eye of the man before him.

"The viscountess and I have wasted enough time with you, Mersham. Feel free to help yourself to the remains of our repast. And now, good day." Without a further word, he steered Marianne out of the room and down the long flight of stairs that led to sunshine outside.

True to his word, the landlord had ordered the carriage drawn up. The matter of settlement was quickly effected by the viscount, who breezily drew out a gold sovereign and placed it firmly in eager hands. The landlord was effusive in his thanks and was still seen bowing even as the occupants of the chaise had long since forgotten his existence. His brow creased heavily as he made for indoors. It was unlikely indeed that the other young gentleman would be as free with his blunt. It was time to politely remind him of his obligations.

The silence in the conveyance was oppressive. My lord's hauteur had returned, and Marianne was uncomfortable in the extreme. His closeness sent a delicious tingling down her spine, but for the life of her she could detect no such reaction in the stiff demeanour of the person before her.

It was hardly known whether she would have been discomforted or relieved to know that my lord's silence stemmed not from coldness but from far too strong a degree of warmth. The ladies my lord had hitherto dallied with had never been either innocent or ladies, in the strict use of the term.

It had therefore never before been his lordship's lot to devise ways of controlling his own impulses, or of forcing his eye to fix on the squabs rather than on the delicious piece of ankle just making its appearance from under damask skirts.

He scowled. Trust him to be engaged on a lengthy carriage trip with a young woman whose perfume was beguiling, eyes bewitching, and figure entrancing. These factors were not what annoyed him so. What annoyed him was his patent inability to do anything about the situation. For the first time, the hideous spectre of a chaperon made sense to his smitten wits. She was saying something. He'd missed the words.

"Beg pardon?" His voice sounded frosty, even to him.

Marianne's eyes faltered under his gaze. She had the most lowering sensation she was making an enormous mistake. "Why did you tell Mersham that tarradiddle, my lord?"

"Which one?"

She blushed. "The one that we are already wed, my lord."

"Raoul. To stop his tattlemongering, if possible. I thought it might make the tale more likely if he knew you were to inherit, after all."

"He will be livid!"

"I daresay. Can't be helped. The only thing that is now imperative is that I get the special license before dusk. There will be no averting a scandal if I cannot. The man is not the type to keep his mouth long shut."

"I am a trial to you. Are you sure you wish to go through with this?"

The only thing my lord was sure of was that Miss Marianne had an intriguing scent and that her closeness was altogether too discomforting. As for second thoughts . . . his stomach squirmed at the very idea of what he was doing. More and more he felt that Raphael would firmly place it in the "prank" category. And after he'd cut up so stiff about his last flight of fancy!

Raoul's thoughts flitted to the well-endowed hussy who'd nearly cost him his life in a duel. Had she been worth it? He thought not. Looking at Marianne, staring anxiously at him from out of lashes of deep, deep dark, he thanked heaven she was cut from a different cloth altogether. Surely everyone must recognise that? Lady Caiting would, but his mama? Would Lady Sinclair welcome this new daughter? If the deed were done, she would.

Raoul allowed his frosty demeanour to thaw just a little. "Perfectly certain, Maid Marianne!"

Miss Spencer-Pultney's throat constricted just a little. When he was charming, he was devastatingly so. She would have to watch herself, for falling in love with him would be calamitous. Not when he'd so clearly stated for her edification that one female would be as good as another when it came to marriage. She must cease to hold antiquated notions of wedded bliss and sanctity. It was fashionable now to be unfaithful. She was perfectly certain Raoul intended to be so.

"Good. Then if you don't mind, I'll rest a little." She closed her eyes.

To the viscount's astonishment, he found he *did* mind. He minded quite dreadfully. While the thing he detested most was a chattering female, he found himself quite at a loss confronted, as he was, with ruby red lips invitingly closed and just a hairsbreadth from his shoulder.

Worse, he found Maid Marianne's conversations engagingly unfettered by missish restraints. For the first time, he actually enjoyed conversing with a female. He shook his head ruefully. Perhaps he was sickening for something. With a sigh, he closed his own eyes. Sleep did not provide heaven-sent relief. If anything, it evaded him like a teasing gypsy, leaving him discomforted and highly irritable. Once he opened his eyes and found Maid Marianne staring at his chiselled features. She had shut her eyes at once, but he'd not been deceived. The lady was awake and taking the most unfair opportunity of scrutinising him to her heart's content.

Raoul Alistair Griffin Sinclair felt a damnable sense of ill-usage. Here she had initiated the sleep idea, and it was he who was obliged to endure the trip with his alert eyes closed and his restless body composed into the inert lines of slumber. He would not do it! He sat up with a jerk just as the left stallion missed its footing. He was catapulted headlong into his betrothed's delicious lap. He lifted his head to beg pardon, then thought better of it.

Marianne's impure thoughts seemed destined to fruition. His eyes raked her up and down, and Marianne felt little shivers of hitherto unknown excitement run right through her being. Unconsciously, her mouth parted and her hand extended in his direction. He groaned and planted a featherlight kiss upon her lips. Marianne's head reeled, and she found herself losing all sense of well-ingrained propriety.

Just as his lordship was about to renew his acquaintance with her lips, he remembered his vow. Maid Marianne would have to beg him for his favours or she would receive none. He would not be played fast and loose on the whim of a woman.

He sat up and straightened his cravat. "I will *importune* you no further, madame."

Marianne cringed both at his tone and at his acid reminder of the very word she had used to describe his tumultuous advances. If anything, she was honest and knew that such a description was unjustly applied in the light of her own eager reaction. She wanted to apologise, but his lips were so tightly closed and his eyes so forbidding that she simply sank back into her seat.

The rest of the trip was uneventful. The scenery was charming, but neither occupant of the well-sprung chaise had the heart to notice.

Five

Lady Amber Sinclair was not aware of a pair of watchful—and wistful—eyes upon her as she raced wildly across the downs. Her short, Grecian hairstyle perfectly framed her face as she allowed her bonnet to be taken up by the wind.

Her groom reined in and tried to retrieve it, but she only snapped her fingers and laughed. "Leave it, Williams! Let it fly high in the sky and be a slave only to the breezes. It was not meant, I am sure, to be pinned down and tied."

Her groom nodded and settled into a gentle trot. Lady Amber might have strange notions in her noggin, but she was gentle and beautiful and the kindest mistress a groom could ever wish for. If she enjoyed seeing her bonnet flying high like a kite, ribbons unfurling prettily in the gusts, he would not deny her the pleasure. Doubtless there would be some varmint on the estate glad of the bounty cast his way. He would have been surprised to know that the "varmint" who finally did reach out for the bonnet was none other than Raphael Delaware, Marquis of Slade.

In a pensive mood, he deliberated on whether to spur his stallion into a gallop and chase after her. The bonnet would provide a perfect opportunity for furthering their acquaintance. His hand was already on the reins when the crushing thought struck him that the lady might not be pleased to have her bonnet so summarily returned. He would look foolish trying to explain what he was doing lurking on the downs when he was supposed to be working on the repeal of the Corn Laws bill for Parliament.

He sighed and turned the horse around. His consuming desire for Lady Amber Sinclair was becoming ridiculous. She seemed not to notice his suit as he daily found excuses to haunt her family home. Had he not pulled her rapscallion brother Raoul out of the boughs several times on her account? Had he not showered her with posies, escorted her to country dances, and even stomached the delights of bohea tea on her behalf?

He had, and each time she had bewitched him with her teasing smile and the flickering lights that danced merrily in her eyes. Not that they were always merry. Sometimes, he noted, they were sober and etched with the cynicism that beset him, too. Those times he ached to reach out and declare himself a kindred spirit. Did he? No. The redoubtable, most sought-after bachelor in all the land did not. The greatest, wickedest, most rakish flirt in the entire kingdom and beyond felt his tongue tied and his rapierlike wit befuddled utterly. It was a strange and bitterly annoying fact that confronted with society's most glittering diamond, my lord was mute.

For the thousandth time that week he cursed himself for a fool. He tied the bonnet to his saddle and turned his horse around.

"Afternoon, Slade!"

Lord Delaware turned his piercing dark eyes on the portly gentleman just heaving himself into one of the sumptuous leather chairs at Brooks.

He inclined his head with a small smile and acknowledged the greeting. Sir Godfrey Barnham was a mere acquaintance, but reasonably affable nonetheless.

"Good afternoon to you, too, sir!" He dipped his pen into ink and hoped that Sir Godfrey would take the hint. He did not wish to be disobliging, but there was the Corn Law to consider, and keeping his mind on *that* was trying enough. His thoughts kept flitting to the beauty whose heart remained whole despite his several attempts at conquest.

Amber was unquestionably the model of everything he could wish in his life. He was tired of his bachelorhood, of the endless rounds of partying, of the several—and very different—ladies who ended up in his bed night after night. He felt jaded and lonely. At four and thirty that was a terrible place to be, especially where the cure seemed quite unreachable. Lady Amber consistently turned down her suitors. Unkind rumours were now calling her the unconquerable. *Insufferable!* Raphael's eyes sparked at the thought, and poor Sir Godfrey retired to his newspaper, wondering what he'd said to bring on a look so stormy.

For far too long now, Lord Raphael Delaware had watched with jealous interest the pursuit of her many admirers. As he whirled around the dance floor with the pick of the season's beauties languishing at his every gesture and mood, his thoughts had been only for one. One incomparable, whose humour was intoxicating and whose wit was as sharp as his own. At first he'd not minded the steady clamour for her hand by all the dandies of Brighton and beyond.

Every lady was entitled to adulation, but it did not cross his mind that she would accept buffoons like Kingsley or Cross. When more astute men joined the fray, his heart had leaped in anxiety. His own friends, Kilcross and Anthony . . . he could practically not bring himself to speak to them. The relief he felt when she turned them down soon turned to panic. If they, honourable men, were not good enough, how could he be so presumptuous as to hope?

He sighed. The problem was, she saw him as an elder brother. Waltzes where his every nerve tingled to the point where he had forcibly to restrain himself from losing the proper distance were lost on her. Inevitably she would smile her wide, charming, infernally sensuous smile and ask him about the horse sales or Raoul or the Slade estates . . . all worthy topics, but hardly the subjects closest to his heart at such exquisite moments. Of course, his answers would translate themselves into monosyllables as his brain tried fervently to reassert authority over his heart and his superbly masculine body.

At times he would feel a flicker of something electric between them. He would sense her gaze boring into him from beneath her smoky lashes. His being would respond instantly in turn, but when he would look up, murmur some small endearment, or move closer, she would always flush with embarrassment and gently turn his thoughts to more commonplace things. When she lost her self-consciousness, her humour was infectious. She had such a strong sense of the ridiculous that Raphael could not rid himself of the notion that she was a kindred spirit. One sent, at times, to try him.

A few letters slashed across his crisp, cream wafer. The speech was writing itself, it seemed. Several men took up chairs beside him but none disturbed the eminent Lord Delaware. Anyone could see he was grappling with the great problems of the day. For an instant Raphael considered what he had written. Too patronising! He would begin again.

"Raphael!"

Raphael sighed. It was Kingsley. "What do you want, Richard?"

"Good afternoon to you, too!" His friend grinned and took a seat.

Raphael wiped the pen dry and tore up the sheet. The gods, evidently, were conspiring against him.

"Did you see the newest bet laid in the book?"

"Not yet. I had thought to catch up a little on more weighty matters." His friend nodded, but there was a mischievous twinkle in his eye that matched his provocative response.

"Doubtless that was why I found you daydreaming with your head in the clouds!"

Raphael flashed him a comradely smile. "Doubtless! So what was this notable bet, then? Anything interesting?"

Kingsley flushed. "I'm in the devil of a quandary about it, dear fellow."

"Tell me." The marquis's tone was a slight drawl.

"You know that I once cherished a deep affection for Lady Amber Sinclair?"

Raphael sat up straighter and his attention became suddenly alert.

"Possibly I had detected something of the kind."

The irony of this understatement was lost on Kingsley. "Yes, well, I put it to the touch and she turned me down."

Raphael nodded. He would never tell his dear friend how his traitorous heart had leaped at the news.

"And now?"

"And now there is a bet on whether Cardamon has suffered the same fate. The duke was becoming awfully particular in his attentions, you know."

Raphael did know. The good Freddie had come perilously close to having a sword run through his heart. Every day Raphael lived with the dread of an imminent announcement. Surely Amber could not refuse the illustrious rank of duchess? Especially as the duke was so wholly devoid of a single shred of malice. Of course, he was not the brightest star in the heavens, but intelligence was not always seen as a virtue when selecting a spouse.

"What are the odds?"

"Five to one she has rejected him."

Raphael felt himself breathe. "How so?"

"An announcement was expected at the Duchess of Cardamon's ball. None occurred, and rumour has it Lady Amber did not attend."

Relief flooded through the marquis. So that was why Lady Amber had been on pins when he'd suggested offering her his escort. His heart lightened immeasurably, then focused disapprovingly on the more immediate matter at hand.

"It is an execrable bet!"

"I know. Had I been her affianced, I would have scotched it in a minute!"

"Had you been her affianced, the bet would not have been laid."

Kingsley looked rueful. "True. Strictly speaking, Hansford should be apprised of this. I am sure he would not like his sister's name bandied about on the betting books."

Raphael's face looked grim. "Indeed not. Leave it to me. I may have something to say in this matter."

He rose, his demeanour entirely forbidding. Not until he had personally scotched the bet from the book did his features relax. When they did, he took quick leave of the place and ordered his carriage sent home. It was too fine a day to drive.

As he paced the busy street, enjoying for the first time the delights and smells, hustle and bustle around him, he threw a coin to a beggar and of an impulse bought a sweet puff pastry from a street vendor on the corner. Though she threw him a ravishing glance and made a very flirtatious curtsy, my lord did not notice a thing.

His head was too full of thoughts of poor, rejected Cardamon. He was still smiling when he reached his town house off Grosvenor Square. He might not have been so, however, if he knew that new bets were now being placed. This time, speculation focused entirely on himself. Odds were two to one that the Marquis of Slade was in love at last.

"Sir Clive Grandison, ma'am."

"Send him in, Carstairs." The butler nodded and withdrew. Two minutes later, a gentleman in his late forties appeared at the doorway. He was tanned, and time had been most kind to him. His face held none of the revealing little wrinkles of some of his peers. His eyes were intelligent, lively, and warm as they took in Lady Sinclair's receiving room and all the little oddments that she held so dear.

"Good morning, my lady!"

"Good morning, Sir Clive!" Her pretty face broke out into a welcoming smile as she stood up and extended her hand. To her surprise, he bent over it and kissed it. His eyes held more than passing warmth as he retained his grip a little longer than strictly he ought to have.

Lady Sinclair flushed, but her smile was demure as she bade him take a seat near the newly kindled fire. "For I know," she said, "that England must seem passing cold after the warmth of the Mediterranean sun."

Sir Clive smiled. "It is an age since I've seen you, Lady Jane. I must confess that the eastern sun pales into insignificance when I am confronted with your radiance."

Lady Sinclair arched her brow. "Flummery, sir!"

He grinned. "Still a straight talker, I see."

She inclined her head. "Will you take tea?"

"Have pity on me, my dear! The English and their tea! One forgets."

"You will not forget the burgundy I have laid down?"

"I knew there was a reason I love you, my dear. Yes, a burgundy will be perfect."

She was not gone long, for hers was a well-run household and Carstairs had obligingly stationed a footman in the hall. Her heart was beating as wildly as if she were just sixteen. She pulled herself up sternly. He had said he loved her. Again. She shook her head. She was a matron of three and forty, well past the age for wild flights of fancy.

When the desired beverage appeared, she was glad to see that she had not been disappointed in her choice of housekeeper. The salver was laden with cheeses of various descriptions and some of her own plum preserves. The bread laid out upon the plate was as white as snow and freshly baked.

Sir Clive eyed the delicacy with appreciation. "How do you manage so fine a bread? The wheat in London is appalling." He made a gesture of distaste. "Some say it is contaminated with chalk."

"A great deal of it is. That is why this wheat is drawn off Raoul's estates and ground specially. What the household does not use is distributed among the vagrants. It is a good arrangement, for I cannot abide either waste or bitter bread!"

"I love you more with every word you speak."

"Stop this, Sir Clive!" Lady Sinclair's tone was admonishing, but her eyes smiled and there was a whisper of pink to her cheeks.

"Have you thought over my proposition?"

"Which one?"

"The one where I marry you and whisk you off to the wilds of India or the shores of the Cape, or plain Brighton or Bath or wherever the fancy happens to take you."

"Horrors!"

"Horrors to your marrying me?"

"No, silly man. Horrors to Brighton or Bath. If I marry I must definitely be whisked off somewhere more suitable."

"Greece?"

"Greece might do."

"Then you will?"

"This is a hypothetical proposition, Sir Clive!"

"Hypothetical be damned, woman! Have I not given you ample time?"

Lady Sinclair twisted her fingers, and for the first time she looked uncomfortable. "I thought you had, Sir Clive, but it seems I was wrong."

"You do not know your mind, then?" His voice became harsh and a little ragged.

"I know my mind. The trouble is, my daughter does not."

Sir Clive looked puzzled. "What has Lady Amber to do with our marriage? Does she oppose it in some way?"

"Indeed not, Sir Clive! I detect a teasing note of approval occasionally, when she speaks of you!"

"That is a relief. I would not have her feel I was trying to supplant her father or any such thing."

"Not at all. She is too good to wish to put an obstacle in my way. Her papa's memory will always be dear—as it will to me—but she would not deny me happiness if it came my way."

"And so?"

Lady Sinclair swallowed and sat down with a sigh.

"I had thought she would wed this season."

"She has had offers enough!"

"True, but none to her taste."

Sir Clive paced the room, trying to be patient but finding the exertion both difficult and bewildering. "If it is a question of where she is to live . . ."

"Not that!"

"What, then?"

"I cannot marry you, then go gadding about the continent like a free spirit. My daughter must be properly settled before I can think of my own wishes."

"Then your wishes are . . . ?"

Lady Sinclair smiled. "I would be a fool if they were not inclined favourably towards you, Sir Clive!"

He breathed a visible sigh. "Then there is no problem! We have only to marry the gorgeous Lady Amber off to an equally gorgeous . . . who shall we select?"

"I think the lady has some say in that, sir!"

"Has she?"

"She has indeed. Very suitable, too, if I could just get both parties to stop playing ducks and drakes and realise the fact at one and the same time!"

"In short, my dear Lady Sinclair, you wish to forgo the pleasures of matrimony for the wiles of matchmaking!"

Her eyes twinkled. "You have it in a nutshell, Sir Clive, but may I substitute the word 'delay' for the word 'forgo'?"

"With all my heart, Lady Sinclair. If you refuse to marry me until your daughter is wed, so be it. It is better than your refusing me altogether, and since Lady Amber is hardly an antidote, I shall hope for a speedy reversal of my fortunes."

Lady Jane smiled. Neither noticed the young woman of five and twenty who stood stock-still at the open door. When they did look up, she was gone.

Lady Amber took a seat in the library and looked out the window with unseeing eyes. How could she have been so selfish? Or blind? She never dreamed that her dear mother had formed an attachment, or that her own stupidly high standards in a husband might prove an obstacle to that romance.

She thought back to the times when Sir Clive had called in between trips to the Orient, Africa, Italy, Greece, Paris, and Spain. A free spirit, she'd called him, and been glad every time she'd renewed the acquaintance. It had never crossed her mind that Sir Clive had intentions any more than simple friendliness, or that her mother might yearn for more tangible freedoms than the running of her household or the sewing of exquisitely stitched shawls and table linen.

She grew crimson when she thought how she had wickedly teased her mama and made sidelong jokes about his intentions. She had never been in true earnest. Quite simply, the notion of Sir Clive in the marrying category had simply never struck her. Such a confirmed bachelor! Such a noted scholar! And yet . . . what could be more suitable? Her mother was young, alert, and pretty. Beneath the calm exterior there lay an affectionate heart and a frothy sense of humour. Why should she not have her happiness?

Lady Amber sighed. The whole thing led round in circles to herself again. If only she could have accepted Freddie! He was good and kind. She did not consider his rank. If anything, she thought being a duchess too stifling for her independent, often impetuous ways. Still, Freddie would have been an excellent, solicitous husband. She could not—she *should* not—have asked for more.

Yet she did. Thoughts of the urbane Lord Raphael Delaware ubiquitously dimmed the gloss of every suitor she encountered. Even the most modishly dressed paled in brief comparison with his athletic figure and simple, impeccable, stylish good taste. She had heard him speak in the House, and since then every oration she heard seemed uninspired. She had seen him ride with the winds, and from then on every mount seemed a dullard, every rider a poor second.

Lord Anthony and Lord Maracas had both assayed chaste pecks upon her cheek. They had moved her not at all. Several more daring young rakes had laid siege to her soft, pink lips. They had not yielded an inch. And yet, when Raphael looked at her with burning dark eyes, her mouth yearned for a taste of his kisses and her cheeks flushed at the very thought. They were hot now, just thinking of him. She put her hands to her face and sighed. If only life were simple, if only her mother were right. But how could she be? Lord Delaware was everything that was proper and nothing more. He treated her with the friendly civility of a sister. Maddening, maddening, maddening!

"Engrossed in your thoughts?"

"Mama! I thought you were with Sir Clive."

"He left a few minutes ago and sent you his compliments."

"He is a lovely man."

Lady Sinclair nodded decisively. "That he is."

"Mama, I have been thinking."

Lady Sinclair looked at her dear only daughter and chuckled. "Excellent! I was beginning to wonder if you would *ever* make use of your prodigious faculties!"

"I am serious."

"So am I. Dare I hope you have been pondering our little discussion?"

Amber coloured. "That and other things. I've decided to set up an establishment of my own. I am five and twenty now, well able to do so without the proverbial raised eyebrows."

"In your dotage, in fact."

"Mama . . ."

Lady Sinclair raised her hand. "Don't talk such fustian

to me, Amber! You are a highly beautiful, highly intelligent diamond of the first water. If you think to be donning mobcaps and hiring some ancient companion to while away the rest of your spinsterish days, it simply won't fadge!"

"It shall not be like that. I shall have my own carriage, my independence. . . ."

"What of a certain Lord Delaware?"

"Mama, I am convinced you are mistaken in his feelings."

Lady Jane felt a most unladylike urge to shake her dearest daughter. Instead, she vented her spleen upon an intricately wrought fan that promptly snapped under the traumas of such ill-usage.

"Is this yours? I am sorry, Amber, but that is the price you must pay for talking such utter nonsense."

Lady Amber stared at her mother openmouthed.

"Yes, stare if you will! Your stubborn refusal to see what is in front of your very eyes has caused this most—I cannot stress it enough—*most* undignified outpouring from my lips."

Amber grinned. "I know you to be capable of far worse, Mama! Don't forget I have often enough stood by when you've been apprised of Raoul's latest pranks and misadventures."

"True! My failings catch up with me, but when the dear scamp will learn, I have no notion! Thank heavens he has been extricated from the clutches of that devilish Dunning woman."

Pleased to turn her mother's thoughts away from her own trials, Amber agreed. "I wonder what he will be up to next?"

Lady Sinclair shuddered. "Even the speculation calls for a restorative! Join me?"

Amber nodded. The remainder of the afternoon passed

in quiet contemplation of possible brides for the young Viscount Hansford. Both ladies would have been astonished to know how futile were their reflections, or how imminent their meeting with the newest Viscountess Hansford.

Six

"Well, we have the special license!" Raoul's tone was triumphant as he fingered the precious paper.

Miss Spencer-Pultney dimpled at him. "True, by dint of a little trickery!"

"It is not trickery to state that the banns have been posted this age."

"Glaston might have something to say to that!"

Raoul chuckled. The thought of foiling his blustering, nipfarthing, sanctimonious old skinflint of a relative greatly encouraged him in this, his latest—and possibly last—little foray into the realm of the female sex.

"The Earl of Glaston, my dear, is not coming!"

"Thank heavens for that. Raoul?"

"Yes?"

He was smiling, and Marianne felt her heart skip a beat. The chilling atmosphere of the carriage ride had given way to something a lot more congenial on both sides. Perhaps it was the relief of securing the license without hitch; perhaps it was their equal desire to score a point off the miserly earl. Whatever the reason, amity had been restored, and Marianne's only real concern was that her heart performed unaccountable somersaults on each occasion she caught the viscount's eye.

"You are certain about this?"

Lord Sinclair noted the anxiety in her tone but waved it away with a vague and airy nod. "I've been in worse predicaments, I can tell you that!"

Marianne was not sure she liked being categorised as a predicament, but honesty compelled her to face the truth of his statement. She must never forget that to her handsome new husband, that was all she was. The latest and very newest kind of scrape. She sighed, but if Lord Sinclair noticed, he did not comment. Instead, he cheerfully pointed out that if they continued their excellent pace, they might even make it home in time for dinner.

Marianne was appalled. Dinner with Lady Sinclair? The thought had not yet crossed her mind, but now it did, and her anxiety increased triplefold.

Raoul took pity on her and patted her cheek. It felt deliciously soft in his hand, but he sternly refused to dwell on this point. Maid Marianne had made her feelings perfectly clear in this regard. He would not play the role of a moonstruck husband only to be thwarted at every turn. No, if there was a lesson to learn, she would be the one doing the learning. It was a promising start that she appeared to blush at his every caress. He would dwell no further on the subject.

"My mama will not eat you, you know."

Marianne did not know, but she managed to sniff bravely. The sun streaked across his lordship's jaunty blond locks as he nodded his approval.

"There, that is better! I daresay my sister Amber will be in high grig when she makes your acquaintance! She is forever on at me about finding a wife, though I must say it is really a bit rich, since she seems to make a habit of turning down ardent admirers."

"Is she very pretty, then?"

Raoul grinned. "Devastating! She has golden guinea

hair and bright green eyes. She is irresistible, in short, to all mankind."

Marianne thought miserably of her own dark features and midnight hair. She did not reflect on how her wide eyes glowed or on how her long tresses shone like satin. The fact that her lashes curled delightfully and that her lips were a wide, provocative ruby red did not seem of consequence. What mattered was that Raoul deemed his sister magnificent and *she,* little Maid Marianne, was the reverse of everything he described.

His lordship settled back into his seat, wholly unaware of how unsettling his words of comfort had been. Marianne stole a glance at his youthful features and wondered, not for the first time, how different this marriage would be had it been motivated by something other than convenience and rather too large a degree of impish devilry.

Had she but known it, my lord was occupied upon similar reflections. Her scent was tantalising him, and he longed to brush a tiny wisp of hair from her dense, black, and utterly unfathomable lashes. With an effort he maintained his position by the window, dispelling his agitation with more than a passing interest in the ladies and gentlemen of fashion who tooled along the busy London road. From time to time he bowed or waved or simply inclined his head. His acquaintances, to Marianne, seemed prodigious.

She shrank back into the squabs, unwilling to be noticed by society. People would think it unconscionable, indeed, for her to be riding unaccompanied in a closed chaise with his lordship. She still had difficulty in believing that in a few minutes she would have every right to be riding in such a scandalous manner. As the Viscountess Hansford, she would be beyond reproach.

"Sit back!"

"I beg pardon?"

Raoul, for the first time, looked anxious. "I see my dearest friend Raphael Delaware not two carriages away. I most particularly wish to avoid him before we are wed."

Marianne did not ask questions. She had a horrible feeling that the dearest friend of her husband-to-be might not be too enraptured at the viscount's latest scheme. Truth to tell, she would not blame him in the slightest. Marrying on such scant notice was the most harebrained notion that had ever beset her. She wondered now why she had agreed.

"Double damnation!"

"What?"

"He has seen us!"

"Us?"

"Me. Us. Oh, what does it signify? Sink down deeper and cover yourself with the travelling blanket."

Marianne did not demur. She took up the blanket and sank down as low as she could, nobly oblivious to the ache in her ankle and the indignity of her position.

"He is waving up the carriage!"

"Will the groom stop?"

"He will if he sees it is the Marquis of Slade! No one ever denies him, you know." There was an element of pride in this utterance.

Marianne's heart sank as she covered herself with renewed fervour. True to Raoul's speculation, the carriage was being drawn up, and it was less than a few moments before Lord Delaware had ordered his own equipage sent home.

"Raoul!"

The viscount shot a glance at the blanket and cleared his throat nervously.

"Good day to you, Raphael! Awfully sorry not to stop, but I'm in a tearing hurry."

The marquis looked at him sideways. Raoul was behav-

ing with transparent guilt. He wondered, for an instant,
what lark his young friend was kicking up this time.

"Take me up with you, then. I've just sent the curricle
on and could do with the company."

Since this was patently true and the viscount could not
desert his friend upon a bustling London track, he dis-
piritedly opened the door and made room for the illustrious nobleman. His demeanour, however, could not have
been gloomier. Lord Delaware, taking a shrewd glance at
the lad, sighed. Another scrape, or he was not the Marquis
of Slade, born and bred.

"Why the hurry, my pigeon?"

"Hurry? Did I say hurry?" Raoul looked at him from
guilty eyes. "Perhaps I could just set you down at Grosvenor Square. . . ."

The marquis nodded, his suspicions confirmed. His
keen eyes made out the travelling blanket, and he grinned
quietly to himself. He did not deny the young buck his
fun, even if he had rung a peal over him at the completion
of the Dunning affair.

Marianne sneezed. The marquis's shoulders shook as
he sternly ordered her out.

Abashed, she emerged from the blanket crimson with
embarrassment. She felt Lord Delaware's eyes raking her
over with a practiced stare and felt chagrined in the extreme.

"So *this* is the reason for your urgency, Raoul?"

Raoul nodded. "I can explain—"

The marquis held up a hand, laughing. "Believe me,
Hansford, there is nothing to explain other than how my
roving eye could possibly have missed such a perfect specimen of femininity."

Marianne gasped. The creature was insufferable!

"You do not understand—"

"Indeed I do! You and Miss . . ."

"Spencer-Pultney." She glowered at him.

He responded by kissing her fingertips with the gentlest of caresses. "As I said. You and Miss Spencer-Pultney were otherwise engaged when I so rudely interrupted you. Please forgive the gauche intrusion, but next time, dear boy, I beg you remember to close your carriage curtains if you do not wish such incidents to recur."

At last Raoul was risen to fury.

"Unhand the lady, Delaware! You have the honour of making the acquaintance of my future wife!"

Lord Delaware's eyebrows shot together as he took in Marianne's ruffled appearance and shabby attire.

"How so, my dear Hansford? I do not recall having the honour of the lady's acquaintance. More particularly, I *do* recall having a certain conversation with you regarding scrapes and scandals. No offence, but I rather believe the lady falls into precisely that category!"

The viscount opened his mouth to explain. He was fore-stalled, this time, by Marianne, who had transformed in a twinkling from a delightfully harum-scarum hoyden to the absolute pink of gentility.

"If you look for an explanation, my lord, then I am afraid you must look to me."

My lord did look, and what he saw made him instantly revise his initial opinion of her. Her quiet, well-bred tones, her imperious bearing, and, above all, her forceful eyes made him aware that he was dealing with quality. If any-thing, the knowledge disconcerted him, for if Raoul had made such a lady an offer, he was honour-bound to wed.

"I cry pardon, Miss Spencer-Pultney. The circumstances were . . ."

". . . strange, and you leaped to the natural conclusion. I can forgive if you can." Her eyes smiled of a sudden and Lord Delaware felt his features softening.

"I am certain I may, Miss Spencer-Pultney, if you care to enlighten me."

She did. As her story unfolded, Raoul was moved to interpolate here and there until Delaware's head was swimming and there was only one fact he knew for certain: if Hansford was in a scrape, it was one of his own making. Possibly, he thought, noting his affianced's shrewd teasing and easy humour, the scrape would turn out the best it possibly could.

At all events, being apprised of the gist of the unlikely tale, Lord Delaware determined to hold his peace. It struck him that unorthodox though the arrangement might be, there was something very likable about the future viscountess. She embraced all of Raoul's youth and vigour; she was quarrelsome and witty; she was beautiful, well-bred, and wellborn. As scrapes went, this was probably one Lady Sinclair could come to bless and Amber delight in. Amber . . . His thoughts took a new turn.

"So you will do it, then?"

"Do what?"

"Support me at my wedding."

"Certainly I will. Lord knows I am as bored as sin! Brooks and Whites are as dull as dishwater, and there is only my speech burning a hole in my pocket."

The offhand agreement was greeted with delight by Hansford, who took no offence at Slade's lighthearted treatment of the matter.

"Excellent! We shall have the ceremony performed at once."

"My dress!"

"Bother your dress! You will have time enough to buy a whole new wardrobe when my mother lays hands on you!"

"But—"

"Hush!" He turned to Raphael. "The chit looks well enough, don't you think?"

Lord Delaware *did* think. If he were not so besotted with the adorable Miss Amber, his eyes might well have roved to the voluptuous curves that lay hidden beneath the unappealing gown. He was surprised that Raoul, notorious for falling in and out of love a dozen times an afternoon, did not look more smitten.

He held his peace. Perhaps it boded well for the future that the match was not based on passion. Lord Sinclair's passions were as easy to extinguish as they were to arouse.

"Come then. I know an excellent clergyman at St. Christopher's. It is the place Lady Catherine was wedded and quite above reproach, I assure you."

The duo thanked him. Raoul became notably more cheerful now that the most difficult hurdle was over. If Marianne could win over his mentor and escape without so much as a scold, convincing Lady Sinclair would be a foregone conclusion. He leaned over and winked at his bride-to-be. With an impish grin, she allowed herself to return the favour.

"What is it, Tilford?"

Lady Sinclair clasped the pearls about her neck and checked the time on the ormolu clock. It was fifteen minutes before the dinner gong, a strange time for her housekeeper to seek an interview, especially in the privacy of her personal chambers.

"Ma'am, I am sent by Carstairs."

Lady Sinclair noted Tilford's strained gaze and ill-suppressed excitement.

"Yes?"

Tilford smoothed the invisible crease in her well-starched apron. "I must announce, ma'am, the arrival of the Marquis of Slade."

Lady Sinclair smiled in satisfaction. "Excellent, Tilford! You may lay out another cover at the dinner table."

Tilford coughed nervously.

"He was not alone, ma'am."

For the first time a little frown flitted over Lady Sinclair's sanguine features.

"How very odd! I daresay he will have some explanation, however."

"I daresay, ma'am. Viscount Hansford accompanies him."

Lady Sinclair's face cleared. "Raoul? Excellent, Tilford, but you need not announce my own son, you know!"

Tilford looked apologetic. "I know that, ma'am. It is just that . . . that . . ."

Lady Sinclair raised her brows. "That?"

The housekeeper looked so completely out of countenance that Lady Jane became concerned. The butler had been part of the household since Raoul was in short coats. If Carstairs had sent her, something must be very amiss. She sighed and paid Tilford her full attention.

Tilford could contain herself no more. "It is master Raoul, ma'am!"

Lady Sinclair rose from her chair. The use of her son's Christian name alarmed her no end. No one was more punctilious than Tilford when it came to matters of etiquette.

"Is anything wrong? Has he been in a duel? Overturned his curricle—"

The housekeeper hastened to reassure her. "He is perfectly safe, ma'am. I should tell you, however, that he is accompanied by the Viscountess Hansford."

Lady Jane stared at her servant in concern. "Have you lost your wits, Tilford? *I* am the Viscountess Hansford."

Tilford coughed politely. "The *dowager* viscountess, your ladyship."

Her eyes widened. "You don't mean . . ." She clasped her hands to her face. "You *couldn't* mean . . ."

Lady Amber burst into the room, her eyes shining with ill-suppressed mirth.

"Mama, you will never *believe* . . ."

Lady Sinclair regained her composure and smiled at Tilford. "Thank you. I trust you will see to the ordering of dinner?"

She curtsied and withdrew from the room just seconds before Lady Jane reached for her smelling salts and cast pleading eyes upon her traitorously smiling daughter.

"You are not going to tell me that in the space of one afternoon your scapegrace brother has managed to find, woo, and actually marry some hitherto unknown specimen of womankind?"

Amber chortled. "I do not blame you for fearing the worst, but truly, Mama, the bride is unexceptionable!"

"Then he *has* married?"

Amber dimpled. "Indeed, yes! It is a great joke. . . ."

"I am delighted you have so hardy a sense of humour, Amber!" Lady Jane's face was uncustomarily brittle as she set down the sal volatile and reflected, for the first time, on the nature of her new daughter-in-law.

"Don't look so pucker-faced, Mama! I assure you she will lead Raoul a regular song and dance. Just what he needs!"

A small moan emitted from the dowager viscountess's comely lips. "He has married a hoyden, then?" Unthinkingly, she reached for the smelling salts.

"Oh, *do* give over with that detestable substance! Just now I will mistake you for Lady Beechley or Madame Helcombe, and you would not, I feel sure, like that!"

Since these two ladies were society's most notable tragedy queens, Lady Sinclair relinquished the bottle at once
but retained her doleful air.

"You like her?"

Amber's bright eyes danced in amusement. "She is not
like Miss Wentworth or Lady Mary or—"

"Spare me, Amber! All those were divinely suitable can-
didates for our Raoul. You yourself selected them, if I recall."

"True, but they were pattern cards of insipidity. Raoul
would have been bored with them in no more than a fortnight."

"Insipid? Stabilising, more like."

Lady Amber offered her mother one of her wide, open
smiles. She adjusted the cameo that peeped neatly from
her collar and dropped a kiss on her mother's frowning
forehead.

"Do not worry, so, Mama! Tell me truly, would *you* have
liked a stabilising daughter-in-law?"

Lady Sinclair's eyes danced for the first time since she
had heard the shocking news. "Indeed, no! I would not
abide it, I am sure! Neither you nor Raoul nor your dear
papa could ever be described in such terms!"

"Exactly so! Imagine having your life ordered and struc-
tured and sober and stable. I imagine Sir Clive would shudder at the thought, too."

Lady Sinclair threw her daughter a sharp glance. "Sir
Clive? What has he to do with it?"

Amber smiled openly. "A great deal, I should imagine!
Shall I wish you happy?"

Lady Jane coloured so prettily that an answer was hardly
necessary.

"How did you know?"

"Never mind that, Mama! Shall we brave the lion's
den?"

Lady Jane wavered for a moment, then inclined her head resolutely.

"If Raoul has truly done this thing, then we have no choice but to welcome unreservedly his new wife."

"My sentiments exactly! I wager, however, that Raoul has met his match in more ways than he might think."

"Whatever can you mean?"

"Only that she was delivering an almighty set-down when I inadvertently stumbled into the room. Raoul was looking chagrined, and Lord Delaware . . . well, his eyes were brimful of laughter!"

"I must say, if *he* countenances the match it cannot be so very bad despite the hugger-mugger fashion in which it was performed!"

"Indeed not. It is the very thing for my sibling, unless I miss my guess."

When Lady Jane finally did make the acquaintance of her new daughter-in-law, all doubts were instantly suspended. Confronted with huge eyes, dark hair, and an irrepressible twinkle, she found herself moving forward and embracing her with none of the stiffness she feared she would feel.

It was not until the covers were cleared and dinner well and truly over that his lordship dismissed the last servant and conversation could turn to the events of the day. Marianne had eaten with delightful relish, and Lady Jane had been pleased to observe she showed none of the signs of a simpering debutante too filled with ennui to eat.

Neither, of course, did she show any signs of a blushing bride on her wedding day, but then, her own son hardly looked as besotted as he ought. True, he threw his wife mysterious glances from time to time, and Lady Sinclair's perceptive eyes could detect a hint of colour on Marianne's cheeks when their eyes intersected, but that was all.

When the explanation was finally unravelled, largely with the help of Lord Delaware, whose ordered logic made more sense than the multitudinous interpolations of the viscount and his newly acquired viscountess, the whole business suddenly made more sense. Marianne's blushes allowed Lady Sinclair to hope she was not altogether indifferent to her young scamp of a son. The darkling glances on his part afforded her similar speculation. She caught Amber's indecorous wink and smiled. As always, her daughter had the right of it. The pair would suit.

Seven

"Good night, Maid Marianne." Raoul's eyes kindled as he took in the long, shining locks, well brushed and tumbling in delightful confusion to her waist. The dresser had correctly taken her leave when the knock had sounded on the other side of the interleading partition. It was right and proper that his lordship make the proper acquaintance of his wife on their wedding night.

Marianne's heart had plummeted, but even she could see that if gossip was to be averted, the customs had to be observed. She looked about for a shawl to cover her night attire, but could find only a flimsy piece of lace to stand between her and modesty. Still, beggars could not be choosers. She snatched up the shawl and hugged it to her closely.

Raoul's eyes were mocking as he noticed the gesture. They changed to something more as they lit upon the ill-concealed curves and enticing lines that strained against the nightdress loaned by Amber in haste. It was a little long and hopelessly tight in certain intriguing places, but still, it had answered the purpose. In the morning there would be shopping aplenty.

Raoul felt a familiar tightening of desire as his gaze moved from form to face. Her lips were faltering, stammering good night with uncustomary shyness. He wanted to hold her and kiss away the words. Perhaps she noticed the thought and inclined to it in an unconscious way, for instead of shutting the door she stood back, the better to allow her husband to enter. He looked quizzical at the gesture, and a gleam of triumph became definitely detectable to Marianne.

Too late she changed her mind and made to shut the door, her quick temper rising at his audacious assumption of compliance. His fingers stopped her, and before she knew it, the door was shut with a finality that made her at once ill at ease and deliciously aware of his presence. Beneath his sapphire robe of blue velvet she suspected there was precious little to protect her from the slightly bronzed skin and even, well-toned muscles. It was clear that the Viscount Hansford had no need of his very expensive tailors, for extra padding and corsetry would indeed have been a sad and unnecessary waste upon his person.

Even while uttering epithets of indignation, Marianne had the good sense to recognise this fact, and even fleetingly to wish to touch the blond, silken curls that just touched his brow.

His lordship brushed them impatiently away and made towards her, all the time reminding himself of his vow to make the good Maid Marianne pay for her insults of earlier.

She had described him as "importuning her," the baggage! It still rankled with the viscount's pride. He resolved again that no matter how delectable the temptation, it would not be he who begged for the marriage to take its proper form. Still, there was no harm in teasing the wench. She was, after all, his wife.

His lordship smiled a little at the thought. He had assumed his wedding day would be the dreariest day of his life. Instead, it had turned out to be the most marvellous scrape, with promise of yet more trouble to come. He stepped a little closer and fancied he could hear Marianne's breathing grow a little more ragged to match his own. When she didn't move, he reached out his hand and took a long, black curl in his fingers. He pulled at it and stretched it flat in the palm of his hand. When he let go, it jumped back in a long, tight curl. He might never have touched it, for all the effect he had on the strand.

Marianne sighed. "It is no use, my lord! When I was younger and sillier I used to take an iron to these ridiculous curls. Try as I might, I could never get them to lie straight."

"You could have been burned!"

"I was! See, here is the mark." She smoothed away some of the hair, and Raoul could see a faint whitening at the base of her neck. He lifted the gleaming mass, and before she knew what he was about, he stooped to kiss the offending spot. If Marianne had felt burned all those years ago, she could not have felt more so now. My lord's lips upon her skin were dreamy, heavenly, and quite out of the question.

"My lord!"

My lord was too engaged in the interesting business of investigating the patch of skin. Even as she wriggled, his lips audaciously followed their path until they nearly reached the lobe of her delectable ear. Truth to tell, his lordship was finding his virtuous vow rather difficult to keep. Marianne's scent was intoxicating, and he could see her shoulders beneath the shawl that seemed destined to slip. While his pride scolded, his mind told him that he was merely taking the best path he knew to make his own dear wife more aware of his obvious charms. Since they were well and truly wed, there should have been no real impediment to the marriage bed.

But there was—reproachful eyes and a stinging slap across his face. Amazement was followed by wrath.

"That is the second time you have done that! I thought you said you were not a shrew?"

"I thought you said you were a gentleman?"

The words stung more than the blow. "I am, my lady, but you have to admit I am faced with more than a little provocation!"

"Provocation? It was you, my lord, who chose to enter my bedchamber!"

"Would you have me ignore you?"

Marianne bit her lip. She was too honest to deny she would have been embarrassed by any obvious lack of attention on his part. In a large household the servants were bound to gossip, and she had no wish to be the object of their musings.

"I am grateful to you, my lord, for what you have done."

Raoul's temper abated as quickly as it had flared. He grinned.

"You have a precious strange way of showing it! I will take good care not to regularly incur your gratitude!"

Marianne breathed a sigh of relief. The grin was infectious, and she found she had no desire to bear ill will towards the delightful stranger who was now her wedded husband. If things had been different . . . but no, they were not! She drew herself up sternly.

"My lord, I really must bid you good night."

"Must you? If I were to follow through on that wish I wager I will be nursing more than just a smarting cheek!"

Marianne blushed. "Why must you twist my words so? Perhaps I should rather have said 'good sleep.' "

Raoul's hand brushed her cheek lightly before he made an obliging though slightly mocking bow. "If that is what the lady wishes, it is what she will get. My own wishes for you are along the same lines, yet slightly different, I feel."

Marianne's curiosity made her fall immediately into the trap of his setting.

"What are those wishes?"

Raoul allowed himself another of his broad smiles and raking stares.

"I wish you sweet dreams, Maid Marianne."

When the door clicked shut his scent lingered. Deep into the night the new Viscountess Hansford tossed and turned. Sad to say, his lordship's wishes for her were not met at all. Dreams were out of the question, for sleep was elusive. It would have been a comfort to Marianne to know that rest escaped not one but two people that long and lonely night. In the event, she did not. When morning finally came, she breathed a sigh of relief. Raoul was gone.

"Where is that wretched boy?" Lady Jane must have repeated this remark for the tenth time that morning. Shopping with Lady Amber and the young viscountess in tow was a rare treat, but exasperating in the light of the absence of her son. Every person who was anyone made an excuse to stop and pass the day with the trio, curiosity being at a fever pitch about the mysterious person who had so rapidly and effectively managed to capture the heart of the debonair and quite renowned Alistair Raoul Griffin Sinclair.

No one would guess from the self-assured way that Lady Hansford accepted her felicitations that all was not as it should be in the ancestral residence. To put none too fine a point on it, his lordship had not been seen since the intriguing moment he had jauntily wished his spouse sweet dreams. This event in itself was no cause for alarm, for Raoul had long been known among his kith and kin as a venturesome spirit, seldom bound for too long to one spot, no matter how comfortable the lodgings or how amiable his obliging relatives.

That he should choose this, of all times, to indulge his taste for horseflesh and make the tedious journey to a promising stable near Trent was, however, the very outside of enough.

Even his most adoring mother had to express her annoyance at this untimely state of affairs. As she reiterated, to Amber's heartfelt agreement, if Raoul had not the sense to be back for the Countess Mollington's ball on the morrow, or the regent's fireworks display the following week, they would all be in the basket. It would be odd indeed if the honeymooning couple were not seen together at such an event. Already speculation was rife about the marriage. Lady Sinclair prayed the speculation would not progress to scandal.

Marianne twisted an errant curl and forced a cheerful shrug of the shoulders.

"Think no more of it, Lady Sinclair! Your son and I have an agreement and I intend to abide by it. He is not, I assure you, honour-bound to escort me as if I were in leading strings!" She was determined not to reveal the chagrin she felt at being ignored. She felt sure her scapegrace husband was keeping his distance simply to irk her and make his point. Well, if he could be stubborn so could she! Not by the flutter of an eyelash would she reveal that she was at all perturbed by his absence. If she did not sleep at night for fear she would miss his return, he, at least, would never be allowed to suspect it.

Her slight pallor could only be described as fitting for one newly introduced to the joys and duties of marriage. Marianne smiled bitterly at the irony, then brightly at her new mama. She, at least, was all that she could ever wish or hope for.

In the space of a few short days she had been made

to feel like family. More, she had been cosseted and cherished, something she had not experienced for a long time. Raoul's shortcomings had more than been made up for by the ministrations of his mother and sister. She was amused and touched at how indignant they felt on her behalf. Even the haughty Lord Delaware had unbent beyond recognition and offered them ready escort to the mantua makers, Astleys, and any other place Marianne happened to express a wish to see. That his eyes rested a trifle warmly on her new sister piqued Marianne's ready interest.

She was all too happy to have something to divert attention from her own thoughts and inward musings. So annoying how her mind kept reverting back to the heady scent of her husband's cologne, the sapphire blue of his entrancing eyes . . . the tantalising lengths of bright hair that fell to his shoulders and was the despair of his valet. . . . Marianne sighed.

Her thoughts must be disciplined. She shook her head brightly at the ivory fan Amber was suggesting for purchase. She had already acquired more trinkets and furbelows than she knew what to do with. It amused her how much attention Lady Sinclair the heiress attracted, relative to plain Miss Spencer-Pultney, possessor of a genteel annual stipend. She would not have been human if she did not find herself revelling, just a little, in all the fuss. Still, there was a limit, after all, to the number of fans one lady might ever need or wish to possess. Besides, quite a number from the inner circle slowly gathering around her like butterflies to the flame had laden her with morning gifts ranging from floral posies to—yes, it must be said—fans of delicate silk and rich, dark ebony.

No, she had no need of fans. Or jewels. As she regarded her reflection in the tall glass that evening, she was able to quell with satisfactory decorum the sudden panicked

thudding of her heart. The image that looked out from
the glass was one that she could hardly recognise: poised,
fashionable, and understatedly elegant. The low-cut bodice shimmered faintly, but otherwise remained strikingly
plain in comparison with the current mode. Raoul might
not be present to witness her little social triumphs, but
in truth his wife would do him no discredit. The thought
that she was not, at least, an antidote, buoyed up Marianne's jangled nerves as the horses drew up for the evening's entertainment. His lordship the viscount still had
not returned. With a whisper of a sigh for what might
have been, she gathered her muff and strode confidently
down the stairs.

It did not take more than the opening moments of the
evening for Marianne to shake herself from the doldrums.
In the short break between the quadrille and the commencement of a rousing country dance, she idly allowed
her thoughts to focus, once again, on the way the land
lay between Mistress Amber and the gorgeous Lord Delaware. He, handsome in shining silver buttons and a stark
evening jacket of midnight blue, was effortlessly command-
ing the attention of all who surveyed him. Lady Jane and
her daughter were far too discreet for such overt attentions, but Marianne was not deceived.

Possibly more in tune with the hopeless fluttering of
love's confused call than she would like to have admitted,
Marianne could feel quite clearly the tension that lay between her two newest, dearest, and most valued allies. As
the night drew on, the impasse became more and more
obvious to her sensitive, generous nature. It *exasperated* her
that Lord Delaware offered his hand to her rather than
to Amber for the commencement of the supper dance.

Equally annoying was Amber's animated smile at Lord Crewe when it was as plain as a pikestaff that her inclinations lay elsewhere. Since Marianne was never one to dwell too long upon herself, it was natural that she began bending her mind to what could be done. If she had tumbled into a marriage not strictly of her choosing, then she must at least have the delight of conniving to match make for someone else. It seemed Lady Amber, sensible in all but the obvious, would make the ideal victim. She looked at Lord Delaware speculatively and could have *sworn* she saw a twinkle of amusement. On second glance, however, his face was impassive.

"My felicitations, Lady Hansford!"

It took Marianne a startled moment to realise he was referring to her. She opened her eyes wide.

"Felicitations?"

Raphael lowered his voice and spoke in an ironic undertone.

"You have been regarding me all evening as though I were an ingredient for some special potion. Am I?"

Marianne dimpled.

"Perhaps, my lord. But I warrant it will be a spell of your own choosing!"

Lord Delaware laughed. His voice was throaty and engagingly deep.

"I do not think I will venture to question you much further, my dear viscountess!"

"Pray do not, my lord, for the answer you get may be too enigmatic for a gentleman of your ilk to understand."

Lord Delaware lifted his eyebrows. It was a long time since he'd been quizzed by the fairer sex.

"My ilk?"

Marianne's answer was prompt. "Top-lofty, proud, and incapable of seeing what is under the very nose."

Lord Raphael looked grim; then his face relaxed into a smile of lazy amusement. He bowed whimsically.

"I grant that in your instance, you were proved correct. I *was* too hasty in my judgment."

"*Indeed* you were!" Marianne coloured at the memory of what he'd all too readily thought of her. He saw the flush and continued smoothly, although his shoulders shook with unchivalrous laughter.

"I would be surprised, however, to find my wit too *often* at fault."

Marianne nodded. "I, too. Unless it be of some matter of great moment. *Then,* my lord, I think you might be blinded to the obvious."

"I take it you have an example of this mental decrepitude I fear I must display?"

Marianne laughed. "Decrepitude is hardly an epithet easily applied to one such as *you,* my lord!" Since half the ladies ambling in the moonlit garden were lingering with the specific intention of catching the marquis's well-practiced eye, Marianne felt quite justified in making this assertion.

"You relieve me greatly!"

"I am sure I *do!* Shall we go in?"

"You have not answered my question!"

"Nor do I intend to!"

Marianne smiled at him impishly. Let *him* work out the meaning behind her words. It was as plain as a pikestaff that Lady Amber and he were a match made in heaven. If it took a few choice hints on her part to make the two realise that salient fact, then so be it.

Her thoughts flitted back to the beginning of the conversation.

"By the by, Lord Delaware, to what do I owe the honour of your felicitations?"

Raphael grinned. Two could play at the game he was

very sure the young Viscountess Hansford was embarking upon.

"Perhaps after your cryptic words, my lady, I should not say!"

Marianne was indignant.

"But that is not fair!"

"No?"

"No!"

He relented and the shadow of a smile played on his dark, handsome features. Just inside, Lady Amber caught a glimpse of the small patch above his mouth that was so distinctive and so intriguingly arresting. Her heart gave a faint lurch for she willed with uncharacteristic passion that smile to be directed at *her,* not at Marianne or any of the dozens of obliging females dotted around the lawns and great hall.

Lord Raphael felt her gaze but did not trust himself to meet it. Instead, he lifted Lady Hansford's hand and kissed the delicate white kid in which it was encased.

"My felicitations," he murmured with an irrepressible twinkle, "for putting my scapegrace young friend quite out of countenance. When I saw him this morning he was looking decidedly below the weather and placing the blame, I might add, squarely at your door."

"You have seen him?" Marianne could not quite hide her astonishment.

"Indeed I have and not a pretty sight, I assure you!"

"Where was he?"

"Helping himself to eggs and ham as bold as brass in my own breakfast room!"

"Well!" Marianne could not quite hide her indignation. "I take it the horseflesh he purchased was well worth the trip?"

"On the contrary, my dear! I have never set eyes on two such mealy mouthed high steppers in all my born days!

You may rest assured, my lady, that Raoul is well served for his mean spirited absence and so I told him!"

"He will not thank you for that!"

"Indeed not, but the least I can do is proffer a good friend advice when he needs it."

Marianne felt her eyes prick with a sudden blur of unshed tears. She brushed them aside impatiently before extending her arm. The long line of lanterns all seemed very dim as she made her way down the tree-lined path and tried to convince herself that it was the situation, not her husband who was to blame. Raoul had rescued her from the clutches of Glaston and she could—and would— honestly expect no more.

She nodded intently as he handed her over to a waiting admirer. The speculative gleam in his eye, though, did not tally with his seeming acquiescence. Raoul, he thought, had met his match. It needed time only to show that his merry minx of a wife could—and certainly, he hoped, would—expect much, much more.

His eyes flickered to Amber's and finally held. The marital concerns of the young viscount and his bride receded with unconscionable speed.

Eight

"Lady Amber, I bid you good evening."

The woman in the Grecian gown of shimmering blue looked up and willed herself to smile. Though she had waited half an evening for this moment, when it came, she still found herself tongue-tied and unprepared. With an inward shake of annoyance she schooled her features to a serene smile and made the requisite curtsy, her lips tremulous and intolerably endearing to the man who addressed her.

"Thank you for your posy, my lord."

Raphael waved away the summer roses he'd procured with such difficulty.

"If I said beauty for a beauty it would seem like arrant flattery, would it not?"

Lady Amber nodded decisively.

"Nevertheless, honesty compels me to say it. Beauty for a beauty." Raphael put his hand to her lips as she made to protest.

"Do not deny me the pleasure of saying what is uppermost in my thoughts! You do me a great honour by wearing the little token."

"I could do no less after the obvious trouble to which you have gone to!"

Raphael smiled. He knew full well that Lady Amber's

bowers would be crushed full of floral tributes. That she had chosen to wear his own was a circumstance that caused the pulses at his neck to quicken slightly.

"May I hope that your gratitude extends to a waltz at the very least?"

Amber's heart soared. "Undoubtedly, my lord!"

"And may I hope that after you will join me in the green room for lemonade?"

"The green room? I do not think . . ."

Lord Delaware could have cut his tongue out. The green room was a notorious little chamber conveniently set away from the rest and known to be a sanctuary for the more ardent of courting couples. He himself had made use of its privacy several times, the more salacious of these encounters having been with their voluptuous hostess herself, the Countess of Mollington.

Amber's shuttered gaze spoke volumes.

"I did not mean . . ."

"No?" Raphael stared at her hard. His lady love's colour was delectably high as she avoided his eyes and concentrated hard on the stem of her fan.

"I *did* say for lemonade, you know!" His voice, though dry, held a hint of amusement not lost on Amber.

"No! That is . . ." Her voice trailed off in a misery of embarrassed silence. His lordship allowed an uncharacteristic grin to spread across his dark, sublimely handsome features. Could he, *could* he have detected a hint of disappointment in her tone?

He shook himself. His imagination must truly be playing unfair tricks if he dared imagine such a response. He cleared his throat and looked hard at the golden headed vision before him. Demure enough, but he could trace her heartbeat with his finger if he chose. Suddenly he chose to. He chose very much indeed and were it not for the wretched piece of gossamer-like film that stood between him and the fair, creamy skin below, he was certain he would have succeeded.

Even so, his hand lightly skimmed the top of her gown, causing a shudder to run through Amber's frame. Something flashed into her eyes that gave him cause for sudden, soaring hope. It disappeared in an instant, but the memory lingered on, warming the room and the meaning behind every playful gesture and remark she chose to make thereafter.

The lively chords of the waltz reverberated through the ballroom too soon for Lord Delaware's taste. He had a fancy to stay and explore his newfound insight, yet the music was calling, her dance card was full, and crowds were already threatening to envelop her in the steps of the dance. This, evidently, was not the most propitious of times.

With a sigh he bowed and took her hand. He would have to submit, he supposed, to the pleasant torture of holding her in his arms, exactly three correct inches between himself and the warmth of her fair person. Even to a hardened rake like himself, the thought of breaching those three inches was tantalising. Tantalising and deeply unfair! Amber belonged firmly in his arms, not delicately at arm's length. The heady scent of her perfume was overshadowed only by the promise of what lay beneath the subtle sapphire sheath she had chosen to effect.

She could have no notion of how alluring a prospect she presented, for if she did, common modesty would have forced her into one of the hideous pink muslins he'd been assured was all the rage. A smile glimmered in his eye at the idea, and Amber caught it, her own lips starting to twitch, though she could only guess at the source of his amusement.

"Don't they look elegant, my lord?" Her eyes alighted

on one of the Rochester twins, resplendent in lace, powder, and gems of all colours and earthly description.

"Indeed they do, my lady!" His tone was so dry that Amber was not deceived. A devilish imp within her bade her pursue the subject a little further. Perhaps it was not such a very bad thing, after all, to have her mind distracted from the tiny black patch that hovered above subtle broad lips . . . not a bad thing, too, to have her thoughts redirected from the piercing warmth that persisted in searing her waist with every step. . . .

She could not count the number of times she had traced and retraced the simple steps of the waltz. First with her dance masters, then with the very elite of society, several of whom would have married her at the drop of a dance card if she had so wished. Why, then, did she feel so terribly aware of this starkly broad-shouldered man, this godlike creature who paid her precious little in the way of flowery speeches, and who was more likely to cut a dash with Raoul than to pay her any kind of court?

She could think of countless occasions when Raphael had shaken his head at her and refused her bidding. He had balked at taking her to see the famous Elgin marbles, he was stubborn about his horses, he had refused to take her even for a sedate trot up St. James. . . . She should have been harbouring a strong sense of ill-usage, rather than daydreaming like a lovesick kitten! And yet daydream she did, all the way through the waltz and halfway through the third minuet of the evening. If she had known what was in Raphael's mind, she would have daydreamed longer.

Across the balcony and in one of the four chambers leading off from the ballroom, another, not dissimilar scene was unfolding. It seemed that Raoul, Lord Sinclair, had finally remembered his wedded state. Marianne's heart did an unaccountable little skip as she took in the deep blue eyes so unexpectedly quizzing her. My lord her husband surveyed the sea green muslin and soft underdress of shimmering amber with appreciative eyes.

"My dance, I believe?" His voice was like velvet, and Marianne had the ridiculous sensation of being swept up into its folds. Suddenly the sophisticated cut of her gown felt too revealing. Had Madame Fanchon failed her? The light in his lordship's eyes spoke volumes and left the viscountess annoyingly breathless. Definitely too low-cut. She mistrusted the gleam that sent a dizzying rush of unfamiliar warmth through her traitorous being.

Her new husband had no right to be so devastatingly attractive. Especially not when she was furious with him and more than a little out of sorts. Her peace of mind would have been better served had he been bald and avuncular in manner. That sort of convenient marriage must surely be more tenable than this daily fluttering of nerves she was ceaselessly forced to endure. Her irritation made her churlish.

"I fear, my lord, I have no place on my dance card." Marianne extended her card, and her tone held a note of triumph.

It was clear that her husband had not anticipated such a setback. Strange to tell, he had not chosen to make his presence felt at the Mollington ball. His idea of an interesting evening would have been a bout at Gentleman Jack's, followed by a cockfight or even a curricle race till dawn. It was Raphael who had coerced him to attend and threatened him with all manner of dire consequences if he did not at least put in his bow.

This edict had been strengthened in no uncertain terms by a wrathful Lady Jane, who had painfully pointed out his duty and all but ordered his attendance. Gloomily,

Raoul had submitted to the ministrations of his valet and allowed himself to be decked out in casual elegance, a large cabochon ruby completing his impeccable toilette.

Now, however, he was faced with unexpected opposition. His good intentions were being rewarded by a haughty glare and a triumphant refusal. Bad enough in the best of times, but untenable when the lady in question was quite the most ravishing woman in the room. The transformation from harum-scarum hoyden to regal viscountess left Raoul's head spinning. His spirits would have been utterly dampened had he not encountered a sudden self-satisfied twinkle behind the golden, dulcet eyes. His lady wife might appear respectable, but Raoul would wager a farthing her thoughts were still as endearingly reprehensible as when he had first encountered her.

He was beset with an overwhelming urge to take her in his arms and spin her round the room until she was giddy or, at the very least, breathless. Besides, that irrational stubborn streak he seemed to have been born with was now gaining an increasing hold on his normally amiable person.

"Let me see that card."

Marianne extended it primly, her eyes challenging and full of triumph. It would not be a bad thing for her errant husband to see she was in high demand. She spoke naught but the truth when she said her card was full.

Raoul examined the delicate blue card, etched exquisitely in gilt and pencilled in with the names of a good many of his peers. Not least among them was St. Eversleigh, Earl of Balluch, and Martindale, Duke of Clyde. Raphael's name had been duly inscribed and, he noted, a good many of his own elite circle of friends. If he did not merit a dance with his wife he would be the laughingstock of the ball. Anger and an unfamiliar spark of—what was it? Not, surely, jealousy?—overcame him for a moment. The card blurred in the candlelight, and he could see the delicate tips of Marianne's pale satin gloves as she held it up for his perusal.

Raoul surprised himself by extending his hand and wrenching it from her grip. Spying a pencil on a salver nearby, he snatched one up and hastily deleted the names of three of his bosom beaux—one earl, a baron, and a mere "Mr."—without a shadow of a pause. When Marianne gasped in indignation he took her hand and marched her up to the dance floor as if she were a recalcitrant child. The music struck up a waltz, and Raoul smiled in grim satisfaction. He extended his hand, and with the eyes of the entire polite world upon her, Marianne could do no more than sink into a graceful curtsy and extend her hand.

A powerful one closed over hers. Marianne felt a strange thrill despite her annoyance at the man's high-handedness. A moment later, a strong arm encircled her waist and she was lost. The dance seemed to go on forever, and she floated across the floor, aware only of a pair of brilliant blue eyes fixed upon her face and open, slightly stunned mouth.

A slow smile fixed upon her husband's face as the music stopped and he realised he had no need or call to return her to a waiting chaperon. Instead, he took her hand and led her through the throngs of interested people to the cool air outside. Raoul, who had balked at attending, who had grumbled all through the finicky business of tying his necktie, who had looked daggers at Raphael when he'd scolded, begged, and pleaded that he attend, now was well pleased with himself. The tabbies were no longer pushing their simpering debutantes in his path, and the dance with the lady who was now his wife had been strangely exhilarating. Perhaps marriage was not to be as gloomy as he'd anticipated. He resolved firmly that between engagements he'd escort his wife around town should she so desire.

Feeling quite noble and virtuous, he grinned at Marianne, whose soft curves and tantalising flesh were just visible in the shadows. He leaned forward and felt a tremendous pain shoot through his elegant top boot.

"What in damnation?"

Marianne dimpled, but her meek tone did not belie the sudden flash of anger as she related sweetly, "That, my lord, was my slipper!"

"Dashed near my toe, too!" Raoul began to look resigned. "I suppose you must have an explanation of sorts, my little termagant?"

"Do I need one?"

The question was forthright, and the straight gaze she cast him made the Viscount Hansford squirm more uncomfortably than the recent onslaught on his person had done.

"Have I been neglecting you, Maid Marianne?"

She dropped her eyes. The remorse in his tone was balm to her hurt pride. He had, after all, rescued her from a terrible predicament and offered her the comfort of his name and dignities. It seemed trifling to quibble over matters of smaller moment. And yet . . . her heart ached to be set a little higher in his esteem than his horses or his gaming, or even, she suspected, his little barques of frailty. Now she answered his question.

"A little." Her voice was small, and the understatement spoke volumes in compromise. Raoul must have understood, for he cocked a quizzical brow, then let all his objections slip from his tongue unspoken.

"Cry compromise then?" She nodded. "I will escort you to all the routs, balls, and infernal soirees you ladies deem fit to attend."

"And I?" Marianne was sure there would be more.

"And you?" For an instant his eyes gleamed, and Marianne felt that strange warmth creep through her body, leaving her eyes bright and her colour suspiciously high. If Raoul noticed, he made no comment, but a light lingered at the back of his eyes as he announced his terms.

"You will refrain from hurling abuse at my head, doing injury to my physical person, or otherwise glowering at me with those passionate honey eyes of yours."

"I do not glower!"

"You manage a fine imitation, my lady wife!"

"I would not if you were not so infuriating!"

Raoul sighed. "What did I tell you? There is to be no scolding, Marianne!"

"I won't scold if you stop being so high-handed! How could you have scratched my dance card?"

Raoul grinned. "The greatest fun I've had all evening, and the best of it is not a soul can call me out!" His smile was infectious.

Marianne found herself relenting. More than that. She knew very clearly she was in terrible danger of falling in love with her scapegrace husband. She found herself smiling in spite of herself.

"You are a dreadful rogue, but I vow I like you the better for it, sir! That is why I threw my bandboxes at you in that . . ."

". . . depraved fashion."

"If I was depraved then so, my good lord, were you!"

Raoul flashed her a devastating grin that even the hardiest of matrons must have found irresistible. "True enough. I would dearly like to become more depraved, but I assume you will not countenance it?"

Marianne was of two minds over how to answer. Part of her was yearning for a little of the depravity her charming young husband promised. Pride, however, made her cling fast to decorum. She shook her head and watched the sudden kindling in Raoul's eye die.

He afforded her a mocking bow. "A pity, my lady. If you will excuse me, then, the gaming tables call." Before she could respond, he turned on his heel and made for the warm throngs within.

The night felt suddenly chilly to Marianne, who remained silent and still a long while after he'd gone. Left to linger on the terrace, she felt her thoughts were far more melancholy than might be expected of a young bride on a balmy moonlit night. They might have become gloomier still if she had noticed the burning eyes of the Earl of Glaston fixed intently upon her person. He did not usually receive invitations to this type of event, but the Countess Mollington owed him a favour. As it was, Marianne had no time to remark on his malevolence. Her hand was solicited for the quadrille, and the strains of the harpsichord were most insistent.

"The green room!" The words were whispered, so Amber was not sure she had caught them correctly. The steps changed, and with them, her partner. She was obliged to cover half the dance floor with near on a dozen eligible young men before she could clarify the words. In answer, a rare, heartwarming grin and a cocked eyebrow to the arch that led off from the main hall. Raphael, Lord Delaware's back looked impressive as it receded from her view, towards . . . yes, she was sure of it, the notorious green room he had so indecorously mentioned earlier. Lord Penryth stepped on her toe, and Amber had to force herself not to wince. Instead, she smiled melting reassurance at the apologies that followed but listened with less than half an ear.

Was it possible that Raphael had decided to trifle with

her? To engage in a dalliance? Her heart lifted and sank at one and the same time. Honesty compelled her to admit that a dalliance would be more than tempting . . . she was past her first blushes, after all, and if one did decide to indulge in such things, surely the Marquis of Slade must be considered the handsomest, most able, most charming, delectable rake in all of London. Her thoughts flitted to the uncompromising features set off by jet black hair, the patch above his lip that she longed to trace under her finger, the lips she had studied. . . .

"Beg pardon, sir!" Amber had the grace to blush. It was not like her to stumble in a minuet. The gentleman dressed all to the rig gravely forgave her, though his foot must have been smarting from her uncustomary clumsiness. Despite herself, her thoughts wandered again.

No! He was surely not thinking of a flirtation! Not with her, after so many years of friendship, after the stern way he handled Raoul, after the care he obviously had for the Sinclair family . . . after the fact that he was a known connoisseur of womankind . . . Amber's thoughts were in uncharacteristic disarray. Disappointment and what? A flutter of hope?

You are a widgeon, Amber Sinclair! The words could have been Raphael's own. When they were children, he'd always scolded that way. The scolding had been deprived of sting, because it was inevitably accompanied by a fond twinkle and brotherly warmth, though he was only a neighbour and older at that.

Go to the green room! The words pounded in her head, drowning out the music and causing yet another stumble upon the long, white marble.

"Are you all right, ma'am?" The solicitous voice was guiding her off the floor.

"Perfectly, thank you!" She was pleased to hear that her voice sounded firm, quite unlike the jelly she felt inside.

"Shall I stay with you? Fetch some orgeat, perhaps? The rigours of the evening . . ."

Amber waved him away. "I will be perfect in just a moment. Thank you." When the curly-haired gentleman showed signs of staying, she waved him away with an airy sweep of the arm. "I do believe Miss Kimble is watching you! I daresay she has been yearning for a dance all evening."

"Do you think so?" The voice was unflatteringly eager.

Amber smiled. "Cross my heart, sir! A lady can tell, you know!"

"And you are recovered?"

"Perfectly! Now I do insist that you leave. . . . Mr. Kirkpatrick seems to be heading her way. . . ."

It took no more. With a perfunctory bow her partner was off and Amber was at last alone. Out of the corner of her eye she could see Lord St. John bow in her direction. If she did not move fast, he would be upon her. And would that be such a bad thing? she wondered. Perhaps Raphael had only been funning . . . perhaps . . . She caught herself up short.

Perhaps she would just march in and see what his cryptic words were all about. Her mother was right. It was time that she settled. Once and for all, she needed to know whether the incomparable was attainable or not. She vowed that if the answer was no, she would find a way to live with it.

On the other hand . . . her mother's words haunted her. "You will never get anywhere if you persistently send him away . . . if you just offer him *tea*. . . ." Amber shook her golden head at the recollection. *Mama!* Sometimes she was most improper. With a sudden wave of decision, she smiled. Tonight she would cast aside her good behaviour. Tonight she, too, would be reckless. Why should Raoul, after all, have sole claim to that family trait? Damn it, tonight she'd throw caution to the winds. Raphael wanted her in the green room? Well, in the green room he would find her!

His lordship, the honourable Marquis of Slade, stared mesmerised at the inviting, deliciously flirtatious, and perilously uncharacteristic eyes of his lady love. The green had changed to amber, closer to her namesake, closer to the wild soul only he detected restless behind her impeccable breeding. Amber seemed always a pattern card of perfection, correct to a nicety, though a trifle aloof. Raphael knew otherwise, for he had glimpsed freedom in her eyes, on her wild rides, in her indulgent, vicarious enjoyment of Raoul's peccadilloes and scrapes. Now, however, he saw the depths in living form and he was stunned.

An Amber of wisdom he already knew. An Amber of compassion he deeply loved. But this? This was an Amber of passion, an Amber of magnetic depth, an Amber whose very wildness drove him wild. She said not one word, yet he knew and he saw. Her eyes were sultry. She closed them for just an instant, but that instant was enough. Raphael finally knew that as afflicted as he was, so, too, was she.

With the newfound knowledge came confidence. All the doubts, the gnawing jealousies, the insecurities were gone as if they had never been. Amber was the woman for him, and by heaven, by the light in her eye, Amber was his. Miss Sinclair was not a tease. If she teased him now—and she did—he could be certain, certain beyond doubt, of the outcome.

His eyes travelled to her mouth and onwards . . . the blue dress continued to tantalise him, but this time . . . *this* time he would brook no interruption. His lips curved into the dashing smile that broke the intensity of his features and had set many a young lady's heart aflutter. Amber was no exception. Truth to tell, she was having difficulty breathing. Slowly, deliberately, Raphael closed the door of the green salon and took a step closer. Amber did not move. She could hardly hear the steps he took, for the pounding in her ears.

Raphael. She had whispered the name so many times in her head it seemed etched for eternity in her brain. Unconsciously, she whispered it out loud now, just as he took her face in his hands and gently bent his head towards her.

His lips were light—feathery. A kiss, but not a kiss. Amber reached out for more, forgetting diffidence, clasping her hand about his warm neck to savour the intimacy of what she hoped would occur. She was not to be disappointed. One glance at her long, closed lashes and the last vestiges of the marquis's self-control were abandoned. His kiss became a crushing, questing embrace. Amber did not mind the hard, uncompromising lips against her soft, untried curves. Her mouth yielded in a sweet delight of untrammelled joy. She heard Raphael groan, and the sound was echoed in her own mind a thousand times and more.

His fingers began to roam farther than modesty should allow. Amber cared not a whit, so lost was she in the rapture of the moment. The conviction that Raphael really, truly loved her overset all other considerations. Indeed, it brought out a veritable imp in her that must have lain dormant all her life.

"Curses!" Raphael mouthed the word, but Amber was too busy with his neckerchief to make a response. Strong hands encircled her own in a tight grip. A flicker of enjoyment crossed the marquis's face as he looked down at his lady love.

"Curses, I said!"

"Afraid I will muss up your necktie? À la waterfall, I

believe." Her lips were a deep pink, wide, and deplorably inviting.

"Beg pardon?" For an instant the marquis was bemused. Then he realised Amber's meaning. "Lord, no! Easiest thing in the world to do! See here." He dropped her hands and briskly tugged at the two ends of the pristine cloth. In the twinkling of an eyelash he proceeded to do a series of convolutions that left Amber bewildered.

"I collect that is the famous Delaware delve?"

Raphael cocked a dark, infinitely handsome brow at her. His lips twitched.

"And what do you know of such trifles, my pretty?"

"Only what Raoul chooses to bore on and on about every breakfast for a month, I am sure!"

"That cannot be allowed to be! Remind me to have a word with him about table etiquette. The knot, however edifying, was not designed to *bore*, I assure you!"

Amber's tone was dry. "I warrant not! Not judging by the interest you evince every time you enter a room!"

Raphael chuckled as he tweaked her nose. "I hope it is not simply my neck attire that causes such a stir?"

Amber pouted. Raphael's eyes lit up in ready laughter. "Not jealous, my pretty?"

Amber smiled. "And if I am? A kiss for reassurance?"

Raphael complied. When he had done, both seemed equally shaken. Lord Delaware was the first to speak, his voice dangerously dark, his eyes kindling with a fire of Amber's making.

"Which brings me back to 'curses!' "

"Oh, yes . . . curses! Why curses?" Amber wrinkled her nose. Far away, the orchestra was tuning up, but she was oblivious to all but the beloved face before her.

Raphael grinned, the patch above his jaw dark and strangely inviting.

"Curses because I'd best stop before I disgrace myself!"

"Disgrace yourself?" Amber's lips were provocative as she made her reply. "My lord, you can do better, I am sure!"

He bowed and grinned delightedly. "There are some that say I can, my lady, but now is not the time. . . ."

"And why not, pray?" Amber could hardly believe her audacity as she reached her long, slender fingers up to trace the patch. He endured it for a moment, then cursed and bent his head toward her once more. Amber made precious little attempt to stop him.

When at last he pushed her from him, she was ruffled and unkempt and blissfully unconscious of the shocking sight she must present. It was up to Raphael to gently set her gown to rights and straighten out the short Grecian locks that threatened to tangle from their thorough tussling.

"I would not be doing this—setting you to rights, I mean—if I did not happen to know this room has been booked for a . . . uh . . . similar assignation sometime soon."

His eyes danced at Amber's panic. "You mean . . ."

He nodded. "There appears to be a premium set on small rooms like these. Much as your lips are enticing, my angel, unless you shortly wish to be joined by another amorous pair . . . and I mention no names, mind . . . we had best repair back to the main ballroom."

"I don't think I could tolerate another quadrille!"

"Neither, my dear, can I!" Raphael's eyes darkened once more. "I have to say, however, that I can equally not tolerate another moment in here with you."

"And why not?"

"Shall I show you?"

Amber was sorely tempted to nod. Instead, she forced herself to think of the unknown gentleman who would shortly be joining them.

"I regret not, my lord!"

She dimpled at him, and Raphael felt his throat constrict. He fiddled with the impeccable necktie that adorned his white starched points.

"A postponement, then?"

Amber nodded. A postponement.

"Shall I call on you?"

She curtsied. "That would be the respectable thing to do, my lord!"

Lord Delaware looked her slowly up and down from top to toe. Despite what had just occurred between them, Amber could feel a rosy blush steal to her cheeks. Under such prolonged, sustained, and obviously impertinent scrutiny, she felt unequal to the challenge of Raphael's rakish ways. His voice was almost a whisper as it reached her ears.

"I am not always quite respectable, you know!"

She nodded. She knew. Only too well, since she had followed the romantic exploits of my lord the marquis with much interest over the years. Bad enough all the respectable dalliances . . . the less respectable ones she had heard of through Raoul. Quite a lady's man, was Raphael. She was hardly sure if she was up to the challenge.

"You know that and don't care?" It was suddenly important to Raphael.

Amber threw caution to the winds. "I know and don't care!"

Raphael nodded, the imp in him gleaming through dark, suddenly bright eyes.

"Perhaps I'll be calling on you then."

Amber nodded, then effected a court curtsy. "I'll be expecting you!"

"Will you, my poppet?" The words were wistful and strangely tender. Amber liked the endearment. She'd been called *amazon* and *goddess,* but never *poppet* before. The marquis's mood changed as suddenly as it had come upon him. Now he was jaunty and arrogant, the Raphael the world knew and loved.

"Best expect the unexpected, then. That is always the way, they say, with the Marquis of Slade."

Amber opened her mouth to reply. Her words were stopped by a gesture from the tall, darkly handsome man by her side.

"I warn you, though, I'll brook no interruptions the next time. . . . Hush!"

He gestured to the door. The brass handle was slowly turning. Behind him, a curtain fluttered in the evening breeze. He gestured in its direction and put his finger to his lips. Amber nodded and took the hint. It would not serve her reputation well to be discovered alone in the green room with the likes of Raphael. She stepped back, behind the heavy brocade and out through the French door leading to innumerable steps and far below, Lord Mollington's gardens.

Nine

"The infernal impudence! Send them away, Carstairs!"

"Very good, my lord. I shall simply say her ladyship is not at home."

"Stap me if I don't say it myself! The impudence!"

Marianne set down the dubious watercolour she was daubing with some relief. Her eyes met her husband's and she felt a flash of something indescribable.

Since Raoul's defection to the game room, she had seen little of his lordship save in the presence of others. She'd heard wild tales of reckless nights and frolics, and even the whisper of an opera dancer in his keeping. She had begun to suspect him of being bored, possibly even wearied by his newly acquired marital status.

Now the fire in his eyes disabused her of these melancholy reflections. The odious Mershams were encroaching yet again, and he was gallantly taking up the cudgels in her defence.

Her heart warmed as she brushed aside a jet black tendril of silken hair and patted down the soft muslin of her skirts.

"I will see them, my lord."

Raoul looked indignant. "After the way they have treated you? I think not."

Marianne bristled, loath to have her will crossed even

by so handsome a man as her husband. She tilted her
chin and looked at him with such a haughty expression
on her impish face that my lord, caught between frustration and anger, had to laugh.

"If you treat them to a dose of *that* kind of civility, perhaps it will answer!"

Marianne flashed him a pleased grin. "Indeed, my lord,
it is as I intend. The Mershams will be forced to curtsy
in my presence, and for that even *I* can be civil."

Raoul smiled. "Excellent, my lady! I shall do all I can
to set you up in your own consequence."

Across the table, Lady Amber and the dowager Viscountess Hansford changed meaningful glances. Anything
would be worth having Raoul and his lady on terms again.
Lady Jane delicately set aside her stitchery and watched
her daughter do the same. Amber's eyes were suspiciously
bright, her cheeks glowing with good health and with what
Lady Jane strongly suspected was a good dose of happiness.
Praise be! She would make use of this unexpected moment
to tax her on it.

Raoul was not as sensitive, his eyes only for Marianne.
He turned to Carstairs, who still stood, stiff as a ramrod,
at the entrance to the morning room.

"Let them kick their heels in the gallery for a while.
It will do them good to have a fair dose of my ancestors.
Lord knows, they used to scare me silly in my youth with
their jaw-me-dead looks."

Carstairs bowed. If he was disapproving of Hansford's
negligent attitude to his noble forebears, or of the cant
language his lordship chose to effect, he did not reveal
so by a single admonishing twitch. Over the devoted years
of his service, he had resigned himself to the deplorable
fact that my lord simply did not stand enough upon his
dignity. He and his delightful sister would always be the

first to chatter to the servants, haunt the county fairs, romp through drawing rooms. . . .

"One more thing, if you will."

"My lord?"

"See to it that my lady is served in state this afternoon. I shall expect no less than six of the liveried servants to be in attendance. You know the sort of thing."

Carstairs almost choked. Though his face remained as wooden as ever, his old butler soul heard in crystal clarity the very harps of heaven. Oh, for pomp! Oh, for a little circumstance! Hansford, it seemed, was handing it to him on a plate. Of the old school, Carstairs deplored the modern custom of being lax in propriety and in the formality that befitted the honourable rank of peer of the realm.

To his reckoning, the house of Hansford had long lacked the fastidious attention to detail and precedence that was expected of one of the finest titles in the land.

True, it had a warmth and happiness about it that spoke volumes for the master and mistresses that made it so, but nonetheless, dignity was dignity. Offered the opportunity of standing on ceremony in grandiose style, Carstairs believed truly he had been confronted with the answer to a heartfelt prayer.

He knew that Mistress Farnley in the kitchens would feel the same way. A kindred spirit was Mistress Farnley. Forever bemoaning the fact that only three dishes and two side orders were ever ordered up of an evening. Dressed lobster and truffled quail were but distant memories for her; the dowager viscountess was more likely to order up a side of beef or plain devilled kidneys than anything more challenging as befitted her elevated station. Now, however, he did not by the flicker of an eyelash show that he was remotely pleased. Instead, he nodded his head in a portentous manner and withdrew with exacting finesse.

Truth to tell, none of the party paid much thought to

the emotions they were engendering in the servants be-
lowstairs. Marianne felt a faint pulse at her throat and
lifted her hand to still it. She was too late.

Raoul was at her side and gently stroked the base of
her neck in a studied effort to calm her. It had the opposite
effect, for the knot of excitement in the pit of her stomach
changed, suddenly, to something that had very little indeed to do with the Mershams. Far from stilling, the pulse
fluttered even more wildly. Though it was but a second
that the hand lightly lingered at the base of her throat,
to Marianne it seemed a moment suspended.

Lady Jane coughed, and Marianne was recalled to her
senses, a little breathless but otherwise calm. "I will leave
you to your visitors, Marianne. Doubtless you will know
how best to deal with them." She bestowed upon her new
daughter an encouraging smile and, with a meaningful
tilt of the eyebrow, withdrew from the room.

Amber smiled in Raoul's direction. "I trust you will do
your best imitation of Papa at his grandest, Raoul, dear!"

Raoul's lips twitched. He bowed in his sister's direction.
"To be sure, Amber, dearest!" There was a mocking
gleam that discomforted her somewhat. Her brother was
unpredictable but not often angered. The strange light
she detected in his eyes appeared, to her, both unfamiliar
and formidably compelling. The Mershams, she thought,
were not going to have a pleasant visit. With a last quick,
encouraging look at Marianne, she gathered up her work
and departed from the cosy chamber grandiosely referred
to as the morning salon, but in truth no more than one
of the many comfortable chambers decorated for ease
rather than ceremony.

Alone with Marianne, Raoul looked down at his wife,
a small smile of tenderness lurking behind his usually exu-
berant mouth. "Are you ready, my dear? Be brave, for I

assure you that as my viscountess, the Mershams can no longer hurt or harm you."

"I know that. And I thank you." The admission cost much, given the trials of the past week. Still, Marianne was fair and knew of a certainty that Raoul would live up to his promise to protect her with the mantle of his name, if not the more precious one of his love.

He seemed to read her thoughts, for he drew her close, and the gentle perfume of roses and lavender wafted into his nostrils and took a grip on his soul. He wanted to drop all resistance then and take her into his arms and kiss her into submission.

Raoul was no fool and sensed the passion behind his lady love's honey gold eyes and deep, inviting, thoroughly entrancing cherry red lips. He ached to run a finger through her dark curls and down to the base of her long, soft neck. Beyond that . . . his eyes drifted to the soft curves beneath the demure bodice of lavender and gold. He ached as he had the night past and the one before that. In fact, he could not remember the last time he'd had a moment's peace since he'd first caught sight of her tantalising ankles making their dangerous way down the ridiculous linen rope.

He sighed in exasperation at the fleeting memory. He would not give in. He had endured two stinging slaps, and though he was more than up to defending himself against his dear damsel, he was disinclined to do so. Nonetheless, the memories of her rejection were humiliating, as were her ill-chosen taunts.

No, though the blush that stained her cheeks indicated she felt no small desire for his person, he would not be the first to yield. If she wanted to taste of the fine fruits of his passion, she would have to be the first to ask. The first to beg, in fact. A determined light came into his lordship's eye at this resolve.

Marianne, reading some few of the thoughts that flitted across his brow, felt her heart constrict. His lips were lazy and sensuous as they looked her over. She wanted them so badly she felt giddy. His eyes glinted and she knew that he knew.

"Wretch!" Marianne could not stop the word slipping off her tongue.

Her husband understood and laughed delightedly. They had a long path to traverse, he and his lady love, but at least it would not be boring.

"You look adorable, my dear. There is just one thing amiss."

"What is that?" Marianne fluttered back to the present in a tremor of anxiety. If she was to face the Mershams, she wanted her dignity to be intact. "Is it my hair? I had Fraser do it to the latest style but perhaps—"

He put a finger to her lips and the touch burned like fire. "It is not your hair. That, my dear, is perfect."

"My gown, then?" Perhaps I should change into the topaz brocade. . . ."

"You look as regal as a queen. Lavender suits you, and the gold is the exact match of your honey eyes. Your taste is to be complimented."

Marianne could not help a glow of pleasure. "I am glad you are pleased, my lord." She cast her eyes down primly. Raoul felt a burst of laughter twitching at the corners of his mouth.

"Are you, Maid Marianne? Then I am doubly pleased." His words were brimful of meaning, and Marianne could not help the ready blush from staining her cheeks.

"Come, then, my lord! What, I ask you, is wrong?"

"You have no jewels, my love. There is no time to get down the caskets that belong by right to the viscountesses of Hansford. Remind me to speak to my secretary. He will see to it that they are delivered safe to your hands."

"I have no need. . . ."

Raoul cast a stern eye upon her. "Indeed you do, lady wife! It is fitting to your station!"

"Since when do you care what is fitting to your rank?"

"Since I have acquired a hoyden wife it is my duty to protect!" Raoul would have bitten back the words if he could have helped it. Marianne looked suddenly lonely and woefully abashed.

"I am a sore trial, am I not, my lord?"

"At times, kitten, but I swear I would not have it any other way." He took her chin in his hand and looked firmly into her eyes. For an instant Marianne thought she was to be kissed, but the moment passed.

"Here! I have a notion!" Raoul withdrew from his cravat a single pin of solid gold centred by a stone of striking size and hue. "A sapphire, my dear. I suspect it will not look amiss with your lavender." Before Marianne could protest, he'd deftly thrown her frothy gauze shawl over her shoulders and affixed it with the shimmering pin.

Marianne felt breathless but radiant. The gift was such an unexpected treasure that she was led to the hope that he must, after all, care.

"I cannot—"

"Indeed you can! There are advantages to being married, you see! Were I a mere suitor a posy would have had to suffice."

"A gift like this would have called my morality into severe question!"

"It is an unfortunate fact of our marriage that your morality never has had cause to be questioned." Raoul could not help the quick retort that sprang ruefully to his lips.

Marianne gasped, her eyes flashing fire. She made to withdraw the pin. Raoul's arms were quicker. They gripped her hands in a viselike grasp and held them, motionless, against her breast.

"You will wear it, my dear, because I will it." His eyes met hers and Marianne had not the strength to resist. She nodded and he released her, though his eyes did not waver from hers for a minute.

"Good girl! It looks admirable, I assure you. And now, shall we?" He held out his arm. After a moment's hesitation Marianne slipped her hand into it. She forced herself to take the few steps to the door, though her body was giddy from a new and unfamiliar desire.

Dear heaven! she thought. *Am I to feel this every time the man comes near?* Her question was still not answered by the time she reached the stairs.

"His lordship and his viscountess, the Lord and Lady Hansford!" Carstairs bowed low as he swung open the great double doors and stepped aside for Raoul and his Marianne. In neither countenance was there a trace of the devilry and mischief that habitually shone from sparkling blue and honey gold eyes.

If anything, the light in his lordship's eyes was glacial, frosty enough for Lila Mersham to take two surprised steps backwards and hastily revise the diatribe that had been spinning around her head ever since she'd heard the terrible, oversetting, and incalculably bad news that Peter had burbled into her incredulous ears some few weeks before.

Her mama, possibly more astute than she, pinned her lips tightly together and effected a grudging curtsy. Marianne barely inclined her head in acknowledgment.

For her trouble, Marianne heard an ill-suppressed hiss that in former times would have boded ill indeed. Delphinia Spencer-Pultney had never been particularly sparing with the long, reedlike cane she habitually resorted to when her will was crossed. While it was true that Lila and Peter had both, at times, been forced to bend for its unsparing application, there could be little doubt that Marianne, with her proud, defiant airs, had ever been the one to take the harshest of its unrelenting strokes. The new viscountess had good reason to wince at the memories, for beyond the remembered pain to her derriere lay a host of humiliations and outraged angers.

Now, however, she took great satisfaction in extending her hand regally and indicating the small occasional chairs that were scattered sparsely across the vast expanse of the receiving room.

"I do apologise for not inviting you to stay. We are entertaining such illustrious guests tonight that I declare I am quite fagged to death! The prince is vastly amusing, of course, but one does so tire of all the ceremony! I believe I shall have to set aside this afternoon to rest; otherwise, of course, I might have offered to take you for a turn in one of the curricles."

The young Miss Mersham cast her mother an anguished stare. The prince! Curricles! It was all too much to bear! She opened her mouth to provide Marianne with the vituperous tongue-lashing she deserved, but was forestalled by the acid sweetness of her mother, who recognised defeat when she stared it in the face.

"To be sure, Marianne dear! We would hate to interfere with your little pleasures! You must, of course, rest, if you wish to preserve your complexion! Such a pity it is that you are not blessed with Lila's peaches and cream, but there it is. I've said it over and over . . . we can't all be gifted with beauty, and one has to make the best of what one has, to be sure!"

Marianne gritted her teeth, determined not to take up the bait. Her eyes flashed, and Raoul decided it was time he stepped into the fray. His sapphire eyes caught hers and he held them for just a whisper longer than was strictly etiquette. Such a smouldering glance as he sent her was enough to turn her knees to jelly and shake her from the sad acknowledgment that the Mershams were right: her looks were unfashionably dark, her complexion intolerably blemished by being sultry rather than fair. The glance cast her way was bold, bordering on the indecent. She felt a blush creep to her cheeks. Her husband smiled audaciously in response and allowed his hand to steal up and lightly, almost carelessly, touch her satin gold skin.

"*Au contraire,* my love! Mrs. Spencer-Pultney must jest, to be sure! A lady of fashion such as she must know that dark is all the vogue! Ever since Brummel was heard to remark that roses have become tiresomely insipid and blondes cast into the shade by more exotic blooms, you must know that brunettes are to be cultivated. He would have had the likes of you in mind, my dear, for beneath the bloom of your delicate complexion lies a true exotic."

His voice was husky with longing, and Delphinia Spencer-Pultney felt herself quake with fury. So it was a love match, was it? *The little trollop!* She was still mystified to know how Marianne had contrived to form so eligible an attachment.

Raoul took a step forward and negligently snapped his fingers. Almost instantly the doors were opened once again and eight liveried servants stepped in, all bearing crested salvers of ornate wrought silver and handles gilded liberally with gold. There were macaroons and sweet pastries and an exotic confection that wafted delectably to the nostrils but remained elusively difficult to identify. Fresh oranges, hothouse grapes, and peaches in abundance added colour to the spread. The servants laid down their burdens only to shortly return with trays of Dresden china, judiciously interspersed with Sevres jugs and delicate teaspoons inlaid with the ancient crest of Hansford.

Lila, unused to such a show of pomp, allowed her mouth to slacken and hang open with wonder. Marianne contrived not to notice, though she, too, was secretly bemused by the sudden show of hauteur displayed in this hitherto cosy household. She nearly choked when Raoul offered his apologies for the slackness of the repast and assured her that in the future, his staff would not be so niggardly in their offering.

"It is just, my dear, that we do not have much time available to us. Kingsley and Scott are due to arrive, and you know what jewellers can be like!" He threw his arms up in the air in mock despair.

"I have several pieces in mind for a bridal gift, so we will not, unfortunately, be able to host your delightful"— he bowed elegantly—"relatives for very much longer. I am sure Carstairs will be able to see them out when they have done? Perhaps they would like to stay a while and view some of the portraiture? The Gainsboroughs are vastly pleasing, I believe."

Mrs. Delphinia Spencer-Pultney blanched at the treatment she was receiving. She was too experienced a player to be deceived by his lordship's veneer of civility. Inwardly, she bristled with fury at being treated like a common sightseer when she had planned on becoming an integral part of the aristocratic household. The viscount's offhand charm failed, as he knew it would, to win her over. The man was neither vague not indigent. She suspected him of being as calculating as herself, and the thought rankled.

Besides, she had personally witnessed the state her drunken sot of a son had returned home in, and although the clodpoll had no doubt had something of the sort coming to him, it was a bitter pill indeed to think that the immaculately garbed gentleman before her could be such a bruising fighter. In point of fact, the infuriating boy represented an eminent obstacle to all her plans and cherished dreams.

The best Delphinia Spencer-Pultney could hope for

right now, was a semirespectable position on the outskirts
of her stepdaughter's circle. The life she had planned for
herself was rapidly dissolving before her very eyes. It was
clear that Viscount Hansford would brook no interference
in his domestic schemes. Whereas the Earl of Glaston
could undoubtedly have been "managed," the viscount's
stubborn chin and haughtily raised eyebrows belied this
possibility.

An intriguing thought flitted into Delphinia's mind. Lila
would just have to step into the breach and marry Glaston
in Marianne's stead. That way she would take precedence
over the galling Hansfords, supplant their pretensions by
producing an heir, and at one and the same time take
the insufferable couple down a peg or two.

Jewels indeed! Marianne needed a smouldering back-
side rather than gems! The thought made her fingers itch
for the cane, but she stilled them as her thoughts flitted
to Lila. The widgeon would have to mind her manners
and curb her tongue, but the deed, she reckoned, could
be contrived. Rumour had it that the earl was spitting fire
to revenge himself of the slight upon his person. He was
unused to being thwarted, and Marianne had certainly
managed *that*. Half of London was whispering behind his
back, and the *Tattler* had featured an unamusing line on
the society pages that related quite clearly to this matter.
It was hardly to be supposed that his lordship would miss
the unsubtle reference to his dilemma splashed in bold
across the paper and available in the lobbies of all the
men's clubs he frequented: "A certain peer has been
thwarted in his matrimonial plans. A case of beauty before
age, you see—better fortune next time, the Earl of G—?"
He was said to be seething.

Decisively, Delphinia curtsied and gesticulated to her
daughter to do the same. Declining the offer of the gallery
tour, she regally announced that it had never been her

intention to stay, "what with Glaston eagerly expecting them at any moment." Lila choked, but was silenced by a particularly quelling stare from her mama. The Hansfords might have won the first round of the genteel battle of wills, but the war was hardly beginning! With a grim frisson of anticipation, the Spencer-Pultney woman marched her daughter out.

Raoul looked across the room at Marianne. His lips twitched with mirth at the proceedings. Marianne's eyes held an answering twinkle. It was a marvellous moment of amity between them—besting the enemy, albeit in the most civilised of fashions, in the most fashionable of places. For an instant the frostiness that had plagued them since the night of the Mollington ball dissolved.

All Raoul saw before him was the curvaceous, mischievous, and positively naughty young scamp he'd so impulsively offered his name. More than that, perhaps, for her eyes had an unsettling way of arousing him to unforeseen and definitely unwanted passion.

Marianne saw his eyes darken and impulsively moved towards him. She loathed the estrangement between them but was too proud—far too proud—to admit her mistake and beg the pleasure of his favours.

Favours they were . . . her eyes travelled to the shapely outline of his masculine hips, then up again to his wide mouth and the faint circles beneath blazing blue eyes. Perhaps he, too, had not been sleeping. His hand involuntarily pulled her closer, and she could feel the warmth of his body just inches away from her traitorously yielding flesh. She closed her eyes, unaware of how long and velvety her lashes were, how creamy her skin against the pitch darkness of shining hair. Though it was braided up in a fashionable chignon, long tendrils escaped their clips and drove the viscount to a desire that held no equal despite numerous past—and pleasurable—romantic escapades.

He was just busying himself with the delightful task of pressing her close against his white lawn shirt when he detected a movement that boded ill for this delicious new arrangement.

Marianne drew her arm back, not from any reason more sinister than the desire to change positions, the better to feel his back, lean and muscular in the simple, elegant, and excessively well fitting morning coat created for him by Weston. My lord, misinterpreting the gesture, felt that his handsome countenance was once more in danger of being slapped.

Instantly he stepped back, remembering his resolve. The delicious moment was lost, replaced by a mocking need to hide the tenderer emotions he very nearly had been trapped into displaying. Until Marianne herself begged for his passion, she'd have none of it, not even for a second. He caught her arm in a steely grip that almost made her wince.

"Not so fast, my lady! It might possibly seem strange to you, but I find I grow weary of having my face slapped!"

If his tone had not been so insufferably superior, nor his grip quite so viciously hard, Marianne might have tried to explain. As it was, she straightened her spine in a manner that would have pleased the most exacting of her governesses and afforded him a marginal curtsy. Then, tears stinging behind her lovely dark eyes, she tossed back her head and marched out of the room.

Ten

"All in place?" The honourable Earl of Glaston leaned back and squinted at his secretary. Though he balked at purchasing a new pair of spectacles, he did produce a quizzing glass of tolerable quality from his voluminous coat pockets. With this he surveyed his poor employee until the man was forced to avert his gaze and shift his weight from one foot to the other.

"Yes, milord, all is in place, I can assure you."

The earl nodded in satisfaction, his gray eyes glinting just for an instant.

"And the Duchess of Doncaster? I take it you have made arrangements for her?"

The secretary nodded. Though he despised the earl, his work was thoroughly efficient, a matter both of self-preservation and personal pride.

"She is to be transported to Tavistock Inn this very night. She is in company with the Baroness Winsome, who, as you know, is the greatest tattler this side of London."

"Good! Does Lord Rhaz travel with her?"

"No, milord! The duke has only just arrived back in England. I understand he is residing at his country estate."

"Pity! All the same, there is nothing like a woman's tattling tongue to ruin a reputation!"

"I believe so, milord!"

"I collect the dowager duchess and her companion will not be short of suitable gossip?"

"All going well, milord, they should not!"

"Excellent." His lordship indicated the decanter.

His secretary moved to unscrew the crystal top, carefully pouring the golden liquid into a tarnishing silver goblet. It was a pity, he thought, that Glaston was so mean. He handed the substance to his employer and once more took up his position by the hearth, his hands firmly behind his back.

"And Peter Mersham? He was amenable to the plan?" There was a small silence before the earl received his answer. When he did, he found the tone of his employee dry and a little uncomfortable as the affirmative was murmured.

It was one thing arranging a young lady's downfall in society—it was quite another, in his opinion, to arrange her downfall in virtue. That Peter Mersham had plans not strictly part of the arrangement forged by the earl had been evident. For an instant, the secretary wondered if the earl guessed the young man's intent and sanctioned it. He would not put it past Glaston—the man was cunning and notorious for the grudges he held. For now, though, he had a question to answer.

"Indeed, sir! The gentleman agreed with alacrity. I had hardly any need of haggling, though he did specify he would need a coach for the purpose."

"He may take the barouche." The earl's brow furrowed—he did not like having to meet demands, particularly those of the likes of Mersham.

"The barouche? I had thought perhaps the landau. I fear the barouche will make for a bumpy ride. The springs . . ."

". . . are perfectly in order!" The Earl of Glaston's voice was sharp. "Does for me, did for my father. No need to mollycoddle the rascal, whatever Delphinia might think."

The secretary cleared his throat. "I collect, milord, that the lady is more interested in her own comforts than her son's."

"I suppose she hinted that a private room be reserved for her?"

She did more than that, milord! I daresay hinting is not in her repertoire!" The secretary looked suddenly nervous. "That is, if I might offer an opinion."

The earl glared at him, ready to decline him this privilege. On second thought, however, he simply harrumphed and resumed his perusal of the papers in front of him. "I daresay! Tenacious woman, that! And as for her pudding-faced daughter . . ."

"Milord, pardon the presumption, but I was given to understand . . . that is . . ." The secretary's voice became a stammer, then subsided into a misery of silence. What he had meant to say was that Delphinia Spencer-Pultney had, in the ten minutes he'd spoken with her, convinced him that her daughter Lila was soon to be the next Countess of Glaston. Surely even she would not possibly imply such a thing if it were not true? The secretary longed to have some confirmation of this strange turn of events, but propriety did not permit him to ask.

Truth to tell, the earl was mulling over the very same question. If he'd not such a downright aversion to Delphinia, he might well have wed her brat in a fit of pique. It was clear from the ingratiating, servile, and utterly sickening call he'd had that morning that this was Mistress Mersham's intent. The idea had merits . . . it would have taught Marianne a good lesson if Lila, of all people, were to take precedence over her. Better still, if he could beget an heir . . .

He sighed. He would love to put an end to Raoul's chances of the earldom. From the minute he'd been born he could not stand the little toad—how much less now that he'd served him such a rotten trick and married the heiress from under his nose.

Well, he would pay dearly for the folly. The earl allowed himself a sour smile as he turned once more to his stammering employee.

"Best spend your talents on what you are paid for, young man! I will brook no speculation in my household, if you please!"

The gentleman reddened at this reprimand. For the tenth time that month he resolved to cease his employment with the earl. Yet, without a letter of recommendation, who would employ him? He could do no more than agree docilely and bow himself out. If the lovely Marianne was despoiled that evening, his hands were tied. There was little he could do, and the matter was in no way certain. Peter Mersham might do the decent thing and return her to the bosom of her family. . . . The young man sighed. Only a fool would believe that.

There was nothing he could do now. The letter to Lady Sinclair had been delivered. Undoubtedly she would think it romantic that Raoul would wish to meet her at Tavistock Inn rather than in the comfort of their own home. Women were so silly that way. The secretary sighed. It had been a stroke of genius to sign the letter with nothing but the initial *R*. That way, Marianne would have no chance to consider the handwriting suspect. She had not been married long enough to recognise Raoul's hand in anything except, possibly, his signature. Now, of course, she would know nothing. And the postscript? Reminding her of her wedded state simply sealed her fate.

Amber stared into the glass as she brushed her hair and for the tenth time fiddled with the bow of her nightdress.

Her eyes seemed very green against the gleaming gold of her hair. Her lady's maid hovered anxiously nearby.

"Are you sure I can't do that for you, ma'am?"

"Beg pardon?" Amber was brought back to reality, though the memory of dark eyes and a warm, masculine scent lingered enticingly on.

When would she see him again? Uncertainty began gnawing at her soul. He had said to expect the unexpected . . . but really, by now she would have thought he'd call. Tomorrow? He'd promised soon, but she was tired of hoping for tomorrow. Tomorrow and tomorrow and tomorrow . . . she was starting to feel wretched. It did not help that Raoul knew even less than she did. Beyond a shrug of the shoulder and a passing "Raphael's out of town; he had his knocker removed only yesterday, I believe," she could learn nothing from him. Lord Sinclair was never particularly communicative over mouthfuls at breakfast. Not when he had Marianne to distract him . . . Amber sighed.

Her maid coughed. "Your hair, ma'am! May I do it for you? I am excellent with curling papers."

The vision receded. Amber chuckled inwardly. The girl before her was no more than thirteen, but already she was sounding like a lady's maid of solid account. Miss Sinclair's good nature and kindliness were well known to her staff. Despite her housekeeper's grim disapproval, she'd agreed to allow Meg to practice on her with sublime disregard for the possible consequences. Curling papers seemed rather excessive, however, since Amber was famed for her short, straight, cropped look. Her ladyship had no wish to disappoint . . . her tone became gentle.

"I am sure you are, Meg! You have had excellent teachers."

Little Megan blushed and bobbed a curtsy. "Then I may?"

"Curl my hair?" The maid nodded eagerly. Amber

laughed. "Perhaps another time. Now don't look so disappointed! My hair needs to grow a little, I think. . . ." Her voice faltered.

Megan's hand had brushed against her skirts, and she emitted a tiny squeal of dismay. To Amber's bewilderment and consternation, the dismay turned to sniffles and then to the production of two round, wet tears.

"What is it?" The tears turned to a spate of outright weeping. Instinctively, Amber knelt to comfort the little servant girl. She appeared inconsolable.

"I forgot, ma'am."

"Forgot what?" Amber was bemused.

"This!" Out of her pocket, the young girl withdrew a note. It was addressed in an impeccable yet unfamiliar handwriting.

"He axed me to give this to you this mornin', he did."

Amber's heart did a strange lurch.

"Who did?"

The girl wiped her eyes. "Dunno his name. Gave me a penny, 'e did." The refined accents were lost in her distress. Amber hardly noticed, for a frisson of hope was shooting through her being.

Raphael. Could it be . . . no, surely not. It would account for his tardiness. . . . It *was* unexpected. . . .

She patted the girl's head and handed her a sweetmeat from the delicate Sevres jar at her table.

"May I see the note, my dear?"

The girl nodded and extended her hand. The epistle was duly exchanged for the sugar plum.

> *Come live with me and be my love. . . .*
>   *R*

Scrawled beneath, a hastily drawn map and a clear depiction of the Tavistock Inn, not five miles from Sinclair

Manor. Amber could not help laughing at the postscript: *Do not worry: we will be respectable!* The rascal . . . she recalled all the things they had discussed about respectability. He was teasing her! If he wanted her at Tavistock Inn, at Tavistock Inn she would be. She trusted Raphael with her reputation implicitly. No doubt he would be waiting for her complete with an entourage of chaperons and aging doyennes. She grimaced. When it came to the proprieties, Raphael could be a real bore at times. That is . . . in the past he had. With Raoul he was . . . with her he had been . . . with himself? Amber grinned.

The good Raphael had a notorious reputation of his own to uphold. She bit her lip. Which would be more important? Her reputation or his own? Marlowe's words implied the former, for she could not dismiss the rest of the verse: *and we will all the pleasures prove.* She blushed. *No!* The postscript was reassurance. How thoughtful of him.

In her heart she knew it was her own reputation that Delaware would cherish. Raphael loved her and would never do anything to harm her. An inner voice whispered that even if he were trifling with her honour, she still would leap at the summons. She half smiled at the irony of it.

After all her prattling and scolding, she was very like her scatterbrained brother after all—about to throw her cap to the winds, and at a notable rake at that! So be it then! There was Sinclair blood coursing through her veins, and the Sinclairs had never, so far as she could remember, *ever* blindly kowtowed to the conventions. She was five and twenty after all . . . practically on the shelf!

She smiled. The wait had been worth it. Raphael! Raphael . . . her heart sang as Megan, forgotten, sniffed forlornly. The sound recalled her to Amber's attention.

"Good heavens, child! No need to sniff! Here, take my

handkerchief and dry your eyes. There is no harm done, after all."

"No?" The girl shyly took the exquisitely laced kerchief and dabbed her eyes. "Thank you, ma'am!" She curtsied and handed back the cloth.

Amber smiled and waved her away. "Keep it, my dear! It might come in useful sometime!"

Megan's eyes widened in pleasure. "Cor! I mean, thank you ever so graciously, ma'am!"

Amber's eyes twinkled. "It is a pleasure, Megan. And now, leave me, dear. I have a few errands I need to attend to."

"Now?" Meg seemed bewildered.

"Now!"

"I thought you was to have an early night, milady!"

"So did I, Meg, but I have suddenly changed my mind!"

"But—"

"No more buts, Meg!" Amber made her voice as stern as she could. The maidservant bobbed, then nodded, then finally, to Amber's profound relief, withdrew.

Lady Sinclair peeked out of her curtains. *Good!* There was still light—more than enough time to reach Tavistock Inn without raising too many brows. Well, her stablehands would have something to say, but she could live with that. . . .

Raoul rapped on Amber's door. She was the dearest of sisters. Of the pair, she was undoubtedly the brains. Whenever the viscount had some serious thinking to do, his legs led him to Amber's calm, comfortable chamber. Her furnishings were plain but of impeccable taste and quality. Cherry wood armchairs, a single firescreen of embroidered turquoise silk, and a shining candelabra of silver added softness and beauty to the simplicity. Across half her wall were hand-carved shelves containing an abundance of books of all description. Hardly necessary, since the Sinclair library was just a corridor away.

Raoul would never house books in his wing—his housed a motley assortment of oddments that randomly pleased: snuffboxes, heavy black mezzotints in Brazilian frames, a Chinese epergne, Gothic-style furniture, and a huge bed draped in crested velvet. For the interested viewer of his cluttered collection, there was even a gargoyle solemnly attached to his eastern window frame. This, truth to tell, was more a whimsical joke than anything else, but his lordship had become sincerely attached to his gargoyle over the years, resisting all attempts by other, more discerning Sinclairs to have the ghastly thing removed. Fortunately for him, his private chambers led out to a little-used courtyard below, so his mother and sister desisted from pestering him too often in this particular matter. He sighed, wishing they were equally forbearing in other matters, too.

His family was incredibly dear to him, but he found them tiring. First they hounded him to death to select a bride. Now that he had done so—albeit in a most unorthodox manner—they were not satisfied to leave him alone and let him be. No, on the contrary! Raoul had never felt so hounded in his life. The more he thought on it, the more hard done by he felt. He could not remember the last time he had spent a satisfying evening among his cronies, drinking licentious spirits and gambling recklessly to boot. Nor, he thought wrathfully, could he remember the last time he'd bedded a well-rounded wench. He knocked again upon the door. Perhaps Amber could sort out the fit of dismals he'd fallen into. It was not to be expected that she would understand the intolerable magnetic effect Marianne had upon him, but she could, he hoped, proffer a little balming sympathy, view matters from his light for a change, possibly offer some advice from a feminine perspective. . . .

"Amber?" It was unlike her not to respond. Raoul unceremoniously pushed the heavy mahogany door open a fraction. No sign of a maid. He pushed it open a little farther. He had no wish to disturb his sister at her ablutions, but the silence was alarming. He had it from Carstairs—the best of authorities on these matters—that the lady Amber had retired. He'd taken specific note of this fact, for whilst it in no way impeded his decision to consult with his sister—it had not crossed Raoul's mind that Amber might prefer solitude to a comfortable cose with himself—it meant he was certain of having her undivided attention without fear of interruption. Where the devil, then, *was* she?

With a swift and careless movement he was in the room, noting the pristine state of the coverlet and the untouched chocolate that stood in a tall china cup beside the bed.

"Amber?" Raoul felt a little foolish as he pulled back the drapes to disclose a charming view of the countryside, but precious little else. He turned back toward the bed, half shrugging his shoulders in puzzlement. Perhaps Lady Jane would know. His eyes caught something creamy on the dressing table. A wafer from Great-aunt Norris, in all probability. He picked it up and fingered the sheet idly before allowing his eyes to roam over the words, not the habit of a gentleman and certainly not something he would have done to anyone else's correspondence, but Amber and he had no secrets. His eyes grew round at the words that jumped out at him.

R . . . R . . . Something niggled at the back of his brain. Raphael! Raphael Delaware, the Marquis of Slade . . . it had to be! He was not paying much heed, but it seemed to him Lady Jane had mentioned something of the kind to him only the other day. He'd dismissed it as errant nonsense, of course . . . hard to think of Amber in an amorous light—harder still to think of Raphael as a serious suitor . . . Raphael the rake, not Raphael the riveted! Yet there was the letter, and as sure as he was standing, Raoul knew his friend would not dally with Amber without serious intent. Lady Jane would be thrilled.

His lordship pocketed the wafer, intending to return it to Amber in due course. He had wits about him enough to know the missive should not fall into the hands of the servants. Good heavens, Raphael's proposal was positively improper! The more he thought of it, the more indignant he felt. The correct form, of course, would be for Delaware to apply to *him* for Amber's hand.

A slow grin lit up his marvellously handsome features at the thought of Raphael finally putting a step out of line. Raoul had endured too many lectures to be complacent about such a fact. This time Raphael was suggesting the improper. With his sister, too! He pulled the letter out and read it again. The grin turned to a frown. *No!* He was not such a nodcock as to let Amber be compromised. She needed protection in this crazy exploit, and protection she would get.

It did not take Raoul long to return to his chamber, exchange his top boots for more practical riding Hessians, and thrust a fashionable beaver upon his head in a manner that would have made his valet cringe. With only the slightest hesitation he knocked on Marianne's boudoir adjoining his own. She was not within, and there was no sign of her maid. A faint scent of honeysuckle lingered invitingly in his nostrils as he walked briskly across the room and opened one of the French doors leading to the terrace. Raoul had used this shortcut for a good many years, especially when avoiding tiresome tutors—a habit he had become adept at. This route down the outside stairwell was so much quicker than the conventional path through galleries and entrance halls. As he reached the last stair, his steps turned to a sprint. It was not long before he reached the stables.

A quick word with the head groom relieved his mind of his major concern: Lady Amber had only recently left, taking with her the Sinclair carriage, rather than the sleek Arabian that was swifter than the wind, a match for no man with an interest in catching her.

Very little time had passed before the viscount himself had the Arabian saddled. As he set off toward Tavistock Inn, he thought on the great irony that his dearest friend and mentor could be in such terrible breach of etiquette.

He was not a quarter mile down the track when he turned round in sudden decision. The marquis was more likely to be in residence than kicking his heels at the inn. He spurred the stallion to a gallop and headed east toward Grosvenor Square.

Eleven

Peter Mersham looked at the ormolu clock on the mantel. His tasselled boots tapped angrily against the drab pastel colouring of the inn's carpet. Not a sign of Marianne, and he had had his minions posted for four hours at least. Was it possible she had not received the note?

Possible, but not likely, he reflected. The servant wench had been well paid for her services and could have no reason not to deliver it as required. Perhaps Marianne had burned it unread. Again, hardly likely, given her ladyship's known curiosity. What then? Peter bit his lip. Fate could not be so unfair! He had the opportunity for revenge most sweet, and he intended to seize it if it was the last thing he did. He did not care a jot for Glaston's agenda, but he had to admit it coincided well with his own. Lord high-and-mighty Raoul Alistair Griffin Sinclair needed to be taken down a peg or two, and what better way than to be cuckolded by his own relative-in-law? Better still, Marianne's disgrace would be witnessed by society's highest sticklers, and in these matters it was *never,* he fondly reflected, the man who was held to account. Marianne would not be able to show her face in polite society ever again, a fact that caused a faint smile to cross his otherwise urbane features. Yes, he looked forward to his encounter with Marianne—very forward to it. The jade had teased him with her beauty, her scent, and her too palpably displayed disdain once too often. She would get what was coming to her or his name was not Peter Daragh Mersham, Esquire. Just one question irritated his nervous disposition and caused a slight twitch to appear around his nostrils: where in damnation *was* the wench?

Lady Amber stepped out of the chaise and directed the ostler to her groom. With fortitude and a lighthearted air of mischief, she dismissed his inquiring stare with a quelling one of her own. True, she was not accompanied by a maid and had no baggage to speak of, but that was her particular business, not his.

She strode towards the inn and fluffed down her exquisite riding habit. For an instant she felt uncertain, standing at the entrance to the taproom, waiting for she knew not what. Then she squared her shoulders and took in the faint scent of cider and roast. The walls were lined with a dark wood, the hearth faintly scattered with ash and the odd pinecone. Cowardice had never sat well with her, and she refused to make an exception now. If Raphael was not waiting for her within, she would eat the feather on her new velvet bonnet.

Suddenly her eyes narrowed and instinct took over. At the far end of the room stood a wafer-thin serving girl with deep, sunken eyes and a cream bun half-hidden in her pocket. The innkeeper was threatening to beat her to a pulp, and, judging by her size and the severity of her tone, the deed would have been accomplished with consummate ease. In two strides, Amber was across the dimly lit room.

"Good grief, woman! Can't you recognise hunger when you see it?" Her eyes flashed as she snatched a silver tea tray off the long, oaken bench and placed it before the unfortunate waif of indeterminate age but undoubted appetite.

The innkeeper reddened furiously, but she recognised quality when she saw it. Instead of venting her spleen upon the newcomer, she turned back scathingly to the original offender.

" 'Ere! Don't scoff, and youse be minding yer manners!" Sally Dawse placed pudgy hands on her hips and shrugged apologetically at the willow-slim young woman who had turned from unexceptional lady of quality into a fierce virago.

"Betsy 'ere is allus hungry, pardon yer ladyship's honour!"

"And whose fault is that, pray?"

The words were like ice, and even the hardened innkeeper felt like wincing at the tone.

"To be sure it ain't mine, ma'am! Girl's got a appetite I ain't seen the like of yet! Eats us out of 'ouse an 'ome, she does, and for what, I ask yer? A bit o' fetchin' an' carryin', that's what! Ain't worth 'er keep, she ain't, an that's a fact!"

Lady Amber Sinclair grimaced. She could guess at the amount of "fetching and carrying" the little scrap of humanity had been doing. For all her pitiful thinness, her arms were like sinews, and the shadows under her eyes told their own sad tale. Betsy, as she was called, was tucking into the plum pie as if it were to be snatched from her instantly. As indeed it would be, the second the fine lady turned her back. Between mouthfuls her eyes darted from mistress to madame, decked out exquisitely in delicate peach cambric, a small feather merrily adorning the day bonnet of cream sarcenet.

Of course, these refinements were lost on Betsy, who knew nothing of fashion's intricacies but everything of being cold and hungry and having pies snatched from under her nose. She sniffed, then sniffed again, one hand clutching the last of the sticky treat, the other moving to wipe her tearstained face. There would be a beating for this, to be sure, but the pie was heavenly, and the kind lady was without doubt an angel sent from heaven.

Lost in these private reflections, Betsy was not to see the ostler beckoning for his pint, nor hear the hooves upon the cobbles as a chaise and four was led around the back. Strictly speaking she should have jumped, for the man would not have time to dally and the horses needed new hay and a good dousing of water. The stables were behindhand with men again, but as Cook was tiresomely wont to say, "there is always Betsy."

Betsy, however, was staring with stubborn eyes at the golden-haired vision who had stripped off her gloves and was now holding out a glass of warm, fresh milk. The milk still had the cream floating thickly on top and was white, as white could be.

Disbelieving in this unlikely luck, the child reached out and gulped down the milk in one swift, deft movement. Brown eyes met green, and in that moment Amber knew the child could not be forgotten and left to her inevitable, pitiable state. Oblivious of the stone floor and the dust from the stream of Hessians that daily made inroads across the entrance, her ladyship knelt so she was at a level with the copper-curled girl before her.

The innkeeper gasped at this latest proof of her ladyship's derangement. "Beg pardon, ma'am, but your gown! I be sure that is the finest trim! From Portoogal, most likely! And what with the soot from the coal and all . . ." Her voice was almost a wail as it trailed off in horrified silence.

"*Bother* the gown!"

Mistress Sally gasped at this blasphemy.

A smile twitched at the corner of Betsy's mouth. She

liked this paragon, who had the courage to put the mighty Mistress Sally in her place.

Amber's eyes twinkled. "And *bother* this inn! You may tell Lord Delaware—I collect he is within—that I wish to remove immediately to Sinclair Manor."

The smile faded from Betsy's face as Amber confronted the innkeeper. Mistress Sally shifted uneasily, then allowed a smug smile to flit across her businesslike face.

"Oh, no, ma'am! You cannot go out looking like that!" She pointed at the smudges on the cambric. "I will fetch a glass directly. Then, of course, you will wish to repair upstairs. . . ."

Amber glared at her, her eyes glowering with unaccustomed fierceness.

"Do you not understand English, ma'am? I do *not* wish to repair upstairs, but I *would* like a word with the Marquis of Slade, if you please!"

The innkeeper looked at her as if she had run mad. Indeed, she strongly suspected the lady of being in spirits, for what else could explain her unaccountable championship of a mere kitchen maid? As for the Marquis of Slade . . . she could well have asked for the prince regent himself. The man was renowned for his fastidiousness and would not be seen dead in an inn such as Tavistock.

"Lady Sinclair . . ."

But Lady Sinclair was not destined to hear her next words. The tableau was halted by a sudden shriek and clammy hands that clutched at her skirts. Betsy had just assimilated the fact that her angel wished to depart. "No, no, no!" she wailed, pounding at Amber with fists surprisingly strong for all their thinness. Her ladyship found her position suddenly changed from kneeling to lying flat on the ground, unexpectedly pummelled by a little hellion in kitchen green.

"Laws a'mercy! Get the smelling salts!" the innkeeper

admonished someone in the small crowd gathering to witness the spectacle.

Peter Mersham stepped into the fray. "May I?" He produced an evil-smelling bottle of sal volatile and opened the lid. Amber had just wits about her to push it away crossly and stand up, brushing the sweepings from the floor as she did so.

"Good heavens, man, I have not fainted! Get that vile concoction away! Betsy, I will not leave this place without you, so I pray you dry your tears. I have hopes that I will soon find you employment enough to earn your keep. There will be no more need to thieve cream buns from the plate." She looked her sternest, and the girl seemed to cheer up at this treatment. Lady Sinclair's benevolence was too much like a fairy tale to believe. A scolding along with the kindness made her promise seem more believable, somehow.

"I be fetchin' and carryin' for you mornin' and night, pleasin' your honour."

Amber bestowed a warm smile on the miscreant. Before she had time to utter another word, however, she was addressed once again by the sallow man in buckskins. He had replaced the stopper of the sal volatile and was regarding Amber with a most discomforting degree of interest.

"Did I hear you addressed as Lady Sinclair, ma'am?"

Amber was unsure of what to answer. She was unused to being addressed by strange men in inns and, while not wishing to be uncivil to the fellow, did not wish to bestow her name to all and sundry, particularly as her unchaperoned position was precarious, to say the least.

As it was, the matter was wrested from her hands by the innkeeper, who loudly proclaimed her to be Lady Sinclair and started a distressingly ingratiating discourse on how delighted they were to have her as a guest. Amber seethed inwardly, but allowed a cool smile to cross her striking features. The man seemed strangely disconcerted by her presence.

Mersham had to think quickly. Lady Sinclair . . . there had been a mistake. The wench must be the viscount's sister rather than his wife. He smiled sourly to himself—it was just his luck, as always. When his appetite was whetted for bedding the voluptuous Lady Marianne Sinclair, he found himself involved in a seedy comedy of errors. He could strangle Glaston for allowing such a ridiculous mistake to occur. Mind you, Venus of the golden hair was not without attractions of her own. The vague air of disdain he sensed acted as a stimulant to his disordered senses.

His eyes turned speculative. Disappointing that Marianne had escaped his clutches, but not irremediable. He could dishonour the sister with no undue effort and *still* avenge himself on Raoul, Lord Sinclair. As he was head of the Hansford lineage, his sister's shame would be his own. Glaston might not be overthrilled, but then it was *his* arrangements that had caused the error in the first place. Marianne could be dealt with at a later date. He checked the time. The Duchess of Doncaster and the Baroness Winsome were due to change horses upon the instant. If he hesitated, the moment would be lost.

The sun's rays were softening as Marianne gently strummed the strings of a harpsichord she'd discovered in one of the antechambers downstairs. The melancholy of the tune seemed to reflect that of her soul. How strange that so short a time had elapsed between the moment she had merrily lowered her bandbox onto the street and now;

she looked into her heart and found it aching with a love that was as unforseen, unexpected, and undesired as it was passionate.

How shocking! Her inner self half mocked the predicament in which she found herself: married, but chaste—viscountess by rank but not by nature. She was trapped in a paradox of her own making, for while she yearned for Raoul her pride scorned to have him.

Theirs was a marriage born of convenience and arrangement—to expect more would be unfair, but to accept less than her heart's desire seemed impossible. Marianne could bear the charade of the wedded stalemate no more. Her fingers plucked idly at the harp, irrespective of the notes. A maid in the next-door chamber winced. Wisely, Marianne set the instrument down and stood up with decision.

She intended to confront Raoul once and for all—for better or worse, she would shake the icy indifference from his face and see what lay beneath. Passion, she suspected, for there were times when his eyes smouldered as he glanced her way, causing faint shivers of excitement to run down her spine and tingle invitingly in the strangest of places.

She smiled faintly at the thought. It had not been difficult to fall in love with her husband. Appallingly easy, upon reflection. But therein lay the rub. That he was attracted to her was beyond doubt. That he loved her? She thought not. Not when there were so many women who, like her, were besotted on first sight. Impossible, too, when they'd known each other so short a time, when they'd married for convenience, not romance. She sighed. If only . . . But no, she was not fool enough not to notice any number of giddy young things casting calf's eyes at her spouse. Not just giddy young things either, she realised with a sigh. It was only yesterday she'd caught Lady Jersey's admiring gaze upon Raoul's unsuspecting frame. If he fell into her clutches . . . Marianne's thoughts became gloomy.

How could she compete with the belles of the season? With practiced flirts like the Countess of Mollington? With a patroness of Almacks even? Impossible, impossible, impossible! Yet the thought that she wanted to compete meant much.

She was not nearly as indifferent to her husband's attentions as she would like to be. When he was not being all grim and cold he was a darling—as madcap, carefree, and unaffected as ever she could require. Apart from that, he was more than passing handsome. . . . Marianne remembered how she thought she would faint at the sight of his bronzed flesh, clad only in the most seductive of dressing gowns. . . . *Oh!* She was going round in circles. Tonight was the night she would confront him. If he rejected her, she would retire to one of the country estates and leave him to his London pleasures. The pain of watching his dalliances—or worse, his cold indifference—would be lessened by a great dollop of distance. At least, she hoped it would.

She left the cheerful, rose-embossed antechamber and wended her way up the front staircase. She was too lost in her thoughts to hear the sound of galloping hooves from the stables or to wonder at the unusual stillness that had descended upon the fashionable household. Upstairs, she seated herself on a comfortable brocade sofa and unbraided her hair. Next to her lay a silver-handled fan that glimmered in the quiet afternoon sunshine. Marianne stared at it idly, making a faint face with her perfect features and delicately rounded eyes.

A long time passed before she made the slightest movement. Had Raoul been mocking when he'd said brunettes were in vogue? She suspected so. Too bad her lips were so wide and sultry—nothing like the adorable pink rose-

buds required of acknowledged beauties. She cocked her
head to one side, allowing soft hair to gently brush her
face. Out of the corner of her eye she noticed a piece of
parchment fluttering idly on the floor.

"Sylvia?"

"Beg pardon, your ladyship?" The maid stepped forward from the closet, where she had been selecting a shawl
to complement the ivory lace gown laid out for the evening.

"What is that on the floor?"

"I can't see. . . ."

"Over there . . . near the drapes!" Marianne half rose
to pick up the offending piece of paper. She sank back
into her chair, however, when the maidservant caught sight
of it herself.

"I will get it, your ladyship." In a deft movement the
woman strode forward and bent to pick up the errant slip.
She glanced at it, and a wave of pink suffused her normally
unruffled face. Marianne was intrigued and ceased playing
with her dark curls.

"Interesting?"

The pink changed to scarlet. Sylvia was a most superior
abigail—able to read and write, though at times like these,
being as discreet as she was, she probably wished otherwise

"It is yours, ma'am! It must have fluttered off the table
in the wind. Who can have opened that door?" She clicked
her tongue fussily and moved towards the curtains.

Marianne dismissed the problem of who, finding the
question of what more interesting. What did the note contain? Sylvia was acting most uncharacteristically coy. "A
note? How mysterious! Let me see!"

Again, the poor abigail blushed. Without a word she
mumbled some lame excuse to leave the room, then thrust
the missive into Marianne's hand.

It was not long before Marianne was perusing it with

a mixture of amusement, exasperation, and exultant triumph. It seemed that Raoul, Lord Sinclair, had come to his senses at last.

"Saddle Black Magic for me, Peterson."

"I cannot, your ladyship."

Marianne cocked her brow in a haughty imitation of Raoul at his worst.

"And why not, pray?"

Peterson looked uncomfortable. He had been with the family for more years than he cared to remember. He had saddled the present viscount's first horse and had mounted him when he was still in leading strings. He knew enough of Lord Raoul to know that something was afoot. If he was hurtling into another scrape, there was no point in alarming the new viscountess by informing her of that fact. No doubt Lord Sinclair would not wish his wife to follow him, and judging by the martial gleam in her eye, following him was precisely what she intended.

Peterson decided that a small lie was forgivable under the circumstances. Smiling sweetly, he informed the new Lady Sinclair that he had strict orders that the prized Arabian was for Raoul's use only.

"He be needin' a strong and steady 'and, beggin' your ladyship's pardon!"

"And *my* hand is not strong and steady?"

Peterson shifted hesitantly under the viscountess's gaze. It pleased him that his master had not brought home some namby-pamby milk-and-water miss, but under these circumstances her gaze was too direct for his comfort.

"To be sure it be steady for a *lady*, ma'am!"

Marianne's eyes flashed.

"Indeed!"

Peterson could not help noticing how her bosom moved

in indignation. A fine figure of a woman, he thought. He smiled, feeling certain that he and the viscountess would deal well together.

Marianne did not wait for any further conversation. Grabbing the bottom of her skirts, she swept inside and marched straight up to the stallion's box. It was empty.

"Might there possibly be *another* reason, Peterson, why I may not ride the stallion?" She smiled sweetly, but the worldly-wise groom was not fooled. Cap in hand, he gazed first at the scattered hay that lay at his feet, then at the dark-haired beauty who challenged him. He sighed.

"It be so, ma'am. Master Raoul—his lordship, that is— he be takin' the 'orse not long since. Tearin' hurry 'e be in."

Marianne nodded. "Did you notice his direction?"

Peterson nodded. Years of service and a strong sense of self-preservation had made him wary of females with tapping feet. He allowed that it might not be wise to prevaricate any further.

"Certainly did, ma'am. Should be 'alfway to Harrow by now."

"Harrow?" Marianne's brow furrowed. It cleared when she realised the direction the man's gnarled fingers were pointing towards.

"Is not Tavistock Inn in that direction?"

The man nodded. "That be what I said, your ladyship. Tavistock be the first change before Martindale, and everyone knows Harrow be but three changes more from there."

He looked at her patiently, as if teaching a particularly stupid pupil how to count.

Marianne opened her mouth to argue, then uncharacteristically snapped it shut. No point bantering with the groom when Raoul awaited her.

The stables had horses aplenty. She chose one sprightly-looking piebald with promising fetlocks, wasted another brief moment arguing with Peterson, who, much to her disgust, recommended her to a sidesaddle, and set off without further delay.

Raoul's gleaming blue eyes dazzled her imagination and spurred her on, making her oblivious to the dust she raised and the approaching thunderstorm from the west. *Come live with me and be my love.* . . . Only those words were on her lips as she cantered down the dusk-filtering road.

"I do feel tired!" The Duchess of Doncaster languished against the soft pillows and looked out at the mellow countryside before her. Her travelling companion, the Baroness Winsome, nodded in prim agreement. The journey from Windsor to Langtree had been a fretful one, fraught with boredom and a singular lack of spice to add dimension to the trip.

True, between the pair of them they had managed to pick out the shortcomings of each and every one of the season's beauties; they had sniffed out every intrigue—real and imagined—they had hinted at Lord Faversham's particular shortcomings, counted back the months Sir Pickersley had been back in England as against the size of his wife's swelling stomach; they had whispered and hinted and offered confidences in low undertones with triumphant, meaningful looks and twitches. They had, in short, outdone even themselves. Still, they were weary of each other's company.

The duchess harboured the most disagreeable suspicion that the baroness was toadying to her because of her rank rather than her person. Of course, this was true, but the truth was not always the most convenient or pleasant of things.

The baroness felt equally disgruntled. She was tired of

answering every witticism of the duchess with ingratiating nods and humble smirks. True, the free carriage ride was a boon to a nipfarthing, cheeseparing individual like herself, but the price sometimes felt a little high. Especially when the duchess glowered at her and reminded her that her nose needed powdering. The baroness had always been rather proud of her pink complexion—she took the remark as a personal affront.

Of course, the duchess, bored and a little crusty, had known she would. She leaned forward with a satisfied sigh.

"I believe we shall stop, Matilda!"

The baroness looked at her as if she had gone quite mad.

"Here?"

"Where else?"

"But I thought you despised posting inns!"

"This is not a posting inn—it is a respectable establishment!" The duchess took out her spectacles. "At least I *hope* it is!"

"Tavistock Inn. Middling, if I recall. Certainly not fitting to your grace's rank!"

"I believe *I* shall be the judge of that!" The duchess adjusted her turban. She was tired of the stuffy chaise; her rheumatic limbs were stiff—though she would never have owned to such a dreadfully aging disorder—and she was hungry. By her reckoning, avocado creoles and a side of ham were reason enough to stop. Besides, she had caught the crest of a coach . . . her interest was piqued, and on a trip of this magnitude, anything of possible interest was worth inspection.

"Matilda . . ."

"I am coming!" The baroness took up her shawl and her finicky stitching. It was some moments before she had retrieved her reticule and lorgnette, but at last the deed was done. The patient footman lifted her down with due ceremony, though she chose to ignore his faint deferential bow. When the duchess was waiting, it paid to make haste. Actually, the duchess was *not* waiting. She had retrieved her stout onyx walking cane and was making her regal way inside. Matilda could just make out the twinkle of her jewelled headdress before the dim candlelight claimed her completely.

Twelve

Peter Mersham dismissed the innkeeper with two fingers and a faint curl to his lip. When she hesitated, he bestowed upon her an ingratiating smile and some small coinage Amber was unable to make out.

"Begone, woman! And don't be so fidgetsome! Lady Sinclair and I are practically related!"

At that, the innkeeper nodded. She was heartily sick of Amber by now and certainly did not see any need to return the largesse that had just been bestowed upon her. It was more than her ladyship had given her, and that was the truth.

Amber looked troubled. The man was vaguely familiar, and she did not care to be put at such a disadvantage. Perhaps it was instinct, perhaps it was simply that she took exception to the cut of his coat, but Amber felt her hackles rise. She was conscious not to create a scene, but her heart pounded hard against the green velvet of her riding habit.

She raised her eyebrows coldly and waited for the man to explain himself. All the time, her eyes remained fixed on the door frame, where she half expected, any moment, the Marquis of Slade.

"Do you not remember me?"

Amber's eyes took in the slender figure and the sallow face. Not memorable, but then she had met so many. . . .

"Allow me to introduce myself. I am Peter Mersham."

Mersham . . . the name had a ring to it . . . Amber simply could not recall. She stared at the man blankly and said nothing.

Mersham felt fury rise to his throat. Of all things, he loathed feeling small. This woman obviously considered him less than a cockroach, for at the approach of such an insect she would, at least, scream. No such sound appeared imminent. Only cold hauteur and a blank look of faint disinterest. Mersham was not to know the effort it took Amber to so school her features. She was not unaware of the danger—if not to her person, then at least to her reputation.

"You may not remember me now, but I assure you that you shall in the future!" He took a menacing step towards her and Amber felt sick. The taproom was empty, and there was certainly no sign of Raphael. Had she been tricked? The gall rose to her throat but she remained splendidly erect.

"Explain yourself, sir."

Mersham strode between herself and her view of the door frame. There was something in the way he looked at her that held her mesmerised.

"I am Marianne's kin. I will have you know that I hold a very particular grudge against her."

Amber swallowed. "Do you, sir? What possible interest can that hold for me, pray?"

Mersham caught the faint stumble in her voice and was exultant. His voice became silky smooth, a little reminiscent of a watchful cat playing with a spirited mouse.

"None that I can think of, except that she is your brother's wife."

"And an excellent one at that!"

Mersham's eyes flashed. "Try not to provoke me, my dear. It might not go well with you."

Amber did not misunderstand his meaning. Out of the corner of her eye she noted the proximity of the fire's poker. When all was said and done, it might serve her well, though she would persist, if she could, in avoiding a scene. A jewel glimmered in the candlelight but Amber ignored it. She ignored, too, the fussy tones of a traveller who had obviously entered the taproom behind her. Her immediate virtue must be safe with these witnesses, but certainly her stainless reputation was in severe distress.

Being found alone in a taproom without benefit of a maid was sufficient to ostracise her from high society. If the onlookers suspected for one moment that she had an assignation with Mersham, she would be ruined.

Mersham could see the thoughts flit through her mind. What he could glimpse of her golden hair seemed particularly bright against the dull tones of the room. He waited seconds, though to Amber it seemed eons, before he strode up to her and placed his hand just beneath the small of her back. Amber went rigid, but still resisted the strong urge to scream. If she attracted attention to herself, she and the proud name of Hansford would be shamed. Worse, Mersham would triumph. She held her peace with a thought to placate the man.

Satisfied, Mersham moved his hand up towards the nape of her neck, just beneath the fashionable edges of her fine French bonnet. This was too much for Miss Sinclair. She moved away fiercely and ducked slightly, just beyond his grip.

"What do you want, sir?" Her voice was hardly above a whisper, but to Amber it seemed a scream.

He licked his lips and smiled strangely.

"What I want, my dear Miss Sinclair, is Marianne. It seems what I shall have to make do with, my child, is you."

Amber shivered, her eyes darting once again to the poker. Though her heart was beating fiercely, long years of training in decorum came to her rescue. Her hands remained still. If she could keep him talking, she could think. If she could think, she could outwit him. Conversationally, she inquired, "Why Marianne? What has she done?"

Perhaps it was not the best of questions. A dark shadow crossed the man's face.

"It is what she has *not* done that matters. Whilst she was betrothed to Glaston I kept my hands to myself and let her be. After all, if Glaston was to hold the purse strings and pay my debts, it was best not to send him spoiled goods."

Amber swallowed, resisting the almost overwhelming urge to shudder.

"And now?"

"Now I still have debts, and the little widgeon has flown the coop. Her husband has insulted me and must pay finely for that, too." He touched the side of his face.

Amber could just make out the dark shadows of a bruise. She knew an instant satisfaction that Raoul could have planted him such a facer. The pleasure was short-lived, for she read fierce revenge in the man's momentarily unshuttered expression.

"But *I* am not Mariannne!"

"More's the pity! However, I am sure Raoul, Lord Sinclair, will be more than a little shocked to find his sister despoiled. Marianne will suffer her fair share of distress, too." Mersham's tone was smug. Amber was providing him with a captive audience. When all was said and done, the mistake was not so very terrible after all. Miss Sinclair would suit his tastes just fine.

He peered over to see whether the duchess and her entourage were arriving.

Nothing yet. Still, there was nothing to say he could not sample the wares before they arrived. It would make her

destruction complete, after all. With a movement that took
Amber unawares, his gloved fingers grabbed the bonnet
and removed it without ceremony. Miss Sinclair slapped
his face. For an instant, Mersham was still. Then he
dropped the bonnet and advanced with such purpose that
Amber was forced to sidestep him. Too late. He caught
her deftly around the waist and pressed his lips fiercely
onto her own. Amber tried to struggle, but his wily body
had her arms firmly pinned to her side. She turned her
head, but his moved with her, trying to force her to open
her mouth. This, she thought wildly, she would not do.

She prepared herself for a wordless, impossible struggle.
Her cheeks burned with the effort to fend him off. As
her hand reached for the poker, her eyes never leaving
his face, she was rescued from an unexpected quarter. Before she could assimilate what was happening, she was vio-
lently released and sent spinning halfway across the room.
In a daze, she noted the events that were taking place.

A loud clang had been followed by a dull thud, a cursing,
yet another thud, and a whoop of glee. Betsy—quiet, forgotten Betsy, who had *not* left the taproom when the innkeeper had, but rather crept silently behind the curtains,
both out of self-interest and an instinctive sense of
trouble—had come thundering to the rescue.

With unusual reticence she had bided her time, not
knowing whether the man was friend or foe to her beloved
angel. She'd been suspecting the latter for at least a quarter of a minute, though his kiss made her wonder. Miss
Sinclair would not thank her for coshing her beau senseless! Still, Amber's resounding slap had acted as a long-
looked-for sign. The man had no business touching her
lady. Betsy was thankful for two reasons—she misliked the
cut of the man's jib, and she was *spoiling* to cosh him over
the head with Mistress Dawse's silver tea tray. This was now
sporting a large dent, but Betsy was not looking overly

troubled. With sublime cheerfulness, she beckoned to Amber.

"Cor, ma'am! I reckon 'e will 'ave a thumpin' bruiser tonight, 'e will!" Amber, unused to cant, could not help grinning. She might not understand the exact sense of Betsy's words, but she was quite sure she could make out the general gist. With an odd twinkle in her eye, she allowed a wide smile to cross her face.

"Reckon he will, Betsy!" This made Betsy laugh. For a split second, Amber looked at Mersham. He was recovering his senses and would need either to be restrained or removed. Just as she was murmuring these eminently sensible thoughts, she looked up.

For the second time that day, Amber's heart gave a lurch. Standing—no, *lingering* in the door frame, a picture of unruffled poise and impeccable panache, stood the Marquis of Slade. Nothing in his demeanour revealed that but seconds before, he had been party to a murderous rage, or that he had just travelled ten miles across an unused track to reach Tavistock before dark. Magnificent as ever, he executed an elegant bow, locked Amber's eyes in a speaking embrace, and languidly pointed to the fascinated Betsy.

The marquis had much to say in private, but that, he reflected regretfully, could wait. For the moment, he had one thing to say to the captive audience, and he said it with due emphasis.

"Adopt that girl!"

Lady Sinclair looked up at him gratefully. "You may jest, sir, but I have already promised something of the kind!"

Raphael smiled, and it seemed as if the gloom of the room had been supplanted by a thousand flickering candles.

"Excellent! She may serve as duenna, for I assure you, my dear, you need one."

The hot look in his eyes made Amber tremble with pleasure. He took her chin in his hands and tilted her face upwards, towards him.

In the shadows, the Duchess of Doncaster looked on, transfixed. Matilda, Baroness Winsome, tittered. She was rapped over the knuckles with a fan and adjured to be quiet. The duchess had not witnessed so entertaining a spectacle for some time.

In the corner, Mersham was fighting a combination of dizziness, nausea, and the familiar sensation of defeat. As Raphael gently stroked the hair from Amber's face, caressing and calming her with the intensity of his stare and the closeness of his lips, Mersham stood up. Raphael paid not the slightest heed. Neither did Amber. Her pulse was racing and she knew it was not from the exertion of her tussle with Mersham. Her eyes locked on the vivid dark patch just above Raphael's deep red lips. How she had longed, over the years, to trace it with her fingers. She did so now. Raphael emitted a throaty groan deep at the back of his throat. Amber felt empowered, lost to all sense of propriety, aware only of his devastating presence and her own ability to ignite his passion.

She closed her eyes, the better to savour his kiss—the first kiss he would bestow upon her, the shadowy kiss of her secret dreams. It was light and tantalising. It promised much, and Amber felt her body move towards him, yielding and demanding more than she had yet received. Raphael put her gently from him.

"Later, my dear Amber, when you are my affianced wife."

For an instant she did not understand. Then she blinked and took in the turbaned head of an imposing gray-haired lady and another, thinner one who did not even bother to *pretend* she was stitching.

Embarrassment struggled with decorum. Bemused, Miss Sinclair blinked as Raphael made an elegant leg to the larger of the two women and bestowed a raffish smile upon them both.

"My compliments, your grace." He nodded towards the thinner one. "Baroness."

The duchess's protruding eyes took on a certain gleam. "You have not, I believe, introduced me to your *friend.*" The emphasis was pronounced and vaguely insulting. Lord Delaware remained unruffled, though his tone brooked no argument.

"Indeed, your grace. May I present to your attention Lady Amber Sinclair?"

There was a moment of tension. Instinctively, Amber knew her reputation was on the line. If the duchess took her in dislike, no intervention by Raphael could help her. She would spend the rest of her days being pointed at and whispered about behind fans. She, who had ever been considered a diamond of the first water! She stepped forward proudly. If the duchess rejected her, then *she* would reject the marquis. Painful though it would be, she would not marry him if the marriage did him no credit. Raphael sensed her thinking and stiffened. He would carry her off and *force* her, if he needed to. He prayed inwardly it would not come to that.

Amber executed an exemplary curtsy and extended her hand.

The baroness lifted her nose and tittered loudly. "I do not think . . ."

Amber's heart sank. They were going to give her the cut direct. Her eyes met the duchess's squarely. The moment passed, and she found her hand warmly clasped in the gnarled one of the duchess.

"For once you are right, Matilda; you do *not* think! And *stop* that cacophony, I beg of you!" The deep voice bent towards Miss Sinclair. "I cannot *bear* a titterer!"

Amber blushed for Matilda's feelings, but it seemed the

baroness was used to such treatment. She simply picked up her stitching and sank back into her seat. The duchess grabbed Amber's other hand and chuckled with self-satisfaction. Her jewels glimmered incongruously in the half-light. "I *thought* I recognised the crested carriage! You must be the Viscountess Hansford's halfling!"

Amber nodded the affirmative. The duchess dropped her hand and beckoned to Raphael. "You may go, my dear sir! No need of you, you know!" The Marquis of Slade emitted an almost audible sigh of relief.

"I will quit immediately, once I have dealt with . . ." He looked towards Mersham. The man was standing with his hands planted firmly on a chair. In the throes of defeat he remained defiant. He pointedly ignored the marquis's menacing expression and turned a sickly face on the duchess. He smiled ingratiatingly.

"Good day, your grace! And Baroness Winsome, good to see you again." The duchess cocked a lofty brow in his direction, but Matilda, to everyone's astonishment, actually simpered. Mersham was not yet finished.

"I should say good *evening*, your grace." He stared pointedly at the clock.

The Duchess of Doncaster looked at him as though he were less than a worm. Another man would have cringed, but Mersham was beyond caring.

"Odd it would be if your grace recognises a young . . . person"—he declined to say *lady*—"who loiters about inns without so much as the benefit of a maid. Stranger still, when that lady has been kissed by no less than two men in the space of a short half hour!" His tone was gloating, for even though the duchess was powerful, not even *she* could gainsay such behaviour. He was right, for Matilda had started nodding her head vigorously in agreement.

"It is true what he says, Duchess! Though Lady Sinclair may be innocent of intent, it cannot be denied that she is not unsullied! We cannot allow her through the portals of Almacks under such circumstances!" Though her tone was gloomy, her eyes had brightened perceptibly. Matilda liked nothing more than watching other people's misfortunes unfold. The duchess, though a tireless gossip and a meddlesome creature, was nevertheless far kinder. She'd taken one of her unexpected likings to Miss Amber Sinclair, and that counted for much.

"Matilda! What *can* you be talking about?" Her tone sounded so astonished that the baroness sat up, feeling very silly indeed.

"No maid? Of *course* the lady has a maid. And an excellent aim she has, too!" The duchess nodded approvingly at Betsy. Betsy blushed, then grinned, then affected a somewhat haphazard curtsy that held more goodwill than grace. Still, the point was made, and Matilda was silenced with a quelling glare.

Mersham did not give up easily. Truth to tell, he was as stubborn as a mule when pushed.

"She *did* kiss—"

He was silenced by the marquis, who grabbed him by the forearms and rammed him hard into the wooden counter of the taproom.

"Yes?" His voice was silky smooth, but Peter Mersham was not fooled. Behind the cool white cambric were muscles of steel. He could feel them rippling with menace. His trapped wrists suddenly felt hot under the viselike grip.

"*Who* did you say she was kissing? I will mince that man into a pulp." The tone was so matter-of-fact that it left no scope for doubt.

Mersham blanched. "Not I!"

Raphael viewed him with contempt. A coward as well as a blackmailer. He released his hands and moved away from the counter; his eyes, however, remained firmly locked with those of Mersham.

"Excellent, for I would not like to feel the lady's virtue was in question. It *isn't*, is it?" He glared at Marianne's relative.

"No . . ."

"You relieve my mind! I am sorry you suggested such a thing even in jest. Fortunately, I will not have to *mince* you."

Mersham looked relieved.

The marquis continued. "Perhaps I will merely blacken the other side of your face. For the insult, you know."

Mersham took up his hat and backed out of the door.

"That will not be necessary!"

Raphael's mouth twitched.

"Indeed, I should think not! Such exertion! Perhaps another time, then."

Mersham did not wait to make a reply. His footsteps echoed sharply across the cobbled floor. The marquis raised his hand and Betsy, recognising authority when she saw it, curtsied and prepared to take her leave. She was called back at the door and granted one of the marquis's dazzling smiles. Instantly, she was a prisoner to his charm. "May I suggest, Betsy, that you pack? I am very sure Miss Sinclair can find some occupation for you in the viscount's household."

"Elevated to a viscount's household!" Betsy was almost speechless with excitement. She bobbed a curtsy and murmured something inaudible that somehow conveyed to her audience that her baggage could be packed on the instant.

When she was gone, the marquis bowed towards the ladies. "I trust matters have now been resolved to your satisfaction?"

The duchess tapped her foot regally. There was an interesting air about her that Raphael could not define but did not quite trust. Matilda was another matter. Cowed, she sought to ingratiate herself with Amber.

"*So* sorry, my dear. Silly mistake, really. Those Mershams are little upstarts when all is said and done—" She was not allowed to finish.

"No! I am *not* satisfied!" The duchess's booming voice made everyone jump. Even the suave marquis was forced to lift a languid brow in inquiry.

"Miss Amber, we've established, was definitely *not* caught kissing Mersham." She paused and pointed her onyx cane in Raphael's direction. "That is not to say, young man, that she was not caught *kissing!*"

The marquis understood the drift of her thoughts at once. If he considered the duchess an amazingly meddlesome creature, he did not for an instant show it. Instead, he smiled sweetly and confronted her head-on.

"I do believe, your grace, you refer—most delicately, of course—to my own efforts with regard to the lovely Miss Sinclair."

Amber, habitually regal, felt a deep blush suffuse her face. The duo were talking as if she were not present. The duchess smiled benignly but with meaning.

"Well?" Her voice boomed. She was in her element, for matchmaking was one of her favourite activities. Raphael smiled and removed his gloves. He walked over to the counter and poured himself a glass of red wine. He tasted it, then set it down in disgust. The duchess snorted. "Serves you right, young man! Good wine is like good breeding—should be refined and drunk only in the comfort of one's home!"

The innuendo was not lost on Raphael, who smiled wryly and shook his head.

"I shall endeavour to remember that, your grace! In fact, I shall humour you entirely!"

He turned to Amber, his eyes softening. She could not

help thinking how handsome he looked in his dark riding clothes and white gloves. Regardless of the dust on the inn's floor, he dropped to one knee and took her hand.

"Well, my dear Miss Amber? Since we are so dreadfully compromised, will you agree to be my wife?" His eyes, though twinkling, yet held an element of seriousness that touched Amber and made her head as light as a feathered cloud. She smiled mistily in return.

"Only if you agree to get off that floor, my lord! I have no wish to so soon be a widow!"

The marquis looked at her inquiringly.

"Your valet! He will kill you if your clothes are soiled on my account!"

The atmosphere in the room lightened considerably. Nothing could alter the duchess's view that it was her meddling that had brought on this timeous betrothal. When Raphael produced a splendid seventeenth-century rose-cut ruby, explaining that fetching it from his countryseat was what had caused the unwarranted delay in seeking her hand, Amber was grateful that this mystery, at least, was solved. The duchess snorted, loath to believe the betrothal was of previous standing. She was so set on believing that it was *her* hand that had caused the union that nothing—not even the ring—could disabuse her of the peculiar notion. With a self-satisfied sigh she rubbed her hands together and announced that the betrothal ball would be held at Kilkenny, the ducal seat of Doncaster.

nodded in approval and surprise. Raoul must have ridden the stallion over, giving orders that the carriage be delivered in case of inclement weather. How thoughtful.

In beaming approval and a little unexpected shyness, and with a heart bursting with budding love, she made her entrance. The cosy fire was just as she had imagined, but the occupants completely overset all expectations.

Seated side by side on a small, striped sofa of soft faded linen were his lordship Raphael Delaware, the Marquis of Slade, and his betrothed. Marianne could not for a minute mistake the happiness that shone from her eyes, nor the strong possessiveness that burned from his. She was just beginning to feel she had stepped into a very private tête-à-tête when she noticed that the room was not empty.

Far from it! It appeared filled with the dominating presence of a very large woman in maroon travelling dress, unmistakable for the number of jewels she sported across both her ample bosom and her turban. A fleeting glance at her companion revealed a patrician-nosed, gaunt-looking personage of middling years. She was engaged in tatting, a singularly prosaic activity given the momentous tone of the event that must have just taken place.

Marianne took in these details in less than a split second. Since she felt no obvious tingling down her spine or sense of breathless anticipation, she inferred in an instant that Alistair Raoul Griffin Sinclair, Viscount Hansford, was not present at the proceedings. Her stomach gave a faint lurch, but she was not permitted to ponder on this fact, for she was being welcomed into the fray, Amber's hands holding her own cold, wet ones.

"Marianne! This is unexpected! Delightful, but unexpected!" Marianne bit her lip. Whilst her affectionate heart was thrilled for Amber, she felt suddenly giddy from confusion and disappointment. Where was Raoul? What of the note he'd sent her? Had he forgotten it? She saw faces in front of her talking, but she could not hear the words. The world was whirling before her eyes, and everything had gone eerily quiet.

The next she knew, she was lying on the sofa and Amber was bending solicitously over her, a bottle of sal volatile and ambergris drifting slowly under her nose. She sat up with a start.

"Don't say I fainted! I deplore and despise women who faint!"

Lord Delaware grinned. It was not hard to see why Amber was so besotted with him. The beauty mark above his mouth was singularly magnetic when his lips curved. He looked very masculine, too, with his coat slung carelessly over his shoulder, and his cravat, usually impeccable, tussled a smidgen.

"Bravo, Maid Marianne! You had us worried for an instant—we'd not put you down as the fainting type!"

Marianne smiled weakly, but her heart contracted. That was Raoul's special term for her, Maid Marianne! Had he been discussing her behind her back? But then, Lord Delaware was his dearest friend. They went back a long way, longer than she had any claim to. Not that she had any claim at all, she reflected glumly.

"Don't tease her, Raphael." Amber came forward.

"Marianne, did you bring a maid? I shall call her if you have need of her."

Marianne shook her head and blushed. "I am sorry. I left in such a hurry. There was a note . . . Raoul . . . I did not think . . ." Amber looked over her at Raphael significantly.

"A note?"

Marianne nodded and blushed.

"Then she must, by some mischance, have received it, too!"

"Received what?"

"Mersham's note. It was intended for Marianne from the outset."

"Not Peter . . ." Marianne thought Amber was confused. The large woman with the thunderous voice entered into the fray and Marianne was lost. She sank into the pillows and allowed the words to fly over her head. Slowly the trio—for Matilda, whilst her ears remained firmly open—could not be said to be an active participant in this discussion—pieced together what had happened. Marianne, listening passively, suddenly sat bolt upright.

"You mean I have been the victim of a trick?"

"Exactly, my dear. One designed to discredit you entirely. Fortunately it has failed dismally. By the way, I am Doncaster. Glad to make your acquaintance."

Marianne had heard of the Duchess of Doncaster. She cut quite a figure in the world of fashion. She cast an awed glance at her face and stood up, the better to effect a deep curtsy.

"Delighted, your grace."

The duchess scrutinised Marianne's face, then smiled. "I believe, my dear, that *I* am, too."

After that, the ice, such as there was, was broken. Marianne felt she could be frank with the room's occupants, though she did cast a hesitant glance at the Baroness Winsome. The duchess rapped her with her fan.

"Pshaw!" she said. "Don't mind *her*, my dear! No one ever pays her the *faintest* heed!"

Marianne thought this a little unkind, but Matilda seemed used to this sort of treatment, for she nodded eagerly and confirmed that this was so. Truth to tell, she was in high spirits, for the drama unfolding before her was better, even, than Mrs. Radcliffe's novel from the lend-ing library. This now lay forgotten at the bottom of her stitching bag, not to be reopened until the morning, at least.

Marianne was shocked to learn of Peter's villainy. A merry girl by nature, she put aside her own disappointment and ventured, even, to imagine what she would have done to the hapless Mersham. She had the party rolling in their seats as she described what might have happened with the red-hot poker. She also rather imaginatively pointed out the presence of a decorative spear upon the wall, something that had eluded Amber's notice entirely.

More seriously, she explained how the note had come at a time when she'd been reviewing rather bleakly the options for her marriage. Amber's throat grew a lump as she consistently defended Raoul's careless treatment of her, his frequent absenteeism, his reckless behaviour at the tables, and the rumours she'd heard of opera dancers in his keeping.

Throughout the recital, Raphael's lips grew tight, for he knew—better than most—how true Marianne's suspicions were. Whilst she made light of it, he could see the telltale signs of strain on her features and the tightly clasped hands in her lap.

Over and over, she kept repeating that the fault was hers—Raoul had married her from chivalry, they had a civil arrangement, she could and did expect nothing more.

Then the note . . . Her eyes blurred with tears, and both Amber and Raphael could instantly see why. The note had been the first intimation that Raoul cared for her, loved her, cherished her enough to lure her on a romantic escapade rather than simply knocking on their connecting door.

Even the duchess was moved to tears at the thought of the disappointment Marianne must now be suffering. Raphael's eyes flashed with fury. Though he had hinted several times to Raoul that he was tardy in his dealings with his wife, he'd had no idea of how far her feelings were engaged.

The strange thing was, Raphael was very certain that the feelings were reciprocated, though the viscount might not yet be at a stage to recognise it. Therein lay the tragedy: two people miserable needlessly. The Marquis of Slade was poignantly aware of the waste, for the same could almost be said of him and Amber. He had always been connected to his feelings, whereas Raoul must be shown . . . He pondered aloud, and the duchess, for a change, was silent.

"I have it!" The duchess was on her feet faster than Marianne could have dreamed possible, given her bulk and her renowned inclination towards rheumatism. She grabbed her stick and waved the onyx cane in the air. The participants in the little drama looked at her inquiringly. Mistress Dawse crept in to lay a table at the far corner of the taproom, but she remained unnoticed. It would have been better by far had the party been able to remove to a private parlour, but this, unfortunately, was beyond the means of Tavistock Inn. No one, however, was thinking of these details when they regarded the duchess.

Her eyes were gleaming with mischief, ever a sign that she had meddling on her mind. The duchess whispered a plan in a loud, guttural voice. When she had finished, everyone—even Matilda, used to her grace's ways—was stunned.

Raphael was the first to speak.

"I could stomach it"—he grinned at Marianne's instant pout—"if Amber can!"

Amber looked at Marianne and her heart was touched. How could she possibly deny her—and yes, her dear, silly, ridiculous brother—the chance of happiness if she could help it? Impossible! She had waited long for Raphael; she could wait longer still.

"I can stomach it, too! Mind you, Marianne is so beautiful. . . ."

Marianne stuck a tongue out at her. There was no chance that the debonair Lord Delaware could possibly fall in love with her. His feelings were too obviously attached elsewhere.

Her outstretched tongue lightened the proceedings, though the Baroness Winsome looked more shocked at *this* than at the suggested proposal.

"We are agreed, then?"

The party solemnly nodded in turn.

"Good! Let the assault begin! Marianne will seduce Raoul in all manner of ways"—Amber looked at her mischievously—"and Raphael will court her. We must take care that no one learns of his—"

"Penchant for you? Adoration of you?" Raphael's eyes gleamed as he regarded his future wife. Amber felt the most extraordinary warmth suffuse her being, but she refused to be deterred.

"You interrupt, my lord! As I said, it is imperative that no one learns of our betrothal. That way, Raoul might be brought to believe your interests have turned to Marianne."

The Marquis of Delaware nodded. "It is fortunate that Raoul is well versed in my bachelor ways. Perhaps it is not quite the thing to mention it, my love, but I am well known in some quarters for my agreeable . . . ah . . . *connections* with married women."

Amber looked him straight in the eye. Her voice grew very quiet. "I can catalogue each one for you, my lord."

Raphael did not miss her meaning. He'd been in love with Amber a very long time and was considered a prize on the marriage mart. It would have been against his principles to engage the hopes of any innocent young debutante, so he'd compromised with a series of very satisfying connections with high fliers and married ladies who could have no claim, other than the physical, upon his person. He was sorry, now, that these actions had so obviously hurt Amber. Inwardly, he vowed to make it up to her. His lady, perhaps regretting her impulsive comment, continued brightly.

"Perhaps a knowledge of what Raoul *has,* coupled with a poignant reminder of what he can *lose,* will serve to wake that stupid boy up!"

Matilda nodded vigorously, her eyes gleaming at the delectable deception she was about to be party to. She gave a yelp as her knuckles were well and truly rapped by the duchess.

"Matilda, one word of this to anyone and I will never talk to you again!" The duchess's voice was firm.

"Oh, no, I mean, certainly not . . ."

"I should *say* certainly not! That means no more carriage rides, no more invitations to fashionable soirees, no more hot bricks and warm baths, no more . . ."

Matilda blanched. The prospect was diabolical, for she knew very well she could not live the life she did on her own meagre stipend. Besides, it was the duchess's sponsorship that gave her entrée into a world she would otherwise only be able to glimpse from the wings.

"Your grace, my lips, I assure you, are firmly sealed!" Nervous, she tittered unbecomingly, but the remainder of the party felt too sorry for her to be irritated. At least they had her promise—there was no need to torment her further.

On this note, the five toasted each other with the inn's appalling red wine and prepared to call the carriages out.

Their good intentions were never carried out, however, for simultaneous with the heavens finally opening in dramatic downpour came the arrival of none other than the subject so vigorously occupying their attention. It was his lordship, Raoul, Viscount Hansford.

Marianne thought her heart would stop as she saw him, wet, bedraggled, and devastatingly handsome. Riding crop in one hand, he cast a glance at her own damp attire and smiled lazily—a heart-stopping, romantic, and entirely unsettling smile that caused Marianne's cheeks to burn and the others to feel that their mission was perhaps, after all, not impossible.

He stepped forward and placed his hand in Marianne's.

"I have no notion of what *you* are doing at this godforsaken place, my love, but, oh, all's well that ends well." He beamed at everyone. "A storm in a teacup, I gather." He flashed a grin at Raphael. "Spent a good afternoon at Watiers, I must say! Bet old Drayton a penny to a farthing piece that Grayson would come up to scratch and he did! Looked over some of Cardamon's horses. . . ."

He was glared at by five pairs of accusing eyes. Suddenly he remembered why he had ridden over in the first place.

He looked over at Amber. "Am I to congratulate you?"

His beloved sister, furious with him at his offhand treatment of Marianne, cast him something akin to a scowl.

"Congratulate me? I can see nothing to be congratulated on except this foul weather and the tedious task of having acted as chaperon the entire afternoon! I, at least, have a sense of propriety!"

Raphael's shoulders shook at this display of outrage. He felt it would be a pity for her meaning to be missed altogether by her blockheaded brother, so he took Marianne's hand in his and looked deeply into her eyes.

"Thank you, Maid Marianne, for a most . . . uh . . . *memorable* day." He touched her cheek gently and bestowed a featherlight kiss upon her hand before releasing her.

Raoul's eyes narrowed in confusion. He felt he was missing something, but could not place his finger on what.

All he knew was that his fingers were clenched and for
the first time he experienced the very real desire to bloody
his dearest friend and mentor's nose. He quelled it, being
a civilised and rather easygoing fellow by nature. Who
cared that Raphael used his own special term of endearment towards Marianne? He wanted them to get on well
together! Still, the sight of his lordship's hand carelessly
creeping round Marianne's waist did seem a bit excessive,
especially considering the predatory gleam my lord
sported in his dark, damnably handsome eyes.

He scrutinised Marianne closely. "Taken to dampening
your skirts, my dear? Rather fetching." His wry, rather disgruntled tone was not lost on his audience. They looked
at each other significantly, and my lord was forced to shrug
his shoulders. He'd sensed a kind of collective smirk that
seemed quite unaccountable.

He turned his attention to the duchess and her companion and made an admirable, if belated, bow. The duchess greeted him regally, but behind her spectacles lay an
undetected twinkle. Though she was loath to admit it, she
positively adored scapegraces, and Raoul was that, if nothing else.

"Hmph!" was all she said, however. The baroness was
more forthcoming, for she found the viscount quite dashing in his tasselled Hessians and riding coat of stiff merino.
His civility in extending his hand to her quite over-
whelmed her, for it was half a minute at least before even
the duchess could get a word in edgewise and testily adjure
her to "stop babbling like a veritable fribble!"

Colouring, Matilda reached for her handkerchief and
apologised, but Raoul afforded her one of his excessively
gratifying smiles and assured her the conversation was of
the most stimulating and elevated kind. His eyes met Marianne's as he pronounced this very obvious falsehood, and
the pair shared a moment of perfect accord. Marianne

was hard-pressed not to giggle, especially as Raoul made the most comical grimace over Matilda's head as he continued to pronounce platitudes in tones of utmost civility.

Matilda was simpering by the time the duchess glared at her and bade her order up rooms for the night, for, as she said, the inclement weather was enough to overset even the hardiest of travellers.

The Hansford groom was assigned the unenviable task of removing himself from the cosy hay in which he had fashioned himself an inviting little love nest, and delivering a note to the dowager viscountess, apprising her of the altered arrangements. Amber felt confident her mother would not mind in the least, Tavistock being no farther than Meadowmead and a great deal better option than risking inflammation to the lungs. Of course the knowledge that Raoul was at hand would offer reassurance to her, though for the life of her, Amber could not see why.

Still, Miss Sinclair had a lot to think about as she fingered the brilliant ruby she had quietly slipped into her pocket on her brother's unexpected entrance. A night away from her observant mama would be the very thing to restore her equilibrium. She glanced at Raphael's profile, darkly handsome against the flickering tapers Mistress Dawse had lit some moments before. He must have felt her gaze, for he turned towards her and his eyes were scorching. Amber felt hot and giddy and quite unlike the cool, eminently sensible young lady she was generally touted as being. She longed to claim Raphael and explore the faint, dark stubble on his chin, the cleft above his mouth, the entrancing black patch so close to firm, masculine lips. She closed her eyes for an instant.

The marquis gave an almost audible gasp before his expression became shuttered once more. Abruptly he stood up.

"I must go." His voice sounded curt, and even Marianne

looked surprised. Remembering the role he found thrust upon him, he made her a very elegant leg and mournfully declared that he doubted he could be trusted under the same roof with one so lovely.

Once again, Raoul's transparent face flashed doubt, incredulity, a hint of anger, and—was it, possibly, envy? Raphael certainly hoped so as he made his adieu. He doubted he could continue with the charade overlong, not with Amber staring at him with her heart on her sleeve. Nothing could be more calculated to ignite his passion more, and little could be more overwhelmingly, unbearably frustrating.

If he had his way . . . but no, he would only have his way when she was his wedded wife. That day could not come too soon for him, so he prayed Raoul would hurry up and set his affairs in order smartly.

Well, he had done his bit for the evening. It was up to Marianne now. Judging from her smouldering eyes, the viscount looked doomed. If her ladyship set out to seduce Raoul, his friend was well and truly done for. With this cheering thought in his head, the marquis felt buoyant enough to lay down the final red rag to the bull.

"Intriguing about the note, my dear Raoul!"

Raoul turned. In truth, he had forgotten about the note. When he'd confronted Raphael about it earlier in the day, his lordship had laughed and told him not to worry his head over it. Amber was not going to be compromised, and if an announcement was to be made he would be the first to hear of it. Raoul, used to accepting Raphael's word as law, had nodded, satisfied.

Truth was, he'd remembered Cardamon's horse sale and was anxious to be off. Having discharged his brotherly duty—as he saw it—he'd ridden off without another thought in his head. Passing Tavistock on the way home

had belatedly reminded him to at least pop his head in.
Which was what he had done—or was doing.

Now Raphael was reminding him about the wretched
thing. Strange if he had been mistaken about Delaware
and Amber . . . he eyed them closely. Nothing in their
demeanour suggested anything out of the common way.
Hands on hips, he surveyed the room, puzzled. And now
that he thought on it, what had Amber meant, she'd been
chaperoning all day?

Raphael's mouth twitched as he watched Raoul muddle
all this through. He decided to add a rider to the pot.

"Odd things, coincidences! Extraordinary how there are
two men with the initial 'R' at Tavistock!" He said no more,
but the seed was planted in the viscount's brain.

Rooted to the floor, Raoul hardly noticed Raphael take
his leave and bravely face the swirling mists and remorse-
less rain outside. The strangest thought kept flitting
through his mind: two *R*s and *two* ladies Sinclair! He
looked at Marianne. She looked demure now, but undoubtedly she had looked brazen before, in her dampened
skirts and slightly mussed hair. Even now, her curls were
falling about her cheeks delightfully. . . .

Raoul felt sick, sicker than he had done ever before in
his whole life. In an instant, a simple flash, he understood
how much his lightly taken marriage meant to him. And
Marianne? She was fetching, alluring as always, but Raoul
for the first time doubted whether this was such a good
thing. If Raphael . . . He swallowed hard. No woman had
ever resisted Raphael. It was one of the things he admired
so much about him. *My god!* If Raphael . . . The thought
could hardly be choked out of his brain. The marquis knew
his was a marriage of convenience. He also had a strong
partiality for married women. Perhaps he thought Raoul
would not mind . . . perhaps he thought he was doing
him a favour, relieving him of the odious necessity of danc-

ing attendance, remembering engagements, attending balls. Raoul wondered how he could ever have been so negligent, or how he was ever going to get himself out of this coil.

Mistress Dawse was returning with some story about a shortage of beds . . . the duchess was looking peeved, the baroness seemed glum . . . Marianne looked perky. Suspiciously, Raoul looked at her. She was in the process of airily informing the innkeeper that her rooms were sufficient after all.

The innkeeper looked puzzled for a moment, but when Marianne patiently explained that she was the new viscountess Hansford, the light dawned. "Well, ma'am! That is right and tight then! You and 'is lordship will be after *sharin'* a bed! I reckon I 'ave enough linen and such after all!" With that interesting comment, she hustled off.

Fourteen

Marianne's heart misgave her. She'd made a great show of settling Amber in and arranging a truckle bed for Betsy, now the official maid. *That* young lady seemed delighted with her lot. Even her pinched face looked bonnier as she surveyed Amber with the type of awe generally reserved for demigods.

She assured Marianne, in her strange mix of youth and pragmatism, that "milady" would be well cared for. She would even nick a piece of Master Dawse's prized ham if she desired it. Amber had to tell her firmly that she did *not*. Betsy had seemed a little crestfallen at this crushing blow, but had perked up almost instantly, to proclaim that the innkeeper's port was known far and wide to be smuggled. She put her hand to her mouth and vowed she would procure some at risk of limb and life if her angel required it. Amber told her quite frankly that she did not.

Marianne, intrigued, asked how the girl knew it was smuggled. Betsy had grinned broadly and announced she had given her pledge not to say. When Marianne looked like pressing her—she was ever one for a lark, was her ladyship—Amber frowned meaningfully and announced she was sure Marianne must be tired. At this, the viscountess rather mournfully understood she had, once more, been in breach of etiquette. Gossip with the serving maids was simply not comme il faut for a lady of her rank. Bother the rank! she thought crossly in her head. In reality, she smiled sweetly at Betsy, patted her on the head, and adjured her to take good care of her benefactress.

Betsy nodded. She needed no one to tell her *that*.

Amber looked over at Marianne. She pressed her hand quietly into that of the young viscountess and gently kissed her on the cheek.

"Good luck, Marianne. I just hope you make my gudgeon of a dear brother see sense! He was lucky to find you."

With tears welling in her eyes, Marianne nodded. She suddenly felt very unequal to the task she had so blithely set herself. One thing to say "seduce your husband." Another entirely to actually do it. With resolution and a firm set of her shoulders she nodded and firmly shut the door.

Not much farther down the old slate corridor, Raoul, Viscount Hansford, was suffering similar misgivings. He desired Marianne intensely but was uncertain of what her feelings were towards him. He was too proud by far to risk being accused of importuning her yet again, but his fingers itched to do just that. He closed his eyes and allowed the soft scent of honeysuckle to drift through his imagination.

He was just coming to the point where his imagination was leading him into far deeper waters when the door opened and the object of his fantasies walked in. She smiled her audacious, endearing smile, and Lord Hansford sighed a deep breath of relief. He inferred he had been forgiven. He maintained this inference when Marianne walked electrifyingly close to him and began untying the elegant sable knot he'd spent all morning perfecting. It seemed strange to him that the action was not one he deplored. Rather, he found it stimulating to the highest degree. He wished her to continue. Of course, she did not.

Instead, she stood back and surveyed him, hands on hips and a deplorable smirk on her perfect, ruby red lips. Raoul wanted to shake her or kiss her, he knew not which. He settled for neither, but said the first thing that came into his head.

"Get that ridiculous dress off before you catch your death of cold!"

Surprised, Marianne looked down and saw what he meant. The cambric was clinging to her shift and was wet through. She'd hardly noticed with the turmoil of the last half hour. Neither, of course, had the rest of the company, so engrossed were they with the various excitements and preoccupations. She hesitated, faintly embarrassed. Whilst it had fully been her intention to throw caution to the winds and cause their marriage to be consummated that night, she felt suddenly shy and a little foolish. To be ordered into her underclothes like a child rather than the woman she yearned to be was humiliating! Worse, Raoul had that militant gleam in his eye that brooked no argument.

"Shall you do it or shall I?"

"*I* will!" Marianne was defiant. She saw the sense in undressing, but deplored the need. She had no desire to be laid up like an invalid the rest of the season—especially when the fault would have been entirely her own. Rather sulkily, she fumbled with the tiny pearl buttons that caressed the nape of her neck and extended down some way below her slender, youthful waist.

Raoul decided that the wedded state had some comforts, after all. In indolent silence he seated himself and watched as his wife fumbled defiantly with the obstinate fastenings. She was aware of his gaze and grew hotter and crosser with every moment. She refused to ask his help, since he'd been so damnably dictatorial, yet she was feeling sillier by the moment.

"I can make that a lot easier for you if you ask." Raoul was teasing. She heard it in his tone and instantly looked up. His eyes had lost their severity and were twinkling. She breathed a heavenly sigh and closed her eyes. Was this not what she had wanted, after all? It was not so very, *very* hard to ask. She opened her mouth to do so but the words wouldn't come.

His lordship wrapped his arms about her and began slowly, infinitely slowly, to remove the cream overdress. She felt her back tingle at every touch of his fingers as the intransigent buttons refused to come loose. Slowly they did, though, and as Marianne felt the dress slipping off her shoulders she felt, too, the first soft kisses that landed just behind her ears and sent a shudder through her being.

She wanted to move, but found she could not. Her whole body was still, wrapped in the single hope that Alistair Raoul Griffin Sinclair would press his lips into her neck and once more send her into a trance of sensuous, breathtaking bliss. He did, lingering a little over her shoulders before moving once more to her ears. She felt him nuzzle them and her pulse began to race quite uncontrollably. Raoul placed his finger on one and timed the beat until it was tumultuous. Then he swung her round and held her a little from him. She flung back her head so that her neck was fully available to be kissed. He ignored it, but moved, instead, to the pink crests that peeped invitingly from her silken small clothes. When she gave a gasp of surprised, abandoned pleasure, my lord stopped and waited for her breathing to subside. She lifted her head inquiringly and he removed the pins from her hair so that the jet black tumbled luxuriously across her face and down her snowy shoulders.

"Ask!"

The word came as a shock, so different was it from the dexterous, gentle caresses to which she had just been privy.

"Beg pardon?" The wonder had not yet left her eyes.

Raoul felt an urgent need to kiss her senseless, but refused, every vestige of his being determined, once and for all, that she beg for his favours. "*Ask* for what you want, my dear Maid Marianne." His tone was husky and slightly mocking.

Marianne blinked. Then the haze of contentment that was wafting over her evaporated in an instant.

"You cannot make me!"

"Can I not?" Raoul's voice was silky as he removed his shirt and gave Marianne a sight of his intoxicating torso. He heard her indrawn breath, for he smiled, then moved towards her, his scent and warmth an overpowering temptation to Marianne, who wanted nothing more than to nuzzle into the athletic curves of his broad shoulders. She grew faint at the sight of his bare belly and curly hair just visible above creamy pantaloons. She wanted to touch, but felt immobilised by the mockery in his eyes.

"No, I don't believe you can!"

Marianne's voice quavered but her resolve was firm. She already knew his lordship was attracted to her. If she wanted, she could allow herself to be lifted in his firm, supple arms and be raised, featherlight, as she had been before, upon the monster four-poster bed that now confronted them. But that, she knew, would be a defeat.

It might not be fair, it might not be quite the terms of their agreed marriage vows, but Marianne wanted more. She wanted Raoul to whisper words of love to her, to adore her, to commit himself to her as he had to no other woman. She wanted him to place her above cockfights and gaming, above his light o' loves, above bachelor pursuits, above, in short, all else. His lordship was making her quiver in undreamed-of places. His eyes, hot and passionate upon her small clothes, were erotic in the extreme. Against her conscious will, Marianne felt herself melting to his unspoken needs.

The tension in the room was electric as he moved behind her and grasped her waist. Then, bending her forwards slightly, so that her hair tumbled over her face and her delightful derriere was tantalisingly exposed to his not unappreciative eyes, he asked her once more. When she declined and made to stand up, he pushed her forwards gently but firmly. The small of her back was imprisoned in one hand whilst his other softly touched the silken fabric confronting him as she bent. Marianne thought she would go mad with unspoken desire.

Again he asked her to speak, and again she refused. The heat was coursing through her veins and she closed her eyes, the better to push aside the heady, intoxicating, and utterly traitorous sensations of her body. Closed eyes just made her predicament more acute. His lordship was now allowing his hands to rove in unspeakable places, his legs hard against her own.

If she was not firm now, the marriage would be consummated, for already a warmth was surging through her that made compliance an inevitable necessity. She could not, *would* not, allow this to happen! Not without first hearing a vow of love from Raoul, for if this thing was done, they would have no chance, ever, of a divorce. They would be locked into a marriage that was at best physically fulfilling, at worst a sham.

She knew it was beyond the bounds of their original agreement, but everything in her ached for more. She wanted commitment; she wanted to be viscountess in truth as well as in name. She would never have that—not for certain—if she gave in to her inclinations now.

Raoul continued to tease her, enjoying the sensations he could see he evoked. Unexpectedly, he lifted her onto the bed, twisted her around, and began delicately untying the laces of her stays. For an instant Marianne fought with herself, but good sense finally won out.

Without an avowal of love, she would never know whether the viscount truly loved her. If he did not, she would lose, with one moment of sensuous madness, the promised chance of freeing him forever. Marianne was too proud not to divorce him if that was what he ultimately desired. She refused to countenance even for one moment, trapping him forever in the charade that was their marriage. Too proud and too in love.

She shook her head and sat up. My lord, not convinced, only laughed and pushed her back.

His hands wandered aimlessly but to excellent purpose. When she emitted a faint sigh, Raoul chuckled a little.

"You cannot say it is not good for you, too, my little maid."

Sapphire eyes bored into deep, liquid honey gold. Frantic, Marianne could think of no way of stopping the viscount, for her response was acting as a powerful, piquant stimulant to his own.

"Raphael, Lord Delaware, would never treat me with such disrespect!" She blurted out the words as loudly and as quickly as she could. They were like a bucket of cold water to Raoul. He released her instantly and swung off the bed, his blue eyes ice cold and grimmer than Marianne could ever have feared. There was a faint twitch in his cheek as he threw her a gown.

"Explain yourself, madame!" His tone was hard, for all the strange jealousies Raoul had experienced earlier came back to him in haunting clarity.

Marianne blushed. She felt miserably exposed on the large four-poster, her one true and intimate love glaring at her as though she were a viper. And she *felt* one. For an instant she doubted the scheme that the duchess had triumphantly devised. It did not do, sometimes, to play with raw emotion. Evoking Raoul's jealousy might serve to make him realise the intensity of his love for her—it might also foster bitterness and disgust.

Marianne feared the latter, for Raoul's breathing was ragged as he gazed at her and demanded an explanation. Marianne felt mute and helpless, appalled by the effect of her devastating remark.

"The note I found . . . it was written by Raphael, was it not?"

Dumbly Marianne nodded. She had chosen this path and would stick to it, no matter that the odds of the gamble were impossibly high.

His lordship shook his head and gave a strangled laugh. "And I thought he'd addressed it to Amber. No wonder he hotfooted it to Tavistock when I taxed him with it!"

The despair that washed over his face was almost too much for her ladyship, who longed, more than anything, to soothe the anguish from his brow and caress him back to a world of normality. If Raoul was suffering, then surely it meant that he loved her? That she had proven what she'd set out to prove? That the marriage of convenience was more than that for both of them? Marianne swung her legs off the bed in sudden decision. She would not allow Raoul to believe he had been cuckolded one second longer.

She raised her hands to stroke the face that had become so dear to her and found herself, once more, gripped in an ironlike vise.

"Don't try it, madame!" His jaw was firm and uncompromising. "I have told you once and I will tell you again that you shall not play your little hellion's tricks with me. You have tried my patience once too often, you little baggage!" He waited for his breathing to subside, then continued in a calmer, more dangerous tone.

"No doubt you and Raphael have found it amusing to dupe me." When she opened her mouth to deny it, he clasped her wrists the harder. "Hush! I shall say no more on the subject other than to suggest that from now on I shall be your escort at every one of your little amusements. I am sorry to cast such a damper on proceedings, but you need not be concerned I shall bother you in the bedroom again." He looked at her contemptuously. "I can take my pleasures elsewhere, thank you."

When he released her, Marianne thought her wrists would be bruised. She did not care, for that was certainly the least of her miserable lot. If she told Raoul the truth now, in this blazing, ice-white mood, he would not believe it. Marianne pulled the wrapper on. She still had her pride. That would have to suffice, for the present.

"I have not, as you put it, *duped* you, my lord! I am merely comparing manners for manners, and I repeat, once again, that the Marquis of Slade has the jump on you in this respect."

"It is fortunate, then, that you did not marry me for my manners! *Au contraire*, I seem to remember *yours* were very much at issue when we first had the fortune—or was it misfortune?—of meeting."

Raoul was seething, and Marianne felt she could push the matter no further. Of course he was right. When it came to manners it would take a lot to beat forcing a perfect stranger to rescue her from a sticky predicament, slapping him for his trouble, and landing him in scrape after scrape to boot.

If she weren't so furious she'd feel guilty. She tried to hold on to her fury. Her wrists ached. She focused on them and pointed to the sofa.

"You might wish to sleep there tonight, my lord."

Raoul glared at her.

"Be damned if I will!" He flung himself up amid the

crisp white sheets and settled down for a night of rest. Marianne was floored. If she removed to the sofa she would look childish. If she did not, it would be an agonising night of painful proximity to the viscount. Wavering, she hesitated until a muffled voice called out from the bedclothes.

"Oh, do get up, you silly widgeon!" Much comforted by this tiny indication that my lord was returned to spirits, she arranged her damp dress neatly upon the rails and climbed into bed. She was not forgiven, but my lord did take the precaution of insuring she had sufficient coverlet and pillows. Though both their eyes remained securely closed for the duration of the long, dark night, neither, it could be safely said, slept a wink.

Fifteen

The Earl of Glaston stared at Peter Mersham in rising fury.

"Were you born yesterday, you idiot? You could just as easily have deflowered the one as the other!"

Mersham, sublime in a blazer of green stripes and gold trim, eyed the earl steadily.

"As to that, my lord, I am tired of your intrigues. I wanted Marianne, and you knew it!"

The earl smiled grimly. "That I did, my lad! I saw the looks you gave her when I came a'courting! Gave me a rare chuckle, it did, seeing you have to . . . ah . . . *curb* your inclinations!"

Mersham viewed the earl with extreme distaste.

"I am glad I afforded your lordship some amusement." His voice was stiff.

Glaston nodded in remembered satisfaction. "Funniest part of the whole affair, I assure you!"

Galled, Mersham picked up his hat and made to leave. "Find some other minion to do your dirty work in the future!"

The earl looked past him thoughtfully. "It would seem I would have to, since I am saddled with a bevy of half-witted incompetents!" He took out an old, rather commonplace tobacco pouch and drew out a pinch of dark snuff.

Mersham turned on him. "I am *glad* Marianne escaped your clutches!"

The earl looked him up and down so long that Peter, for all his cockiness, began to feel uncomfortable.

"I am glad she escaped *yours,*" was all his lordship said. It was enough. In a fury, Mersham made to depart, but not before he'd retrieved a scrawled piece of paper from the table.

The earl's eyes narrowed. "Give me that!"

Mersham scowled. "Why should I? It is a contract between us!"

"One in which you have signally failed!"

"Afraid I might claim my miserable gold guinea?"

"Claim all you like! You'll not get a sixpence out of me!"

Mersham knew it was true, for all his board at Tavistock had cost a cool twenty shillings at the least. The knowledge infuriated him the more, but he felt impotent against Glaston's white-hot glare.

"I'll escort myself out!" He jammed the hat upon his head.

"You relieve my mind!" Glaston laughed cheerlessly, his veined hands clutching at the oaken table with a vigour that belied his years. Mersham's last sight of him was with the snuff to his nose, his liver spots yellowing in the gloomy, ineffective taper light.

Delphinia Spencer-Pultney's voice pierced the air like a quavering shriek. Peter knew that if he had been a few years younger, he would be feeling the effects of a very carefully bestowed punishment on his rear end. He forbade himself to squirm as he faced his mother, but out of the corner of his eye he could see Lila smirking in the background. The sight, for some reason, thoroughly incensed him. He turned on her.

"Let me suggest, my dear Lila, that if you wish to captivate my lord Glaston, you had best desist from eating all that *delightful* confectionary! The last I heard, he was bandying your name about as a pudding-faced brat!"

"And so she is!"

Delphinia threw her daughter a darkling glance of dislike. Such a disappointment she had proven to be! At the morning calls she had managed to inveigle her way into—at great cost, it might be added—all the chit had been able to do was simper unbecomingly and remark that Lord Norris had grown "passing handsome!" Delphinia could see that if the deed was to be done, it had to be done by herself. Her eyes narrowed calculatingly. She stretched out her hand.

"Give me that note!"

Peter obliged—it was never wise to get on his mother's wrong side, especially when one was only halfway through the quarter and knee-deep in debtor's notes.

She perused it carefully, arching her eyebrow haughtily at the lewdness of the tone. Painstakingly, she inspected what remained of the seal. At length, she nodded, a small grimace hovering just below her long, aquiline nose.

"I believe, Peter, it will suffice. Perhaps I have done you an injustice." The smile she bestowed on her only son, while not bonny, was nevertheless sufficient to give Mersham hope.

"Whilst you remain an idiotish dolt, I have hopes that you are not, after all, the absolute codfish I had assumed."

With this ambiguous remark, Peter had to be satisfied.

When Delphinia Spencer-Pultney imperiously called up a hack later that day, she was wearing a day dress of deep

green merino and a cunning little hat of soft kid and swans-
down. True, her gloves were a little shabby and her reticule
rather large for the elegant confection she'd chosen to
wear, but coupled with her best pearls and a tiny dab of
perfume, the outfit made Mrs. Spencer-Pultney feel pleas-
ingly desirable as she sank back into the rather hard
squabs.

A town crier called the time and she nodded. *Good!* His
lordship should be at table, by her reckoning. Men were
at such a disadvantage when their stomachs were involved!
Besides—she looked out of the window cautiously—she
was feeling the glimmer of hunger pangs herself. She
hoped the Glaston repast would be ample, for the hack
was costing her a fine penny piece, and she was not one
to squander good money for naught.

"Sir Clive!"

"My dear Lady Jane! Taking the air?"

The dowager viscountess nodded, her eyes bright from
the small breeze that gently kissed the cycads along
Langtree Avenue.

"May I join you?"

The question was rewarded with a wide, speaking smile
and a gesture to the horse to slow to a simple trot.

"Of course you may! You are looking very dapper this
morning!"

Sir Clive reddened slightly. "I was hoping you would
take this route!"

"Resorting to stratagems, Sir Clive?" Lady Jane could
not help teasing. "Surely you were not afraid my servants
would deny me?"

"Indeed not, ma'am! But how else was I to entice you
outside? A fine day like this ought not be wasted taking
tea, you know."

"Sir Clive!" Lady Jane pouted prettily. "Are you suggesting my tea is not of the very first order? I infuse it from my own herb garden, as you must be well aware!"

"That may be, but you know, my dear Jane, that I believe green growing things belong in *gardens,* not in perfectly respectable cups! Now give me an orgeat or a . . ." His attention was diverted by the sight of Raphael, Lord Delaware, bowling past him in a high-perch curricle of singular beauty.

"Stap me if I won't purchase a gig like that for myself, Lady Jane! What say you? Are we too old to . . ."

But Lady Jane was not listening. She was staring in bewilderment at his lordship's bright-eyed passenger. Smart in royal blue satin with white rosebud trim and a tiny muff to match sat Marianne, Viscountess Hansford. Lady Jane was too far away to note the clenched fists that clung steadfastly to the equipage or the tears that glinted at the back of honey gold eyes. What she did see—and that with puzzlement—was that Raphael's hand lazily rested on her shoulders as his other deftly maneuvered the reins.

Sir Clive coughed. "Don't like to tell you your business, beloved, but it has been April and May with them all week."

Confronted with the dowager viscountess's shocked stare of blank astonishment, Sir Clive cleared his throat once more and looked as though he wished he'd held his peace.

"Does Raoul know?"

Sir Clive stared at the middle distance and bowed to one of his numerous acquaintances.

"I imagine he does. Been to the same routs and balls, practically *dogs* the pair of them, from what I hear!"

Jane's head was reeling. "Raoul at balls? You must be joking!"

"I am not, Lady Jane! He missed the Alberkercky cockfight the other day and did not attend the opera once last week, despite the fact that his fancy bit of muslin—" Sir Clive pulled himself up short and coughed. He'd nearly been guilty of a gross indiscretion and hardly knew how to continue.

Lady Jane's eyes lit up in fleeting amusement. "No need to look so troubled, Sir Clive! I am not a *total* innocent, you know!"

"Indeed, I should hope not!" He was back to his bluff, teasing self.

Lady Jane continued. "Besides, my beloved son has led us quite a song and dance with all his little barques of frailty. I do hope . . . Oh!" She put her delicate hands to her mouth. "I do hope . . ."

Sir Clive looked at her inquiringly.

"I wonder if Marianne knows."

"Possibly her latest flirtation has something to do with it. Hell hath no fury, you know."

Lady Jane nodded thoughtfully. "Perhaps. I am hoping, though, that there is more to all this than meets the eye. Raphael is Raoul's best friend. My son, in his idiotish way, is probably allowing Marianne to acquire a little town polish."

Sir Clive pulled his horse up to a stop. "Much as I would like to agree, I don't think so, my sweet. There are whispers abroad that my lord and lady have had a lover's quarrel. I wouldn't have dreamed of mentioning it. . . ."

"Don't be silly, Sir Clive! You are practically family!"

"Well, I hope to be in the very near future! How, by the by, are Miss Amber's fortunes progressing? I have a most particular reason for the interest, as you are aware!"

Ordinarily Lady Jane Mary Delmont Sinclair would have blushed at this pointed inquiry. She would most certainly have withdrawn her hand, which now, somehow, lay encased in Sir Clive's. The circumstances, however, were not ordinary. Her brow wrinkled in a troubled frown.

"My God! Amber! Does she know?"

"Of Lord Delaware's flirtation?"

Lady Jane nodded dumbly.

"I imagine so, though why . . ." Sir Clive looked puzzled. "Good lord! You don't mean . . ."

The dowager viscountess nodded miserably. "I should not really divulge her secret, but you are so acute, I see that you have divined it anyway. The Marquis of Slade is Amber's chosen husband. She is more than a long way in love with him."

Sir Clive Grandison emitted a low whistle. So *that* was the way the wind blew.

"What the devil are you bothering me at table for?" The Earl of Glaston stared at his manservant balefully. "Deny her entrance, man, and fetch me a bottle of red. Not the seventy-eights either. A glass of the inferior vintage will suffice. And if I find that Milsop has been dipping into it again . . ."

"He was sacked, sir!"

"Excellent! Now pray you hurry, if you don't wish to suffer a similar fate." The earl dismissed the man with a wave and bit into a ham bone. It was fatty and more than a little gristly, but my lord did not appear to mind, other than a passing mumble that the cook ought to be hanged, drawn, and quartered.

The minion knew better than to argue that Cook did the best she could with the meagre housekeeping allotted her. Such statements would earn him the rightabout for sure, for the earl was too mean either to admit or alter his nipfarthing ways. Alistair Sinclair, the Honourable Lord Glaston, took out the *Morning Post* and skimmed the columns in disgust. He did not hold with all the industrial reform that was going on, and he might have to speak his mind in Parliament if the wasteful practice showed signs of continuing. Education for beggars! The earl sniffed and turned the page with a great sweep of his hand.

When he looked up, he was surprised and displeased to see the manservant painstakingly adjusting the brocade on his livery.

"Begone, man! Cannot a man breakfast in peace?"

The manservant bowed. "At once, sir! And the lady . . . ?"

"What lady?"

Glaston was putting on his spectacles and moving to the chess board he'd set up the night before. He surveyed the black with displeasure before taking up a piece of the ivory. It was a bishop, and he moved it in a lazy diagonal across the board, so it confronted the black queen and castle with perfect impunity.

"The one what as is sittin' in the drawin' room, my lord."

Glaston removed his hand from the black queen and whirled around in disgust.

"You have not actually admitted her, I hope?"

The manservant was pleased to deny it. Glaston peered at him through his spectacles and nodded. "Excellent!"

The manservant persisted. "The butler did, though!"

With a sigh the earl moved the queen a square and instantly retaliated by removing the castle with the ivory. That transaction complete, he focused wholly on poor Phillips, who found his feet pinching in his new leather shoes and dared not make a movement for fear of bringing the earl's ire down upon his own innocent head.

"What?" The word sounded like a roar to Phillips, though in fact it was only a very baleful, raspy interrogative.

"Put 'er in the drawin' room, 'e did, sir!"

The earl eyed him with disgust. "That will be all, good man!"

Phillips nodded, relieved. He'd discharged his duty and was more than happy to make his exit.

The earl found his cane, and by dint of a slow and laborious progress, made his way down the huge and draughty hall. The grates were all empty, for my lord saw no reason at all to waste perfectly good firewood on mild mornings like these. Overhead, monumental candelabras flickered with perhaps a couple of candles at most—an inspiring enough reason for Raoul to avoid like the plague the residence to which he was heir.

Glaston turned down the east wing and passed a series of faded tapestries without a second glance. Truth to tell, he was spoiling for a fight, and he knew that in Delphinia Spencer-Pultney he had found a worthy opponent. Apart from being vile beyond belief, the woman had brains enough to appreciate his particular brand of shrewdness. He would give her a run for her money, he would! No doubt she had come, yet again, to foist the lovely Lila on his jaded palate.

He entered the room and looked at Delphinia in disgust.

"Good lord, woman! You've turned fashionable!" The words were uttered in distaste, but Delphinia patted her graying curls smugly and made a slight, grudging curtsy.

"All the rage, my lord, I assure you!" Her refined accents did not fool Glaston, who knew her to be little more than a trumped-up cit of lowly birth. He glared at her, then shrugged. "It is your money you are wasting, so it is hardly a concern of mine!"

Delphinia shrugged coldly but he saw the light of battle gleam in her hard, flinty eyes. Glaston was amused. At least the old battle-ax would afford him a moment's diversion. When he'd finished bandying words with her he'd have her removed. Vile creatures made fascinating playthings, but their interest palled.

"And to what do I owe this unexpected honour?"

Delphinia indicated two of the less worn armchairs at the far side of the room. "May we?"

The earl eyed her suspiciously, then nodded. "If we must! Since you have already inveigled your way here, we might as well make the best of it. But I warn you, Delphinia, I am up to your tricks!" He moved forward slowly, his gout paining him, though for the life of him he would not admit it.

Mrs. Spencer-Pultney smiled sweetly and deposited her overlarge reticule next to the most lavish of the old-style brocades. When she sat down, she winced, for the stuffing was far sparser than it looked.

Miser! she thought. To the earl she bestowed a syrupy smile and placed her arms primly across her lap.

The earl was not fooled for a moment.

"No use trying to hoodwink me with your sly smiles! Save them for someone who is less bang up to the mark."

Delphinia bit back an unpleasant retort. The earl, confident he had won the first bout, sat back in his seat with a satisfied sigh. His spine was so straight that the lack of padding bothered him not a whit.

"And where is that pudding-faced daughter of yours?" Glaston did not mince his words, but glowered smugly at his adversary. "I am amazed you don't have her in tow! And let me tell you, Delphinia, that if you think for an instant I would contemplate marriage to that cabbage—"

"I do not, my lord!" Mrs. Spencer-Pultney brought him up short.

The earl's air of boredom suddenly left him. He placed his spectacles lower upon his nose and looked at Delphinia in disbelieving surprise.

"No? I could have sworn you were throwing the chit at me!"

Mrs. Spencer-Pultney inclined her head slightly.

"I *was,* my lord."

"Ha! Then you don't deny it?"

Mrs. Spencer-Pultney shook her head. "I do not!"

The earl, for once, was floored. "Well!" was all he could think of to say. Then he looked slyly at Delphinia. "Realised I was awake to your suit, did you? I am no bacon-brained, jaw-me-down gudgeon to be taken in by any simpering miss, let me tell you!"

"Indeed not, my lord." Delphinia was being suspiciously conciliatory.

"Don't my lord *me,* if you please!"

"Very well, then!" Delphinia's voice assumed some of its usual authority. "I shall not, Alistair."

He raised his brows. "No one calls me that but my mother, and she is long dead."

"Excellent, for I should hate to share the running of the household with her."

"Beg pardon?" The earl was caught between a gasp of outrage and a crack of uncontrollable mirth.

"You heard me right, my lord! I'm of a mind that we will deal famously together, you and I. Besides . . . I have a notion to be a countess."

"So do half the ladies of England, my dear!"

Mrs. Spencer-Pultney drew her reticule onto her lap. Holding the earl's eagle eye with her own, she opened the clasp and rummaged daintily inside.

"There it is!" she announced with a triumphant smirk upon her lined face. "Half the ladies of England don't hold *this,* do they?"

The earl's eyes narrowed. Whatever was the woman talking about? Reluctantly—for he felt at a decided and unexpected disadvantage—he extended his hand for the missive Delphinia was triumphantly clutching in her grasp.

"Oh, no, you don't, my lord! I have a mind to keep this for safekeeping!"

"Keep *what* for safekeeping?" The earl's tone was testy. He felt a spasm of gout coming on and he misliked the look in Delphinia's eye.

"This . . . this . . . *contract* you had with Peter, my lord!"

"What of it?" Impatience and a little doubt could be detected in my lord's glacial demeanour.

"You ordered the deflowering of an innocent, Alistair, my dear! Exactly the type of thing the gabblemongers would enjoy!"

The earl's face grew florid. "Are you blackmailing me?"

Delphinia smiled at him sweetly. Not exactly *blackmailing* you, my lord! I like to think of it merely as *inducing* you."

Behind the table there was a faint snigger. The earl caught sight of one of the housemaids. Her feather duster looked suspiciously clean.

"Out of here! Out! Out!" His voice was almost a bellow as he grabbed his cane and waved it menacingly in the air. The housemaid did not wait for a second warning. She bobbed a hurried curtsy and fled, blushing crimson at the unholy invectives that followed in her wake.

"The trouble with you, Alistair, is that you simply do not know how to run a household." Mrs. Spencer-Pultney replaced the letter and set her reticule down. "Now if *I* had the running of the place . . ."

The earl clenched his fist and thumped the cane angrily on the floor. "Which you do not."

Delphinia blithely ignored him. She had the upper hand and was enjoying herself immensely. ". . . I'd sack the little jade and deduct tuppence for the uniform she is wearing. Then I'd order up that lazy footman I saw lolling about and order *him* to do the dusting. The brass handles could

do with a polish, too." She looked thoughtful as she surveyed the room. "Too many candelabras, Alistair! You encourage the servants to waste!"

The earl nearly sputtered in indignation. "That I do
not!"

Mrs. Spencer-Pultney remained firm. "Indeed you do,
for every time a taper is changed I will bet my last groat
that some of the wax is kept by the servants for melting.
The more candelabras, the greater the scope for temptation. Common sense."

The earl sat back in his seat, looking thoughtful for the
first time since his encounter with Delphinia. "You have
a point. I will look into it."

"I trust you do! Check every night the length of your
tapers. Staff have an unerring habit of changing them before even half the wick is exposed! Mark my words, you
will find yourself saving."

Considerably mollified by this thought, the earl nevertheless allowed his eyebrows to draw together in a bushy
frown.

"We amble off the topic, Delphinia!"

"Do we?" Her lips thinned in the semblance of a girlish
smile. "I thought we were discussing what an excellent
housekeeper I would make!"

"*I* thought we were discussing illegal blackmail. The
punishment for that, you know, is prison."

"*I* thought we were discussing deflowering an innocent
English maiden. The punishment for *that*, you know, is
death!"

Mrs. Spencer-Pultney's eyes held Glaston's. It seemed
an age before either looked away. Check, but not checkmate. The earl had one more trick up his sleeve.

"The note incriminates Peter, not me."

Mrs. Spencer-Pultney was scornful. "Franked with your
seal? Written in your hand? It is strange, but I have mislaid

the first page. There is nothing to indicate who you were addressing, I assure you!"

The old earl looked daggers at her. "I care not a fribble what the gabblemongers say!"

"Obviously not, my lord, since you are such a cantankerous, curmudgeonly old soul!"

The earl had never been spoken to this way. His eyes narrowed in singular loathing. Mrs. Spencer-Pultney continued. "However, since I am perfectly certain you have no wish to spend the rest of your days in a place like Addersley Gaol, I am offering you a less objectionable alternative!"

The earl opened his mouth to tell my lady what she could do with her alternative. She lifted a regal hand.

"I will make an excellent countess, my lord. Besides, think how annoying it will be to dear Marianne to have to defer to me in public!"

The earl cocked his head to one side. The idea *did* have merits. . . .

The stalemate was rapidly turning into checkmate. Delphinia smoothed down the folds of her emerald gown. Time enough to mention the improvements she expected to be made to this old mausoleum . . . the balls she expected to hostess . . . the gems she had noted in the windows of Messrs. Kingsley and Scott . . . time enough when the old dupe was well and truly trapped. She shuttered her thoughts and turned to the earl.

He was amazed she could smile so charmingly.

over London, retained an aloof exterior throughout until she thought her heart would either burst or break. She was not to know that across the room his eyes never left her, but remained fixed on the sparkle of her spangles and the deep crimson sarcenet that Madame Fanchon had fashioned into a frothy dress of impeccable taste.

She was not to know, either, that his hands clenched over his dress sword every time the marquis drew her towards him, or that his heart, like hers, was as heavy as lead. The realisation that he was not quite as indifferent to his wife as he might wish did not make my lord the viscount feel any better. He'd known an instant's madness when he'd first learned of the attraction between Marianne and his one true friend. He'd been wild with fury at Raphael's note, determined to run him through the instant he laid hands on him. He had spent half a night toying with the idea of challenging him to a duel, the other half convincing himself that he did not care.

Honest as always, Raoul could see how this shambles had come to be. He had announced with due disregard for Marianne's feelings that "one woman was as good as another," he had aired those views loudly and widely to Raphael, he had given both to understand that his marriage vows meant precious little, and he had neglected Marianne shamefully. Couple that with Raphael's notorious penchant for married women, and he must have considered Marianne fair game. Raoul, sick with jealousy, could not, in fairness, intervene.

The marriage was one in name only. He could not dictate to Marianne what her preferences should be, just as she could not stop him seeing Rosamund the opera dancer. His thoughts turned to her and felt strangely flat. All the fun had gone out of those escapades. Another grievance he could lay at Marianne's door if he wished to! He did not wish to. All he wanted was to hold her in his arms and beg—yes, beg!—her to love him. He thought, with a twisted smile, of his very great pride that had insisted on *her* doing the pleading. Well, he was well served for that particular brand of egotism! She hated him, and he could not, in fairness, blame her.

Then there was Amber. . . . She was putting on a brave face, but it was clear to Raoul that her eyes darted to the marquis's excellent features whenever she thought she was unobserved. The viscount, harum-scarum though he traditionally was, nevertheless loved his sister tremendously. It pained him that she should suffer, for whilst he was undoubtedly at fault, she was not. He pushed his way through the throngs of glittering people that seemed to appear from every niche and tried, so far as he could, to ignore the chattering noise. Two violins, a harpsichord, and a double bass were tuning up—the viscount thought the racket would drive him mad. He was tempted to loosen his cravat, but that, of course, was unthinkable.

Finally, by dint of several ungentlemanly shoves and a great deal of "beg pardons," he found himself by Amber's side. She, magnificent as always in a braided velvet with ermine trim, smiled at him cordially and bade him sit with her.

"Not dashing likely!" Raoul was vehement, though Amber was relieved to hear he had modified his language. The viscount's turn of phrase could sometimes be too colourful for comfort—especially in the presence of so many ladies.

"What, then?"

"A walk outside? I cannot bear this squeeze a moment longer." For an instant Amber felt sorry for him. The viscount had doggedly been escorting them to all manner of functions—from whist to morning soirees. He must have been having the devil of a time of it! His bachelor days had been spent dreaming up heaps of wafer-thin reasons why he had to put in his regrets. Some of them were little short of tarradiddles, as Amber had berated him severely. Not that it did any good! He would simply grin his engaging smile and cozen her into offering countenance to all his lame excuses. And now . . . now was a different Raoul, one who grimly attended function after function without the veriest hint of the merriment that usually bubbled just under the surface.

Amber was inclined to think it a good sign, though she wished Raoul would come to his senses soon. Also, she wondered at Marianne, for she looked uncommonly wan beneath her merry social mask. She was meant to be seducing Raoul. Amber wondered how far she was progressing. She blushed at the path her thoughts were taking and looked sideways at her brother. By the looks of him she was failing miserably!

The strain was telling on everyone, for whilst she perfectly understood the necessity for the charade, it was hard indeed to watch Raphael make love to another woman— even if that woman was her own, dear Marianne. She had no shortage of dance partners, but somehow they all paled before the marquis, who had taken her into his arms for one cherished waltz that night before continuing his siege on the new viscountess. A muscle in Raoul's cheek twitched, and Amber could see he was thinking similar depressing thoughts.

"Raoul . . ." Amber thought it might, after all, be kind to offer a hint.

The moment was lost, however, for in the crush of making toward the exits, her gown ripped. Not the calamity it could have been, but sufficient to make her need to repair to the ladies' room for a few makeshift adjustments to hem and heel. The viscount, though a loving brother, thought it beyond the call of duty to have to escort her, once more, through the dizzying throngs of revellers.

He loosened his stifling cravat just a fraction and made for the cool outdoors. Miss Sinclair was not so fortunate. The ladies' room was full to the brim, and she spent the rest of the evening locked in polite conversation with the Eversleigh sisters and the honourable Lady Scarborough.

Sir Clive Grandison was not a man of inaction. He was more used to climbing pyramids than patiently waiting for events to take their course. Of course, when it came to the lovely Lady Jane, he found it within him to make an exception. That did not mean it was not fatiguing to watch the younger generation cut their eyeteeth, and with so much pain! It was as plain as a pikestaff to Sir Clive that something—or someone—needed prodding. It was just a matter of what and whom.

Over the next couple of days, he found himself accepting every invitation that came his way. He even, in energetic moments, endeavoured to follow the elusive trail though London that Marianne seemed to be leading. Interspersed with elegant fittings at some of the more reputable milliners, seamstresses, and mantua makers were visits to Astley's, the British Museum, the Tower of London, and, more puzzling still, several orphanages and offices of law.

Very properly my lady had a maid accompany her, but in all other respects she remained quite alone. That is, she was accompanied by Raoul, Lord Hansford, and Amber and Lady Jane upon occasion, but certainly no rendezvous of any romantic nature could be detected.

Sir Clive felt half ashamed at all his spying, but really, as he told himself, his motives were truly of the highest order. A mystery was attached to the strange courtship of Lady Hansford and the Marquis of Slade. It apparently existed only in the most public of places, under the watchful eyes of all society! Peculiar, since most liaisons were conducted the other way round.

Sir Clive began to ponder. He also set several quiet inquiries on track regarding the orphanages. What he learned surprised him and increased enormously his respect for the new viscountess. It appeared that my lady was quietly donating a great deal of money to the edification of the poor.

Sandwiched between the types of amusement that would seem fitting to a lady of her rank and wealth, she visited the sick, helped in the establishment of a successful soup kitchen, had oversight of a rehabilitation centre for pickpockets and petty thieves, and had ventured into back streets that appalled even the worldly-wise Grandison. Sir Clive was inclined to think she was either a saint or a little fool. Probably a combination of both, given what he knew of her.

Her spending confirmed his original surmise. The heiress retained control of her own pursestrings. Either this was a quixotic gesture of Raoul's, or the marriage was not as simple as it appeared. Given the strange circumstance of the Delaware affair, Sir Clive was inclined to think the latter applied. He chewed his lip thoughtfully as he entered the hallowed portals of Brookes.

Sir Clive usually eschewed such places, preferring the heights of Mount Olympia or the ruins of Pompeii to the starchiness of a gentleman's club. He had to admit, though, that as a measure of society's pulse, one could find no better haunt than the likes of Boodles or Watiers or Brookes. He ignored the comfortable studded chairs and the *Morning Post* that was instantly offered on his arrival. He walked straight past, too, the marble porticoed lounges and the grand portraits hanging elegantly in heavy gilt frames.

On other days he might have given passing attention

to the classical statues that tastefully occupied small alcoves, or to the mechanical train that wound its slow way across a miniature track erected, as a novelty, at the far corner of the club. Today, however, his feet marched firmly across parquet flooring until they arrived, at last, at an Aubusson rug of exquisite detail. Sad to say, Sir Clive did not even notice the luxury beneath his boots. His quick eyes were perusing the betting book with a strange animation. He turned the pages quickly, causing several of the gentlemen to look up from their papers. Again, Sir Clive hardly noticed. He was too engrossed in what he read.

It seemed Lord Delaware's preoccupation with the lovely viscountess had not gone unremarked. The betting books were filled with speculation on all of society's little quirks and foibles—it was only natural they should feature as an item. Sir Clive drew his brows together. Odds were at three to one the lovely viscountess was smitten. Exactly how such a thing could be established beyond doubt baffled the ordinarily acute Sir Clive, but that was the least of his concerns. His first was to see such vulgar rumours scotched.

He turned on his heel and made for the exit. The baronet was uncommonly out of sorts for a man of his sanguine temper. At the door, a sudden thought occurred to him. He walked back to the book and took up a pen. With a flourish, he took up the challenge, betting *against* the prevailing odds.

Several young bucks looked at each other significantly. If Grandison saw nothing in the latest scandal, there probably was nothing in it. He was not a man who parted with his blunt lightly. Besides, everyone knew he had a more than passing interest in the Hansford affairs. Instantly the odds were reduced to two to one. By the end of the day, it was set at evens, and the day after that found the betting closed. There were other, more delicious scandals to chalk up at the gentlemen's clubs.

Lady Jane looked calm, but the base of her throat fluttered with a faint pulse that made Sir Clive long to take her in his arms. Of a sudden, he swore a most ungentlemanlike oath and strode across the room to do just that.

Lady Jane demurred slightly, but Sir Clive would have none of it.

"Ods-bobs, my good woman! If I cannot kiss you in your own drawing room, where, pray, can I?"

Since the obvious reply led to the most indelicate of answers, Lady Jane was forced to concede the point. Settling her on the sofa, Sir Clive proceeded to interrogate her on the activities of her progeny.

Lady Jane sighed.

"Truth is, Sir Clive, I don't know *what* to think! I could swear Raoul is not indifferent to Marianne, nor she to him! Their behaviour seems extraordinary! The odd thing is, Amber, who, as you know, I've worried my head off about, seems in perfectly good spirits." She offered him a macaroon off the tea tray. Sir Clive declined, his concentration torn between the delicious sensation of having Lady Jane so close to his elbow and the interesting import of her words. She continued.

"The darling may simply be putting on a brave face, but honestly, I cannot detect it. She seems perfectly collected when Raphael pays his addresses to Marianne. Why, at times the exasperating little chit sends them off at her own suggestion!"

The pieces were at last falling together for Sir Clive. He smiled a slow, endearing smile and took Lady Jane's slender fingers into his own.

"You hearten me, my little dove!"

"Hearten you? *Puzzle* you should surely be more accurate?"

"I think not! What is more, the day I shall call you mine seems rapidly to be drawing closer. Does a spring wedding suit? I hope so, for I warn you I shall not wait a moment longer than I have to!"

"But—"

"Hush!" The baronet put his finger to her lips. "I have not forgotten my promise. It is only that I predict, really and truly, a most happy outcome for your Amber."

"May I know why?"

Sir Clive thought. Possibly it was better that Lady Jane did not know the outrageous scheming that was taking place under her very nose. Undoubtedly she would give the game away, for she was too honest for such trickery. Besides, Sir Clive was not sure; he only suspected that an elaborate plot was underfoot to make the Viscount Hansford finally see sense.

"Trust me."

His voice sounded so confident and comforting that Lady Jane nodded. It was in much lighter spirits indeed that she sat at the pianoforte and began to sing.

Seventeen

"Marianne!" Marianne looked up from the toast she was biting into. Her heart stopped and her pulse started fluttering with indecorous speed. This was the first time her husband had actually addressed her at breakfast for quite some time.

More than that, he was looking at her in such a way that set her knees atremble and her heart hammering in her rib cage.

"Care for a ride in my tilbury?"

Marianne's eyes sparkled.

"I would adore it!"

My lord breathed a sigh of relief. It had not been so difficult, after all, to bring the colour back to her cheeks and the merriment surfacing to her expressive, liquid gold eyes.

Raoul stood up, a satisfied twinkle in his deep sapphire eyes. The exorbitant cost of the canary yellow tilbury with its matching white stallions seemed vindicated.

"Come on, then!"

"I will need to change!"

Raoul inspected her closely. She was wearing a pale pink muslin scattered with tiny ribbons and a delicate hint of lace at the neck.

"Must you? You look . . ."

There was a silence. *Adorable* had nearly tripped off his tongue, but he didn't want to frighten Marianne. If she was in love with Raphael he must move carefully.

". . . in prime twig!" The compliment must have had a good effect, for my lady blushed, then smiled her saucy smile that set his heart racing.

"Nevertheless, my lord, I must change! A day dress simply won't do for a tilbury ride! We would hate to flout the conventions, you know."

Raoul wasn't at all deceived by the prim look and downcast eyes she chose to assume. The viscountess relished defying convention. It was the prime thing he loved about her.

"Baggage!"

She dimpled at him and curtsied. It seemed to him that the sun filtering into the morning room was far brighter than when he first entered.

He was fagged to death of wallowing in his misery. If he had to win back his own, dear wife then that was what he would do. His thoughts confirmed an uncomfortable suspicion that had been lurking in his mind for overlong. Marianne *was* dear to him. More than that, she was worth fighting for, even if that fight meant taking up cudgels with Raphael, Marquis of Slade. The notion was novel, for Lord Delaware had been a steadfast friend since Raoul was in leading strings. Still! He had neither the advantage of being married to the lady nor the sincere depth of feeling that Raoul finally understood lay deep within his own heart. To Raphael, Marianne was an interesting plaything. To Raoul, she was everything.

He vowed not to get annoyed with her, not to revert to the grand manner, not, above all, to object to her slapping his face. If my lady wanted to, she could kick his shins, for all he cared. So long as she did it for him, with him, and *to* him. With this admirable intention, my lord smiled lopsidedly at his wife. She had already moved toward the door.

"Five minutes, no more!" he called after her departing back.

He could hear echoes of mock indignation as she tripped out of the morning room.

"Amber!"

Miss Sinclair, just in from picking luscious hothouse strawberries, took one look at Marianne and smiled.

"My dolt of a brother has come round, has he?"

Marianne nodded, her eyes shining. Amber dropped the fruit and opened her arms. Marianne found herself biting back tears in the warm embrace.

"I never thought I could be so foolish!"

"Not foolish, Marianne, dear, just in love! Dry your eyes. You don't want the silly gudgeon to see you with tear-stained cheeks!"

Marianne laughed. "Indeed not! I am in a panic as to what to wear! I was thinking the primrose cambric. . . ."

"Excellent choice, but anything will do. You would look fetching in a rag, I believe!"

Marianne giggled. "Do not, I beg, tell Madame Fanchon that!"

"I shall not if you only make haste! Raoul is most tiresome when it comes to keeping his horses waiting."

"Oh! I'd better fly! The strawberries . . ." Marianne looked at them doubtfully.

"Go! I will gather them up."

Marianne nodded and fled to her chamber, where an assortment of clothes went flying on to her bed in such quick succession it sent her maid's head spinning. No sooner had she procured a matching bonnet and gloves than milady changed her mind and the process began again. Finally, though, Marianne settled for a deep peach chintz with honey gold flecks and a large ribbon around the waist. The elegant attire was completed by a high poke bonnet finished with a merry length of matching ribbon.

The viscountess had not time to see whether she had made the correct choice. She was halfway down the stairs before her maid, brandishing a sizable silver looking glass, realised she was gone.

The tilbury had high spoke wheels and was, as Raoul had boasted, a "rare goer!" The morning was crisp, the breeze from the west making riding a little chilly but none-theless enjoyable, for the oaks gently swayed to the rhythm of the hooves and the grass smelled of springtime and peonies.

Raoul had deftly maneuvered them away from the more fashionable tracks of the city and out toward the rolling green hillsides past Tavistock and beyond.

Marianne allowed herself to relax and enjoy the heady excitement of the spanking pace they set. From time to time, her eyes would stealthily wander to Raoul's profile as he held the reins lightly in one hand. His strong jaw and blond, curling hair were a great temptation to her. She wondered what he would do if she just slightly adjusted positions so that she could stretch out and touch them.

Her mouth curved slightly at the thought, for whatever else their relationship held, there could be no doubting the mutual attraction that flowed between them like a river of tumultuous, unstoppable currents. She knew that if she wanted to, she could reach over and stop his breath, con-trol his heartbeat . . . wreak havoc with the horses.

She chuckled to herself. Whatever other designs she had for that day, it did not include being catapulted into a ditch. She curbed her immediate desires, but began, in as cunning and calculating a way as possible, to plan her poor, unwitting, defenseless husband's seduction.

Amber and Raphael had played their part in the grand plan perfectly. Up until now, however, her own role had been meagre and singularly unsuccessful, to say the least of it. Today was her chance, for today, she was determined, the intricate tangle that all their affairs were knotted in would have to be untied. Once and for all, she wanted Raoul as her husband and her lover. She wanted—*desperately* she wanted—him to acknowledge her as his wife—and lover.

The little tilbury merrily rolled on, just missing a couple of rabbits, a particularly large pothole, and a farm gig containing three geese, a pig, and a series of chickens. Each time a collision was deftly avoided, Raoul turned to her and grinned.

By Jupiter, Marianne thought, I do believe he is showing off! By the time they had reached their destination she was convinced, for the wheels were covered in mud, the stallions were panting, and several larger conveyances had been left in the dust upon the road. She, of course, was breathless with excitement. Her eyes were sparkling and her bonnet had been discarded long ago. If she had not tied the ribbons to the bouncing seat it would have been history. As it was, her hair was tumbling in delightful profusion right down to her waist, the deplorable curls deplorably curly—and, in short, exactly the way my lord liked it.

When they finally stopped, he looked at her and her heart started hammering in her chest most painfully. Her only consolation was that hers was not the only one. My lord had removed Weston's fine greatcoat, and through the crisp white cotton of his shirt Marianne could just detect his chest rising and falling in harmony with her own. She remained perfectly still, for, truth to tell, she was transfixed. His sapphire eyes were gleaming dark, a sea of unfathomable, hypnotic blue.

For all her good intentions and cunning plans to allure him, Marianne found she could do nothing. It was fortunate that *nothing* was enough for my lord, who happened to find her choice in gowns—especially the cut of the décolletage above the satin ribbon—quite entrancing. What was more, despite the fact that she neglected to stroke his jaw as she had fully intended, her honey gold eyes were as wide and speaking as they possibly could be through lashes as thick and dark as hers.

My lord seemed not to notice her strange immobility, for his eyes had moved from the tantalising curves he'd been aware of all through their delightful ride to her face and the gorgeous ruby red lips that had been an irksome feature of his dreams for longer than he cared to recall.

"Care to climb down?" She nodded, but his eyes remained firmly fixed on her mouth. "Excellent! I won't be a moment tethering the horses; then we may be comfortable!"

He smiled sweetly, but Marianne was not deceived. Comfort, she considered, was the least of what either of them had on their minds. He leaped down lightly and was amused to find that before he had got round to help her down, she had jumped the distance herself.

"I keep forgetting what a little hoyden you are!"

"I shall take that as a compliment, my lord, since the day is too fine to cross swords with you."

"Too fine indeed."

His teeth gleamed white in the sunshine, and Marianne's heart did a somersault. She watched as he tethered the horses and offered them a fresh carrot to graze. Lady Sinclair was fascinated that her scapegrace husband had actually been thoughtful enough to secure several in his capacious buckskins.

He caught her watchful eyes and grinned an engaging, thoroughly enticing sort of a grin.

"You will probably find more to fascinate you in my breeches, my lady, if you care to explore!"

Her ladyship nearly choked. It crossed her mind that he would be well served if she took him up on the carelessly made offer. On the other hand . . . something ardent in his eyes made her wary.

"No?" His lordship heaved a huge sigh. "How very disappointing!"

Marianne agreed, but she remained firm. Time enough to explore the interesting contours. . . . She blushed crimson at the direction of her thoughts. My lord said nothing, but something about the sudden perkiness of his step made Marianne think her musings were too transparent by far.

"Ready to talk, Maid Marianne?" His voice was gentler as he helped her down onto the long, soft grass. Around them wildflowers sprouted in gay profusion, and a few robins pecked at the acacia berries that lay hidden beneath the spring shoots.

"I think so, my lord."

"Raoul."

"Raoul."

He nodded, satisfied.

"We seem to be in a tangle, you and I!"

Marianne nodded seriously.

"I give you leave to slap my face, if you will!"

Marianne's heart turned over at this patent sign of goodwill. "Thank you, Raoul, but I do not think that will be necessary!"

"You don't?" Raoul looked surprised and boyishly relieved. "Even if I find it necessary to stroke your wild curly locks?"

Marianne nodded. "Even then, my lord."

Raoul was intrigued. He took several strands in his fingers and drew her closer. "Even if I were to find it imperative to remove your gloves and kiss each little finger from beginning to end and all over again?"

Marianne smiled into his penetrating eyes. "Even then."

Raoul removed the gloves and discarded them with not a thought for their pristine whiteness and expensive lace trim. He took each finger gently and systematically kissed it so thoroughly that Marianne felt quite faint at the experience. When he was finished, he started the process all over again. For once, her ladyship was rendered speechless. Encouraged, my lord replaced her hands into her lap and continued his interrogation.

"This grows interesting, Maid Marianne! Would you slap me, I wonder, if I breached those . . ." His eyes fell to the creamy white expanse of her chest and the interesting curves that had been tantalising his senses all morning. The pulse in her neck raced until she could scarcely breathe. He grinned and moved his eyes upwards to her mouth, scrutinizing it with such intensity that again Marianne felt faint. ". . . very rosy lips of yours?"

It seemed to the viscountess that every living creature had stopped its chirruping and foraging simply to stare at her. The world was suddenly quiet. Not even the nearby stream dared bubble and flow with quite the abandon of a moment before. Her tongue passed over her lips in unutterable anticipation. She wanted to nod invitingly. She wanted to lure him with her eyes like a siren in the manner she had planned all through the tilbury ride. She wanted, finally, to seduce her Lord Sinclair.

Instead, she was miserably tongue-tied and incapable of speech.

For a horrified instant she feared her silence would be misinterpreted as displeasure. She saw the flicker of doubt in Raoul's eyes, but at a small, trembling movement of her outstretched hand the doubt was gone. He moved towards her and placed his hand on her chin.

"Do you know," he said huskily, "this is what I have longed to do from the moment I set eyes on your delicious-looking ankles?"

Marianne shook her head. "You were so grim, my lord, I thought—"

"Hush, Marianne! Let us set aside our troubles and enjoy the moment. Perhaps, in time, you can come to love me."

Before his wife could formulate a response to this cryptic phrase, or realise quite fully the import of what he had said, her body felt suddenly alive with sensations she could never have dreamed possible. Raoul's kiss was everything she had remembered and wildly, madly more. It held the teasing, ardent passion that had engulfed her memories and desires ever since their first caress. But this time the teasing, exploring tongue held more. Marianne was too inflamed to know exactly what, or to feel the commitment and yearning that flavoured the kiss with all her romantic heart could desire. All she knew was that she was transported to some glorious heaven, and she hoped fervently the moment would not stop. It did, but just as she was bewailing that fact, she found the kiss was being replaced by a headier experience by far.

The honourable viscount, oblivious of his surroundings, was divesting himself of all his outer garments. Marianne could only gasp as she observed his slim, muscular stomach, invitingly hard and flat. When his hands moved confidently to his breeches, she felt the most unaccountable sensation flood her being.

Raoul must have understood, for he drew her close and began the indescribable exploration that followed. Anyone passing might well have raised their brows at the sight confronting them. It was fortunate, then, that not so much as a passing gig happened their way.

Even the stallions, enjoying their dappled meadow and clear springwater, did not so much as cast their equine eyes in the couple's direction.

Marianne relinquished all reason and allowed her husband to work his magic. His blond head glittered in the sunshine as his hands worked havoc with her mind and body. When his lips moved to her laces, she closed her eyes and neglected to see how deep, piercing blue his own had become.

She was so captivated by his scent, his taste, and his exquisitely expert touch that she missed the murmured terms of endearment, the deep, throaty words of love that escaped from the back of his throat and hung in the air like a bond between them. All she felt was a delicious, indescribable madness that she was no longer able to reject, neglect, or rebuff.

Thus it was that on a fine spring day, becomingly divested of bonnet, parasol, and *all* of Madame Fanchon's fashionable handiwork, my lady Marianne at last became viscountess in truth as well as name.

Eighteen

"Is my lady within?" Lord Delaware smiled at Carstairs, who admitted him at once.

If the elderly retainer thought it strange the amount of time Lord Delaware spent dancing attendance on the new viscountess, he certainly knew his place enough not to show it. Besides, despite his private reservations he *liked* the marquis, who was never so toplofty that he failed to say "please" and "thank you" or tip nobly when the occasion arose.

"I believe not, my lord."

The marquis raised his handsome brows just a trifle.

"Indeed? There must be some mistake! I was positive we had a riding engagement this afternoon!"

The butler cleared his throat.

"I believe her ladyship accompanied Master Raoul—I mean his lordship—to one of the country estates."

Lord Delaware thought hard. What was the meaning of this new circumstance? Had the duo finally come to the sort of understanding he hoped?

"Which estate, Carstairs?"

"I do not know, my lord. They did, however, take the new tilbury. None of the grooms were required."

The marquis smiled merrily to himself. He should think *not*, if Raoul intended any of the activities he suspected!

If it was the tilbury, they had probably not gone too far. Possibly Raoul's estate at Elderberry. At all events, it appeared likely that the riding trip would be postponed or cancelled. By now, he very much hoped, Marianne would have other things to be thinking of!

Blandly, he turned again to the butler, who was waiting patiently for instruction.

"Is the dowager viscountess within?" He dared not ask for Amber, despite his exalted position in the family. Amber, unmarried, still required the aegis of a chaperon. The butler smiled approvingly. At least he did not have to rebuke the marquis, as he had many a young buck seeking private audience with the popular Miss Sinclair.

"I believe so, my lord. She is gathering cuttings for her herb garden. If you will take a seat?"

The marquis nodded and removed his simple though elegant chapeau bras. After the butler had gone, he moved restlessly to the window and looked across the large, well-tended garden. If he hoped for a glimpse of Amber, he was to be disappointed. He caught not a fleeting flash of her guinea gold hair, or her long, swanlike neck. He sighed and fingered one of the crystal figurines impatiently.

"Careful, my lord, that might break!"

He whirled around and was not disappointed. Standing in the doorway was his one true love, a smile of angelic, endearing calm engulfing her like sparkling rays of sunshine.

"Amber."

"My lord." She was suddenly shy, for since the fateful night of the ball, she'd not been alone with Raphael in the sense that she was now.

Lord Delaware absently replaced the crystal.

"I was expecting your mother."

"Indeed, I know! We were busily plucking marjoram together when we were informed of your presence."

"And she sent you, instead?"

Amber compressed her lips thinly but her eyes twinkled. "I have been sent to bear a message, Raphael! My mother is delighted that you have come calling, but unfortunately, *most* unfortunately, is at a crucial moment with her potions. Evidently the chamomile must be mixed this instant with the marjoram or . . . or . . ."

The marquis's lips twitched. "Or the roots will decay, rendering the concoction utterly vile?"

Amber nodded. "Exactly so!" Her tone changed. "Do you know, Raphael, I seriously suspect my innocent mama of meddlesome matchmaking?"

"How so, my little love?" Raphael's eyes never wavered from the lady's lips. Unnerved, she sought to introduce a light tone to the proceedings.

"Because, my dear Raphael, with an alarming glint in her tender eyes, she bade me entertain you in her stead!" Amber put an indignant hand on her hips. "Of all the transparent, conniving —" She was silenced by the smouldering stare the marquis was bestowing upon her person. A hot flush appeared on her normally tranquil complexion.

If the marquis noticed, he was too polite by far to tax her on it. Instead, he idly helped himself to a pinch of snuff from a marcasite box of exquisite workmanship and nodded equably.

"Eminently sensible woman, Lady Jane."

"Raphael! She is a conniving—"

"Just so! My point exactly!"

Amber had to yield, laughing a little uncertainly. The uncertainty deepened when the marquis came so close she could smell his deep, masculine scent and feel his breath upon her face.

"And shall you, my dear, beloved, most unutterably adored Amber?"

"Shall I what?" She was frantically trying to gather her wits against this unfair siege of her senses.

"Shall you entertain me this afternoon?"

"My lord!" Her voice bubbled with feigned shock and laughter.

"Well?"

"Indeed, my lord, I think I shall!"

When the butler passed by some fifteen minutes later, the sight that met his eyes was one that should have shocked his conservative soul. Instead, he cast a glance across the hall to check whether any of the other servants had been edified with the same view. They had not. With an almost imperceptible movement, Carstairs took the unprecedented step of ensuring that they never did. He shut the drawing room door.

Marianne cupped her hands lazily in her chin and watched the bright cornflowers merrily bobbing up and down amid the long, lush grass. The sight of Raoul, Lord Sinclair, bathing without so much as a stitch of small clothes offered an equally pleasing prospect, although she was not unaware of the dangers attendant on their situation.

When she had taxed Raoul on the foolhardiness of their abandon, he had only grinned and rolled over, pulling her on top of him with the strength of a lion. He seemed not at all concerned that they might be arrested for their public display or, at the very least, embarrassed by interested onlookers. He seemed deaf to all reason as he caressed her gently, putting all her own objections entirely out of mind.

When he climbed out of the stream and came to join her, dripping wet and flicking water playfully at her shift, she gave up remonstrating and simply sighed in utter, heartfelt satisfaction.

"I wish we could stay here forever!"

Raoul looked at her closely. Though every moment of the day had been like a small miracle to him, he was not unaware of the herculean task that lay before him. He still had to wrest his wife's affections from his best friend. The thought of Raphael clouded his enjoyment of the moment. Still, when his wife looked at him in that peculiarly happy and hungry fashion, all shadows seemed to flee.

"We can, if you want to!"

"Don't be silly, Raoul! we cannot spend the rest of our days perched by a public stream! Think what the onlookers would say!" Marianne giggled at the thought.

"Be *damned* to the onlookers!" Raoul's eyes were darkening once more to deep sapphire. "Besides . . ." He looked at her a little more seriously. "There shan't *be* any onlookers!"

"And why not, pray?"

"Because this stream is bang in the middle of the Elderberry estate and *you*, my dear, are chatelaine of it!"

"Beg pardon?"

"Elderberry, Huntingdon, and Newstead are all entailed to the viscountcy. I also hold three other estates west of Lancashire, but they are independent of the Hansford title. Won on change to the second viscount in the last century, I believe." This history lesson over, my lord turned his interested attention to matters of anatomy.

Marianne pushed him aside and pummelled him with her fists. "Raoul! You beast! You could have *told* me we were on private land!"

"Could I have?" Raoul grinned. "Would have spoiled the fun! Besides, I had other things on my mind, lady wife."

Marianne decided she liked that title. Just when she was

mulling it over in her head, she had an alarming thought and sat up, plunging Raoul's roving hands into sudden disarray.

"My goodness!"

"What?"

"Lord Delaware! We were to go riding today!"

The light was extinguished from Raoul's eyes. He stood up and began dressing without another word. Marianne could have kicked herself, but the damage was done.

"Raoul . . ." She desperately wanted to explain, but that grim look she so dreaded had returned. "It is all a mistake."

Raoul looked at her with none of the merriness she had so come to treasure.

"A *terrible* mistake," he said. The bitterness and hurt were all too detectable in the lines etched across his mouth and brow. Marianne wanted to soothe them, but the moment for such intimacy seemed to have melted away.

"Let me explain."

"There is nothing to explain. I understand perfectly." Raoul offered her his back as he moved to the horses and connected up the little tilbury.

By the time he had finished, Marianne was more or less dressed, though she was having slight difficulty with one or two of the fastenings at the back. Raoul moved over and helped her, his long fingers bringing back searing memories of the night he had done the reverse.

Finally, when he had finished, he politely lifted her over the high spoke wheels and tucked in the delicious canary travelling rug he'd taken the precaution of purchasing.

Their steady trot back held none of the heady delight of earlier. Still, as Marianne told herself, there was no going back. With the marriage consummated, there could be no annulment. She wondered whether Raoul was thinking the same thing and whether his self-control stemmed from happiness at this fact or bleakness at the prospect. She could have sworn, earlier, that he loved her! And yet . . . there was still this reserve between them.

She peeked at him now. His beaver had been squashed onto his head with deplorable lack of finesse, but for all that, he looked quite dreadfully handsome, his golden skin a fine contrast to his brown riding gloves. His whip hand was light and effortless, and though he was not exactly a member of the Four Horse Club, Marianne found his handling of the tilbury faultless.

"Cry truce?"

She smiled at him charmingly and his heart melted, though his head remained wary and decidedly cold.

"Truce, madame! Indeed, I have to confess to a little jealousy of my Lord Raphael! He appears to be demanding an inordinate amount of your time!"

Marianne bit back the retort that he was *meant* to be jealous. A glimmer of hope flickered in her mind, for whilst she infinitely preferred being called Maid Marianne to *madame,* she could sense a thawing of her unsuspecting husband's defences. So she nodded and remarked with sweet innocence that Raphael was an excellent escort and they were fortunate to have him at their disposal.

Raoul ground his teeth at this, but fairness did not allow him to argue. They *were* lucky, for Raphael had stood by them as a couple and him as a veritable young sprig of fashion, through thick and thin.

He stole a glance at Marianne. She looked so composed and serene. Surely she could not be betraying him with his dearest friend? On the other hand . . . he *had* treated her abominably. He resolved, once again, to turn a new leaf. His task was to win her from Raphael, not accuse her of treachery.

"I am sorry I grew so pettish, Marianne."

Her ladyship glanced up in surprise. There did not seem

to be a hint of the ready mirth that usually accompanied his remarks. Stranger still, she did not think he was mocking her. Lord Sinclair, for once, looked heartachingly contrite.

She was just wildly thinking what to say when she bowled forward and found herself clutching at his shirtsleeves in a most undignified manner. Sad to say, Raoul's inner musings had made his thoughts wander. The stallions, used to a firm and steady hand, sensed the inattention and tried to bolt. Fortunately their efforts were overset by a skillful manipulation of the reins. When Raoul was done, though, he was perspiring from the effort. Marianne was trying to disentangle herself from his lap but found herself firmly clenched to his side.

"Oh, no, you *don't*, Lady Sinclair! Bad driving needs at least *some* compensation!"

"You nearly ditched us, my lord!" Marianne's tone was severe, but her heart, once more, had begun to race.

"It is your fault entirely, and so I will tell any incomparable who happens to ask!"

"How so, my lord?" Marianne wrinkled a puzzled nose at him. Not very ladylike, but then, he had not married her for her ladylike qualities.

"You were distracting me!"

"I was *not.*" Her ladyship was indignant.

"Indeed you were, with your gorgeous hair billowing out of that ridiculous confection! Take it off. It was better tied to the tilbury."

"I cannot! We are entering the city, my lord."

"Decorum? What is this, Marianne? Are you sickening for something?"

Marianne laughed. Her merriment was infectious, and my lord found the corners of his lips twitching in response. Despite the long task ahead of him, Lord Sinclair had hopes he could win his wife. When she continued to giggle, he found his spirits rising immeasurably.

"To hell with Raphael!" He felt a weight drop off his shoulders as he made this silent pronouncement. The marquis could look elsewhere for his pleasures. Marianne, in the future, would be too dazzled by her *own* husband to have the smallest use for him. The viscount smiled, but the pleasure was marred by a trace of bitterness. It still hurt just a tiny amount that his best friend should have chosen his wife as his latest flirtation. Still, to be fair, it was understandable. Who, after all, would *not* be attracted to her twinkling eyes and bonny figure? Raoul's blood stirred at the thought, and if *his* did . . .

"What are you thinking of, my lord?"

If the viscount were to say what he was thinking of at that moment, there would be an accident for sure. As it was, the tilbury was in danger of being overturned from every direction as the crossroads led to a meeting of the stagecoach, an overfull farm gig, and a crested barouche of unknown heraldry.

"Marianne, I swear if you look at me that way I will pull you down from this delightful vehicle and march you off to the nearest haystack!"

"Which, I think, is over there . . ." Marianne's eyes were brimful of laughter as she pointed to a series of neatly stacked piles of straw just off the main intersection.

A retort was made impossible, for Raoul needed to concentrate all his energy on the stallions, which had grown restive from all the activity.

The stagecoach was given right of way, and the little tilbury remained stationary in a cloud of dust as the lumbering vehicle, complete with a range of passengers from all walks of life, made its slow way forward. Marianne could just make out the passengers seated on the roof, clutching tenaciously at bandboxes and bursting portmanteaus.

For an instant she reflected how easily *she* could have been such a passenger, for if Raoul had not rescued her, she would almost certainly have been left to such devices.

She smiled at how very nearly she had become an opera dancer. What fustian! It all seemed such a very long time ago. Raoul's profile—always engagingly interesting—was breathtakingly dear to her now. How fortunate that she had aimed her few possessions at him that fateful day!

For an instant she reflected on other possible outcomes of her actions and shuddered. Raoul, she knew, deserved her love, obedience, and respect. She resolved firmly to be a good wife to him and not to expect more from him than he felt able to give. She sighed a small sigh. How *very* annoying that she did not have a shred of patience in her entire body! Well, she would turn over a new leaf. Raoul, Lord Sinclair, was worth the effort.

Nineteen

"Glaston, I *insist* we hold a ball! We will have the holland covers removed from all the furnishings. I can't think how you allowed them to become so shockingly drab, and we shall call in the decorators to refurbish the fittings. . . . Glaston!"

Delphinia's voice rose to a high-pitched squeak as she addressed the newspaper confronting her. If she thought the piercing noise might shake his lordship from the *Worcester Journal,* she was destined to suffer a severe setback. The earl, on the contrary, dipped his head slightly lower into the pages and appeared deaf to the verbal onslaught that now threatened his digestion.

The lackey on duty silently removed the covers and laid down a small cup of hot coffee. My lord stretched out his gnarled, liver-spotted hand and drank the beverage down in one searing gulp. With a gesture, he indicated for more to be poured. The noise continued in his ears, but he patently ignored it.

"And if you think, Alistair, that this . . . this . . . *decoction* can be mistaken for coffee I will have you know . . ."

My lord continued with the third column of the *Worcester Journal.* Two more hours and he could escape to his club . . .

". . . coffee beans from the New World!" Delphinia nodded decisively and rang for some sweet tea.

The earl carefully turned over the page and perused each item with studied calm. His eyes gleamed with a certain malice, for while Delphinia had bested him on the first round, the new countess was going to find him an implacable adversary. The thought cheered him up somewhat, for there was little doubt he found the perpetual, ceaseless nagging a trifle depressing.

Still, he would regard it as a challenge. *His* would not be the spirit crushed in this imbroglio. The thought of crushing Delphinia's spirit was a salve to his pride.

"I can't think why no one has yet responded to my invitation. I expressly required an answer." Delphinia's brow crumpled in annoyance. The earl did not see the dissatisfied lines around her mouth, for he was busy with the mail that had been offered to him on a salver of tarnished plate. The countess's sharp eyes noticed its decaying condition and she made a mental note to admonish the servants yet again . . . strange how they were all putting in their notice . . . she would have to contact Mrs. Oakley's house of employment.

"Glaston!" Her tone was so sharp that even the earl could not ignore it. His shuttered expression appeared benign, but even the hardened Delphinia shivered involuntarily.

"I hope you have a good reason for interrupting my morning paper, Delphinia, dear!"

The words were sweet enough, but Delphinia was not fooled.

"I . . . I . . . well, I desire a ball, Glaston!" The words came out in an uncustomary flurry, for Delphinia was unused to having to tread warily.

"Do you?" The earl looked at her in sour amusement.

Well, she would pay for her blackmail, she and her pudding-faced wench!

The countess of Glaston was not sure she liked the amused inflection in her husband's tone.

"I do! Lila will need a decent come-out ball, and I do feel we need to celebrate our recent nuptials, Alistair!" She looked at him coyly, and the earl felt inwardly revolted.

"*Do* you?" His mystified tone annoyed Delphinia excessively, but since she saw the need to wheedle him round, she made no complaint.

"Indeed I *do!*" She looked at him slyly. "You will be wanting that hussy, Marianne, to curtsy to your new bride, will you not?" Her eyes met the earl's.

He grudgingly nodded, for on that issue at least, he and his wife were in perfect accord.

He laid down the mail and mused for a moment.

"Lady Simmington is holding a masquerade ball this evening. No need to hold a ball of your own, Delphinia! Think of the unnecessary expense! If you and that . . . that . . ."

"If you call her a pudding-faced wench again I shall scream!"

The earl pointedly ignored her ". . . that pudding-faced wench—"

"Alistair!" Delphinia's fingers gripped her cane convulsively. My lord ignored her. He was beginning to enjoy himself.

"In short, if I were to escort you to Lady Simmington's, Marianne will be forced to pay her respects *there*. No *need* to have a ball of our own." The earl smiled in miserly satisfaction. *A masterstroke!*

Delphinia thought quickly.

"Don't be so absurd, my lord! The Earl of Glaston must be seen to entertain, and entertain you shall! However, there might be something in your notion of Lady Simmington's little get-together. . . ." The thought of humiliating Marianne made her burn with impatience. True, it would have been better with her as reigning hostess, but that would come. "I do believe you are correct! We will attend this evening. The Viscountess Hansford is bound to be there. She positively haunts fashionable gatherings!" Delphinia's eyes gleamed with hatred.

My lord saw this and decided that Delphinia was a better mouse to his cat than Marianne was.

His lips twitched slightly with something very akin to naked malice. He flipped through his letters rather pointedly, then sat back in his seat.

"Alas, my dear it is not to be!"

"Why ever not?" Delphinia's voice was sharp. Once she had set her mind to something, there was precious little that she would permit to stand in her way.

"I have sifted through this assortment of letters and assure you, my dear, that not one among them is franked by Lord Simmington!"

"What is that to the purpose? I was thinking, my lord . . . Madame Fanchon is supposed to be simply exquisite with a needle. I daresay it might cost a bit more, but if we tell her that it is urgent . . ."

Lord Sinclair, Earl Glaston, extended one arm languidly.

"You miss the point, my dear!"

Delphinia looked at him absently. Her thoughts were awhirl with the necessity for feathers and muffs and little buckled slippers and—

"Delphinia!"

The earl's roar brought her back to reality.

"What *is* it, Glaston?"

The earl stared at her unpleasantly. His head was ringing from the sound of her voice pealing over his head all through breakfast. He had had enough.

"There is one slight, unfortunate obstacle to all this gadding about."

"And that is?" Delphinia lifted one brow archly. She hadn't gone to the trouble of becoming countess to encounter *obstacles*.

"There is no invitation from Lady Simmington!"

"Nonsense, Alistair! You must have dropped it! Lady Simmington is notoriously toplofty! A man of your rank . . . of *course* she'd invite you! Now if she hasn't invited *me*, it would be because . . ."

"Because?"

"Because she has not yet been apprised of your wedded state! That reminds me, Alistair . . . we must send a note in to the *Gazette.*"

The earl shook his head. "Forgive me! I thought it must be because of your low birth. As you said, she is a stickler."

Delphinia grew purple. "Fustian, Alistair! As Countess of Glaston I am unimpeachable!"

Excellent, for *I* am not!"

"Whatever do you mean?" Cool brows arched in sudden surprise.

"Did you not know?" Glaston's voice was silky smooth, but his heart beat faster. He was moving in for the kill, and the new Lady Sinclair, Countess Glaston, was like a lamb to the slaughter.

"My youthful indiscretions have put me irreparably beyond the pale. It was never proved, of course, but my name has been bandied about in connection with that dear, sweet innocent, Lady Sophia Martin. But hush . . ." The earl's eyes were filled with grim satisfaction. "I should mention no names!"

"You mean you raped—"

"Despoiled, my dear! Despoiled. Rape is such an *ugly* term, do you not think?"

The countess paled.

"Then . . . ?"

The earl nodded grimly.

"I am not received in the best of drawing rooms, I am afraid!"

Delphinia was silenced. The full import of her husband's words were only now sinking in. If he were not received in society, then there would be no balls, no soirees, no informal little dinners . . . in short, she would be a social leper. Worse off, in fact, than before she had married him. Marianne would never pay her precedence, for they would not be destined ever to meet.

She seethed at the injustice. My lord wiped his face delicately with a linen cloth and indicated that the coffee might be sent away. Revenge, he noted, was sweet.

He thought of his favoured pastime: my lady was in check.

Delphinia glared at him. She strongly considered having hysterics, but thought the better of it. The servants would only gossip, and there was no one in the household to bear her sympathy.

The earl smiled. "Exactly so, my dear."

She could see he had read her thoughts and fumed. Her fury turned to ashen disbelief when his chair squeaked back against the oaken floor and he extended his hand.

"Delphinia, dear, I find that dress most becoming." He did not, but again, my lady Glaston was too shrewd not to see where his thoughts were leading.

"It is the morning, my lord!"

"What odds? You are my wife, are you not?" She winced, and his lordship smiled. He would see her well served for a lifetime of her unceasing chatter.

When she was silent, he took her hand and led her through the great, oaken entrance.

He might have been snared in a parson's mousetrap,

but my lady would yet live to regret her blackmail. He thought carefully. Check? No, Delphinia Sinclair, previously Spencer-Pultney, was solidly and quite firmly caught up in checkmate.

Raoul handed over the reins with a faint sinking feeling in his gut. The Marquis of Slade's elegant curricle was stabled alongside his own crested barouche. There could be no doubting that Lord Delaware had decided to wait.

Marianne noted the same, and her eyes flickered to Raoul's. They were still an exquisite blue, but had lost their sapphirelike qualities. Diffidently she put a hand on his. He looked at her, and it seemed that the troubled expression vanished from his brow.

"It seems your beau is determined to take you for that riding lesson!"

"He is not my beau!"

"No?" Raoul politely helped her down and adjusted her gown.

"No! I daresay the marquis is simply being polite."

"Hmm . . ." Raoul did not comment further, and Marianne did not like to tax him. Truth to tell, the viscount was considering his strategy. If he was to win over Marianne, there was no point in forever raising a dust with her. He simply had to hope that his own charm and undoubted magnetism would win out. The viscount was not a coxcomb, but he was aware that he was not unattractive to the female sex.

Marianne seemed fond of him—he would change that fondness to love and be damned to Raphael!

"Afternoon, Carstairs!"

The butler noted Lady Marianne's hand in his lordship's and bowed approvingly.

"Good afternoon, my lord, my lady!"

Raoul took off his beaver and flung it onto a peg. The butler, outraged, admonished him in the sternest accents.

"Master Raoul! You know you are not to—"

The viscount cast his eyes up in comical dismay. "You ought to know, Marianne, that whenever he 'Master Rauols' me I am in serious trouble!"

Carstairs assumed his former dignity. "Far be it from me, my lord—"

"And when he 'my lords' me I am in even deeper trouble!"

Marianne smiled sweetly at the butler.

"Quite right, sir! How very vexatious it must be for you, having an employer who does not know his proper place! It is fortunate indeed that he has *you* to instruct him!"

The butler bowed. "Quite so, madame! And may I take your bonnet?"

Marianne meekly offered up her hat. She studiously avoided her errant husband's eye, for she knew that if she looked at him she would fall into a paroxysm of giggles that would have poor Carstairs mortally affronted.

"Shall we repair to the front drawing room?" Raoul's eyes smiled as he tucked Marianne's hand in his. If he had to confront Raphael, he might as well do it with the advantage.

The butler cleared his throat, but neither party heard him. They were both wrapped up in their own thoughts. Marianne was terrified that the sight of Raphael waiting for her would stir Raoul to fury once more. She prayed the obliging devil did not flirt *too* outrageously in front of her husband, but she did not hold out much hope. The man played his part with consummate skill—almost, at times, *she* fell into the trap of believing his flowery words and handsome addresses.

Raoul bit his lip as they drew closer to the door. He hoped, too, that he would be able to control his temper.

It was not easy watching his best friend pay court to his wife, but if he did not wish to ruin the fragile understanding he and Marianne appeared to have forged that day, he would have to tread with care.

Carstairs watched their disappearing backs with a slight frown. Should he apprise them of the occupants of the front drawing room? What would protocol demand? Lord Delaware was not usually formally announced, but then the circumstances today were different. Still, as he wisely decided, the viscount would be the first to be apprised of the inevitable news that must await him. He decided to hold his peace.

Raoul flung the door open and marched breezily in. "Raphael, my apologies! I delayed my wife but cannot, for the life of me, say I regret it." He looked meaningfully back at Marianne, who blushed furiously at the bold statement.

The next second, his eyes focused on the room and his head began to swim. Raphael, Lord Delaware, had his arm audaciously around his sister's waist. Worse, her short guinea gold hair was looking more tussled than Grecian, and her bodice was suspiciously loosened.

Amber's cheeks were hot with colour and her eyes sparkled a dazzling shade of emerald that even Raoul, in all the years he had known her, had never before elicited. She seemed dazed in an aura of happiness that to her brother seemed at odds with her very compromised situation.

Raphael, the blackguard, looked smugly, devilishly content, his dark hair gleaming against his snowy white shirt points. In the few seconds Raoul stopped to notice, he saw that his dearest friend's rugged jaw was relaxed, his deep, dark eyes shining with a fervour different from his usual cynical demeanour. His necktie was loosened to a shocking extent, allowing strands of silken hair to be just detectable beneath his shirt.

Given Raphael's dazed state, the circumstance that followed was perhaps unfair. Unfair or not, the impeccable marquis found himself grabbed by the scruff of his neck and pummelled with such force that the wind was knocked out of him. Oblivious to the distressed pleas of his womenfolk, Raoul divested himself of his gloves and coat and utilised his lordship as he would a punching bag.

When he stopped, panting for breath, Raphael staggered to his feet, allowed himself a wry smile, and cried halt. Too late! Raoul's arms were swinging once more. My lord the marquis had little option other than to look a little apologetic and retaliate.

He sent Raoul staggering across the floor with one sure blow. As Raoul, spluttering, attempted to recover, the marquis firmly grasped both his arms and pinned them to his side. Raoul struggled against him, cursing, but the marquis did not say a word.

When he stopped, Amber moved towards him in obvious annoyance.

"Don't be such a gudgeon, Raoul! Just look what you have done to Raphael! His nose is all bloodied, and if he does not get the most *thundering* series of bruises . . ."

"Thundering be damned!" Raoul was furious. "Don't you know what he has done, Amber? Have you quite lost your wits, let alone your decorum? The man has ruined Marianne and he has ruined you! *Ruined,* I say!"

"Fustian, Raoul!" Amber's tone was abrasive. "I'll wager he has done no more than *you* have done with Marianne!"

"Marianne is my wife!"

"You don't love her, though, do you?"

"Of all the scatterbrained things to say! Of *course* I love her, you little vixen! What is more—"

Amber was never to learn what was more. Marianne,

hearing his words, rushed towards him and threw herself onto his tender, aching frame.

The marquis stood back a small distance, a faint smile playing across his aquiline features.

"Ouch!" Raoul sounded ungracious, but in truth he was pleased, for whilst he was anxious for his sister's good name, he could not help being heartened by the strange turn of events that sent Marianne careering so wholeheartedly into his embrace.

"Do you really, truly love me?"

"What is that to the point, my love? Of course I do! Every inch of you, by the way, from the top of your wavy dark head to the tips of your adorable toes! In between, too." He stopped for breath, watching the transparent expressions cross his wife's face.

All at once, Raoul wished the wretched room would empty. He turned to Raphael. "Can you not find somewhere else to kiss my dolt of a sister? If she has not the sense—"

"Sad to say, she has not, Raoul, my friend."

"I should say not! Kissing you with such abandon! Hanging on to your shirtsleeves like a veritable—"

"Watch your words." Raphael's voice was suddenly stern.

Raoul coloured. "Well, you said it yourself, Raphael! She has no sense at all."

"What I *meant*, my dear, deluded Raoul, was that your sister has thrown all caution to the wind and agreed, by a stroke of immense good fortune, to be my bride."

Raoul looked from Raphael to Amber. The day's events were still a deplorable muddle, but there was nothing to be confused about the expressions that transformed their faces as they looked mistily at each other. In bewilderment but dawning understanding, Raoul finally relaxed.

He took a seat, put his hands on his head, and started

to laugh. He laughed so much that he ached, for his body seemed strangely battered. This was not surprising, for his lordship the marquis was a regular at Gentleman Jack's and knew how to deliver a blow of passing strength when the circumstance arose.

That gentleman, it should be noted, had drawn Amber up close and was now absently stroking her arm. When she darted from his light embrace, he felt inclined to complain, but to no avail. Very soon he found himself bullied into the comfiest sofa, his bleeding nose being attended to with every care. My lord was unused to such attentions, but in time found them pleasing enough. Soulfully—and with a cheerful wink at Raoul—he succumbed.

Twenty

Sir Clive Grandison smiled to himself as he skipped off the paving stones. He did not care if several gentlemen of eminence stared at him. No doubt they thought him a trifle tipsy, but this was not the case, unless happiness could cast one into such a state. Sir Clive had never been in his cups before and was not about to start now.

No, what made the man so eminently happy was the fact that he had just won a small fortune at Brookes. Even now, his pocketbook felt peculiarly heavy as he made his way down Ludding Street and up toward Chambertin Square.

He thought with a wry smile that the rumours he had so hastily scotched at Brookes had had an unusual and rather rewarding side effect. Namely, he had won threefold the money he had carelessly set down at the club. To boot, the baronet was no less than three hundred pounds richer.

The money had been conceded unequivocally the day the marquis's engagement was announced in the *Post*. Even the habitually cynical and curious could not doubt the love they saw in Lady Amber Sinclair's eyes, nor the fact that it was requited with admirable intensity on the part of the marquis.

The rumours surrounding Lady Marianne Sinclair were also deemed to be, in the words of the voluble Duchess of Doncaster, "utter balderdash and codswallop," a pronouncement that would have earned her much censure had she not been of such an eminently forceful character and rank. The fact that *she* had been the mastermind behind the circulation of such rumours now seemed beyond the point. If Marianne's character was deemed stainless, then stainless, it was.

So it was that Sir Clive, with perfect ease of conscience, could gaily take the lauded steps of Brookes two at a time and claim his prize. This he had done at the earliest opportunity, having conceived an excellent notion of how to dispose of such unwarranted good fortune.

The baronet had no need of a supplemented income, since he was well enough endowed in his own right. Even the knowledge that his bachelor days were drawing to a rapid close did not deter Sir Clive from his projected action. He was a man of integrity and frowned ever so slightly on money procured through gaming. Since his unexpected windfall fell into this category, he felt inclined to dispense with it speedily. This he did, astonishing a certain viable soup kitchen, an unnamed rehabilitation centre for pickpockets and petty thieves, and several nameless orphanages with the extent of his generosity.

When Marianne privately taxed him on this, he merely winked quietly and allowed her to understand her secret was safe. He also, with a very deep chuckle, allowed her to understand he had spoken—off the cuff, of course—with a certain lawyer friend who would remain nameless. When he mentioned the address, however, Marianne's heart started beating most unrhythmically. It had been Mr. Fettering of Dunning, Fettering, and Company who had first pointed out to her the peculiar coincidence of Lord Alistair Sinclair's having a scapegrace namesake like Raoul.

Of course, he would probably never have suspected the harebrained scheme that had germinated in Marianne's mind from that moment. Marianne herself was uncertain until the second she'd stared into Raoul's fathomless sapphire eyes and been lost—hopelessly lost—to all further reason.

Sir Clive had pinched her cheek fondly and commented that it was just as well she was such a lively lass and such a perfect foil to her husband. If fate had had a helping hand, he was not such a curmudgeonly old spoilsport to gainsay it. Further, he had shopping to do.

Thus it was out of his own pocket that Sir Clive purchased a memorable betrothal ring of flashing white sapphires for his dear, patient, and ineffably sweet Lady Jane.

He bent on one knee, his eyes twinkling as he took her hand and made her an avowal of love.

Lady Jane's face betrayed her happiness, but her lips remained prim as she shook her head and wagged a teasing finger in his direction.

"I vow, Sir Clive, you knew more of my offsprings' little plots and caprices than you cared to let on!"

His face was bland as he slipped the ring onto her long, slender finger.

"How so, my dear, beloved Lady Jane?"

"Just a suspicion, Sir Clive! You looked prodigiously pleased with yourself when *I* thought I was at my wits' end with them!"

"Needed to help the young things on, my dear! Couldn't wait for you forever, you know!"

"Couldn't you?"

Sir Clive ceased kneeling and stood up.

"Not if I could help it! Have done nattering, woman! You *will* marry me, won't you?"

Lady Jane looked demure. "But of course, Sir Clive!" was all she said.

It was all that was needed, for the baronet took her in his arms and kissed her with an energy that seemed surprising for his years.

When the couple looked up, it was to find four pairs of merry eyes rather indecorously surveying the action.

"Tut-tut, Mama! The drawing room is not reserved for such . . . such . . ."

". . . interesting?" Amber chimed in.

Raoul looked at her approvingly. "That is it . . . *interesting* activities."

Lady Jane did not look in the least abashed.

"No?" she asked provocatively. Sir Clive was ever one to take up a challenge, and the couples decided to take pity on the pair.

Too late! Carstairs was marching down the corridor, a peculiar and triumphant gleam in his eye. To his exacting standards, the Hansford household was at last being honoured as it deserved.

With a certain sparkle in his eye, he threw open the double doors and announced in loud, sonorous tones, "Her Grace, the Duchess of Doncaster!"

Raoul threw a harassed glance at Marianne. She looked equally harassed, then pointed to a flight of stairs just beyond the balcony. The guilty pair had just made their escape when the duchess walked in. If the marquis and his betrothed felt a trifle envious of the scapegrace pair, they did not show it. Amber executed an immaculate curtsy, and my lady nodded in urbane approval.

Lady Jane called for some tea, and the marquis meticulously made his bow before producing his snuffbox. Always a gentleman, he resigned himself to the requisite afternoon in her grace's colourful company.

Trapped on the stairway, Raoul grinned at his lady wife and silently offered her a step. She refused, preferring the infinite advantage of remaining standing.

My lord did not object when she boldly ripped the buttons from his shirt and explored the finer aspects of his chest. Neither did he mind when she strategically leaned forward, allowing him an intriguing sight of pale, creamy flesh. What he *did* mind, however, was that my lady seemed content to tease him. He was not permitted to make a sound lest her grace the duchess be shocked within. Indeed, she would have been, given the depraved direction his thoughts were leading.

Presently, however, my lady viscountess took pity on her spouse. With a wicked, thoroughly enchanting smile, she set to work. It was not long before my lady, still dazzled from the sunshine, and bearing a strangely smug smile upon her excellent features, could have admitted to the world—had she wished to—that Lord Sinclair was, at last, well and truly seduced.

LOOK FOR THESE REGENCY ROMANCES

ROMANCE FROM JANELLE TAYLOR

ROMANCE FROM FERN MICHAELS

DEAR EMILY   (0-8217-4952-8, $5.99)

WISH LIST   (0-8217-5228-6, $6.99)

AND IN HARDCOVER:

VEGAS RICH   (1-57566-057-1, $25.00)

YOU WON'T WANT TO READ
JUST ONE—KATHERINE STONE